THE
FRENCH
LOVER'S
WIFE

THE
FRENCH
LOVER'S
WIFE

A Novel

JANET GARBER

SHE WRITES PRESS

Published 2023
Printed in the United States of America
Print ISBN: 978-1-68463-181-0
E-ISBN: 978-1-68463-182-7
Library of Congress Control Number: 2022914327

For information, address:
She Writes Press
1569 Solano Ave #546
Berkeley, CA 94707

Book Design by Stacey Aaronson

She Writes Press is a division of SparkPoint Studio, LLC.

To My Tireless Supporter,
Sheldon I. Hanner

Mais, si tu m'apprivoises, ma vie sera comme ensoleillée.
(But if you draw me close, my life will be bathed in sunlight.)
LE PETIT PRINCE, ANTOINE DE SAINT-EXUPÉRY

The trouble with you, Ma, is . . . you won't let me be boss.
ALEXANDRE, AGE 3

I won't let anyone be the boss of me.
LUCIE LERNER BONHOMME

PROLOGUE

Inside the Walls of La Roquette, 1974

*E*xiting the métro at dusk, I directed my steps down Rue de la Roquette. A crooked little cow path once, it winds down from the Bastille's Angel of Liberty, past the site of the women's prison to Père Lachaise Cemetery, where many who fought for liberty and many who never gave it a thought molder in their graves. At my back, the angel glued forever to his pedestal, in certain lights and in certain angles, gives the impression of impending flight.

Hurrying New York–style in Paris was not an option. A light rain was falling, I had no umbrella, and so was ducking under canopies, peering into shops, a prisoner of the homemade delicacies on display for commuters like me: pickled herrings, carrot and garlic salads, anchovy pizzas, quiches lorraines, Alsatian *choucroutes*, rice pudding pies, and interminable rows of flaky, light, melt-in-your-mouth *pâtisseries* whose names I was still trying to master: *mille-feuille? éclair? clafoutis? flan? pithiviers?*

In New York we just said, "Give me a Danish."

Tearing my eyes and nose away from temptation, I came upon a hardware appliance store: TV sets, radios, hi-fis, tiny refrigerators, washing/drying/pressing machines; then clothing shops, fancy baby dress shops, an Indian shirt store, the US Army Surplus Store; a flower shop; a laundry; and a service center that would bail you out when your mini-toilet jammed. I walked on.

Across the street were dozens of cafés, brasseries, *tabacs*, a restaurant or two, a gas station, a new Vietnamese take-out joint. Unaware of its incongruity or proud of it, Théâtre Oblique squatted in the middle of the action, a square white building bringing arts and letters to the marketplace: Strindberg, Kafka, Ingmar Bergman. And not far from the theatre sat a little brown synagogue made of Jewish stars; its outside walls had been decorated for free by the various competing political groups. Nothing vicious, just free speech taking advantage of every available wall space.

Stopping well before Place Voltaire, in this best of all possible worlds, nowhere near the site of the women's prison or the cemetery, I pushed open the heavy *porte-cochère* to enter the cobblestone courtyard of our hundred-year-old building, turning back to register the scene one more time: How could I have forgotten the horsemeat shop, Kosher butcher, tripery, charcuterie and the chicken, ducks, geese, and rabbits on display; the *magasin de vin* (wine shop); *supermarché*; and the handful of pharmacies, coiffures, shoe stores, and bookstores? *Qu'est-ce qui vous manquait?* Why, nothing. Nothing was missing. You could live your whole life out on this street and lack for nothing.

What was I doing here? A little Jewish girl from Queens? No big deal in my hometown. Sure, I had impossibly thick curly black hair cascading down my shoulders, the porcelain complexion of most twenty-something women, a wide "come closer" smile, and what I was told was a certain "glow." But I was well aware I had hit the jackpot. I bet not one of those snooty girls in my ninth-grade

French class got to marry a Frenchman. Little Lucie Lerner, whose father was a butcher and mother, a secretary, whose "bedroom" was the couch in the living room, little Lucie was living in Paris.

Grad School Intersession,
February 1, 1973

ate pointed her gnarled finger at me. The whole matter, now out of my hands.

For the third night in a row, a guy from my comp-lit class invited me to a party at his house. "Lucie, please come to my *pachanga*! You'll see, you'll have a great time."

Why would I bother? Another in a seemingly endless series of snowstorms had blown through Rochester that morning. With no transportation—too poor to own a car—how could I even get to his house way across town? He was a good friend, but I had absolutely no romantic interest in him. And I was really not the party type: introverted, a hopeless dancer, and too easily cowed by my peers at lunch reciting Chaucer in the original Middle English. I much preferred relating one-on-one.

But I knew I should make the effort to go. Twenty-four already, I still had no one to love me, though I'd looked in all the obvious corners, venturing as far west as Colorado the previous summer to chase a love-delusion. After a "ride" or two when I first arrived in town two years ago, I quickly tired of the English Department's assembly-line dating game. Picture two moving sidewalks, males lined up on one side facing the females on the other. An unseen emcee strikes a gong; the sidewalks move in opposite directions, lurching to a stop at the sound of a second gong. Kerry now paired with Kim, Sari with William, Judy with Kevin, Debby with the Chaucer prof. The new couples peel off two by two, rushing to consummate their newfound passions. I was too much of a romantic, too much a cynic to indulge in this incestuous '70s sex game. Would sexual liberation prove as good a deal for the woman as for the man? Enrolling in the comp-lit class was my way of taking a breather from the English department's hothouse atmosphere.

Saturday night. My roommates were both gone for the weekend. If I stayed home, I could work at making more of a dent in *Moby Dick*, finish comparing the influence of French poets on Robert Browning, straighten out those footnotes in the Beckett research paper, or ponder topics for my dissertation.

I opened the front door and scanned the empty streets, and a strange compulsion overtook me: I *had* to go to the party. I slammed the door, grabbed the telephone, and called everyone I knew, finally managing to unearth a ride from an acquaintance of an acquaintance. I rushed to get dressed. Shaking out my freshly washed, rum-scented hair, I slid the Indian minidress hanging in my closet off its hanger. Maroon-colored with embroidered strands of yellow, green, and red running through it, how deliciously it wrapped around my petite frame. At last, an occasion to wear my new brown leather Frye boots!

After all, I had no idea what cute guys might be hiding out in comp lit.

An hour later I wandered by myself from room to room at the crowded house party, sampling the chili and chips, sipping cheap wine from a Styrofoam cup. As I paused to admire one of the host's many exotic Amate wall hangings, I shivered; someone was shadowing me from room to room. I pivoted to my left and yes, there he was. A man with a beautifully sculpted face. Could actor Jean-Pierre Léaud from Truffaut's masterpiece, *The 400 Blows*, possibly have a twin?

"You must be French," I blurted out. Well, there simply was no other possibility.

"Pierre," he replied, extending his hand. *"Enchanté!"*

We both got an electric shock as his hand touched mine. I let out a little gasp. "Static electricity," I explained.

He smiled. "Statique . . . ah, yes."

Look at him! Silky black hair almost down to his collar, high cheekbones, pale oval face set off by his ragged black sweater. Those deep-set eyes and that slightly mocking expression. He must be a poet, I thought. Immersed in French language and culture since ninth grade, with a double major in English and French, I'd always had a love affair with all things French.

I was a goner.

"Follow me," he said, reaching for my hand again. He led me to a corner of the living room where we crowded in together. Leaning close, he rested a hand on the wall behind me. I felt drunk breathing in his scent, and barely managed to string two sentences together. He continued boring into me with those deep-as-a-well dark eyes. I forced myself to look away, but blushed deep red down to my hair follicles. *What should I do now? What does he want?*

I peeked up through my wispy bangs and saw he was still there, staring, waiting. He smiled, flashing a perfect row of ivory teeth. I made note of his shoe polish—black lashes, pale complexion, perfect V torso. "There you are!" he exclaimed. "Will you come out now and play with me?" He swept his hair away from his forehead.

"I'm in trouble. Big trouble," I muttered to myself.

"Trouble?" he repeated. "Can I help you, Lady?" He took hold of my hands and held them, leaned forward and gave me another deep-sea gaze. His hands were so warm.

I broke eye contact to gaze around the room. The grad school party was going strong. People were pairing up, and on the hi-fi Linda Ronstadt was blasting, "It's So Easy." No one looked our way; therefore, no classmates around to tattle on me. I spotted a skinny blonde girl, most likely an undergraduate, standing at the entrance to the room, staring at us, slightly open-mouthed, a cup of wine in each hand. "Why is that girl giving us evil looks?" I asked. "Do you know her?"

He glanced over at the skinny girl and made a dismissive gesture with his hand. "I came with her, but that is not important now." He grinned, stroked my arm, and began—in a low, sensuous voice—to explain he was completing a master's program in optics, having already earned an advanced degree back in France in solid state physics.

Yikes, double threat. Cute and smart!

"I am a working-class boy who somehow made it to college."

"Obviously you are very bright—"

He responded with the classic French shrug, but I could tell he was pleased.

"So I come from France. Now I want to know about you."

I wasn't sure why, but I started babbling like a brook, telling him family secrets, my uncle who married and divorced the same two women five times, my brother who woke up at noon and gobbled five apples in a row, my father who turned off his hearing aids any time he was at home, my mother. . . .

I stopped midstream and noted how he took it all in. No

doubt he understood only a portion of what I said. His English was a bit limited. I'd have to help him out with language right from the get-go. He seemed mesmerized by my short dress and boots. I caught his eye and this time he blushed. "I love your knees," he whispered.

I tried to focus but resumed my inane chattering: "One of my favorite films is *Claire's Knee*! Eric Rohmer's the director, right? What a film. I love French cinema. So . . . sensuous."

Those dark eyes boring into me, eating me up. I felt hot all over. Thrilled and embarrassed at all the attention. I swept my thick, curly black hair off my shoulders. He inched closer, grinning as he inhaled the rum scent, and smoothed my hair down. He did that thing again with his eyes. I blushed; my whole body, one hot tingling mess.

An hour later when my ride signaled she was ready to leave, Pierre rested his hands on my shoulders—I breathed in his slightly smoky scent. He borrowed a pen from me and engraved my address and phone number on his palm. His hands, so beautifully sculpted, with the long fingers of an artist. He drew me in for a French farewell, four pecks on the cheeks. "*A très bientôt!*"

"Bye, Pierre."

On the ride back I was absorbed by one thought only: *If he doesn't call me, I'll die.* Simple as that.

That very night though he wrote me a poem that he carried to me the next day, walking miles in the slush from the opposite end of the city. A poem!

Quand le bonheur est vrai, je crois qu'on a peur d'y penser. (When happiness is real, I think we are afraid to think about it.)

Happiness? I'd waited long enough. I wasn't afraid. I was more than ready. Bring it on!

Three weeks passed with Pierre stopping by every single day to see me, rarely empty-handed. "Look what I brought you. Mandarin oranges. Good for your health. Shall I teach you how to prepare rice pilaf? Very nutritious."

"I'd love that," I said, but I hoped I was in for more than a cooking lesson, more like a hot and torrid love scene. *Deflower me! No wait, a little late for that.* I no longer needed to put him off, confident my birth control pills would have kicked in by then. I poured some red wine we downed in a few seconds and gave him the sultry Lauren Bacall treatment. He might not have understood the movie allusions or the exact words, but he certainly got the picture.

He appeared happy to oblige, all broad shoulders and wiry strength, lifting me up in his arms and carrying me into my bedroom. He laid me down on my white comforter and stripped off my sweatshirt, jeans, bra and panties, shoes and socks, article by article, until I was stark naked, arranged like an hors d'oeuvre on a platter, just waiting for someone to pluck me. I was breathing heavily, so lubricated an elephant could get in there.

He stepped out of his clothes, climbed in next to me, kissing me, nuzzling my breasts, running his hands up and down my body. My back arched as he crawled down the bed and kissed me *there*. Expertly, with a practiced aim. Within seconds I exploded in my first orgasm ever. Delicious waves of feeling rocked my body. *Yes, yes, yes, this is what I've been waiting for.* I made to return the favor but he lifted up my hips and entered me, thrusting in and out until he too came. With a moan.

Afterwards, we sat up in bed, peeling the oranges, exchanging hot and sticky kisses.

The weeks went by in a blur. The weather warmed. Generous to a fault, a real giver, Pierre insisted on treating me to a new spring coat with his larger student grant. We cooked together, played together, loved together. Best of all, he danced with me in the shadows of early morning, arms clasped around my waist, spinning me around. We stared, fascinated at our images in the mirror. So young. So vibrant. "We make a handsome couple, don't we?" I asked, knowing he agreed. I often caught him staring at my profile.

One afternoon I was brewing us some coffee in the kitchen when he summoned me. "Come Lucie, I must show you something amazing. Leave the coffee." I followed him to the bedroom. He sat on my beloved purple armchair, the one I found at a street sale. I approached and let him draw me onto his lap. "Now listen carefully, Lady. Years ago I drew a picture of my dream woman, 'Sarah.' " He unrolled a piece of canvas for me. "Look! *C'est toi!*"

I picked up the profile sketched in charcoal to get a better look. Sarah, with her long black hair and seductive smile. "Isn't this amazing?" He covered my face with butterfly kisses, getting pretty turned on by his own artwork. I went with the flow. *Overnight I had a boyfriend. A French lover. All mine. Ordered up especially for me.*

"I'm putting my money in this drawer," he announced one after-noon, opening my dresser. "Take what you need. I send some money to my mother every month, but the rest is for us." *Us.* Newly enriched, I was able for the first time to alter my study schedule to explore the city with him. I no longer worried as much about exceeding my six-dollar-a-week food allowance. I'd been existing on scrambled eggs and hamburger meat, but now watched carefully as he prepared onion soup, baked fish, and casseroles for me and my roommates.

"I want you with me, want to walk with you in spring, see you in your shorts and halter tops, sunbathe together in Genesee River Park. Oh, and of course, make lots and lots of love," he'd proclaim, playfully wrestling me onto the bed.

"I don't like it, do you, when couples close themselves off," he said, "put a shell around themselves? Let's not do that." Pierre and I opened up to our friends, shared our happiness with them. We constructed quite a social life. I even hosted an elaborate Passover Seder for twenty people, only two of whom were Jewish. We all sat on the floor around an oversized tablecloth and read the entire *Haggadah* in English. What a magical moment that was.

This handsome Frenchman chose me to shower with affec-tion and attention and love. I learned so much from our talks together about the world, history, and geography. "Do you un-derstand that America uses up most of the world's resources?"

I had no idea. We walked up and down Genesee Park Boule-vard every night after dinner, discussing world affairs, a welcome new habit. "You know, you are more European than American. After all, if your grandparents had remained in Europe. . . ." An accident of fate turned me into an American. I was relieved to learn I was not to blame for any of my country's errors in regard to the rest of the world.

Pierre explained he was raised by his mother, and in many ways had been on his own since he was eight. Though I came from a lower middle-class two-parent family, I quickly saw we shared the same values: hard work, perseverance, discipline, integrity.

"It's impressive that you are pursuing a career," he said. "You are both beautiful and smart." He kissed me on my nose as we headed back through the deserted streets to my apartment.

His lessons were not limited to our conversations. In bed, too, I continued to be an ardent and eager student.

What a lucky girl I was! I only prayed it would last.

My roommates vamped a bit when he was around, striking sexy and alluring poses. But Pierre had no intention of straying. He stuck around even after my cat, Braveheart, scratched him. "From now on, remember," I teased. "Never back a cat into a corner."

ele

The Courtship

*A*fter a few months Pierre decided it was time he met my parents. He accompanied me home on a weekend visit to Queens, New York. I readied myself for battle, sure we'd run into some flak. He was not only not American but his name was Pierre Bonhomme and not Pierre Goldstein. My father, as a rule, looked down on "greenhorns." My mother found something wrong with every guy I dated, yet she felt it her duty to warn them about my "terrible disposition."

I was in defensive mode as we sat down in their dining room for a dinner of roasted chicken made with onion soup mix and marmalade, accompanied by instant mashed potatoes and peas from a can and lots of orange soda. Instead of fireworks, I heard my mother chatting Pierre up on every subject imaginable. "What do you think about our involvement in Vietnam?" she asked.

Uh-oh!

Pierre put down his fork. "Do you realize, Mrs. Lerner, the French were in Indochina for ten years before the Americans stepped in?"

Pierre went over some of the history with her; it became fairly obvious he was opposed to the war. I saw my father bristling. He was a World War II veteran, very patriotic, and definitely a hawk. He disapproved of boys setting their draft cards afire before running off to Canada to hide out, and of girls burning their bras and demonstrating half nude in the streets.

Luckily, Pierre caught on to the need to flatter my mother, her cooking, her lovely home. She became putty in his hands, beaming as she passed him another slice of coffee cake. She showed off her limited supply of French 101 phrases, and he praised her to the skies. My father remained tight-lipped and reserved. As usual. Was it because of his hearing impairment? I noticed his hearing aid in his left breast pocket. But was it turned on? He didn't say much of anything but smiled and nodded the way he tended to do when my girlfriends visited and he wasn't quite able to follow the conversation.

At the end of the visit my mother took me aside. "He's got such good table manners!" My father kept his observations to himself but gave me some extra frozen ribeye steaks from his butcher shop to take back upstate.

Pierre's not being Jewish had evidently become a non-issue since at twenty-four, I was, in my parents' eyes, "over the hill." They'd both been desperate to unload me since I turned twenty.

No obstacles here. I concluded we had their blessings. Strange, I had a sour taste in my mouth. They had accepted Pierre, the rebel, so easily. I was aching for a fight. Maybe I should have told them he was a communist?

In early May we were sitting at my kitchen table, reading and taking notes when he interrupted me once again. "How do you say *insolite?*

"Not sure. Unusual?" I handed him my *Cassell's French-English Dictionary.* "You need to look words up."

He didn't get annoyed. He cracked open the dictionary, but also kept up the how-do-you-say-how-do-you-say song. Little by little his English was improving. I would have preferred to speak more French to him, but his gaining proficiency in English took precedence. I could do a pretty mean French accent, the result being we often amused our friends with a funny little routine that started with my asking, "Ow long av you been in zees contree?" We thought we were hysterical; our audience appeared to agree.

Pierre had finished his coursework a few weeks earlier and immediately received a couple of offers from well-known companies—Kodak and Bausch & Lomb. With his roommates departed for the summer, and without much discussion, he packed up his stuff and moved into the big house I shared where he insisted on buying most of the groceries. We spent almost all our time together, which was delightful, but any time he needed to return to the lab to run an experiment, I silently rejoiced. A little time to myself. We'd been having so much fun I'd been forced to take an incomplete in one course, my first ever! So shameful.

During my two years in Rochester, I had had no time or money for sightseeing or leisure-time activities, my head being stuck in a book, many books. Reading, writing, reading, writing. Now, hand in hand, Pierre and I roamed the city like tourists, visiting the George Eastman Museum downtown, and attending a reading by Lawrence Ferlinghetti and a lecture by the famous French literary critic, Roland Barthes. Once a week Pierre treated me to a romantic dinner in an off-campus pub. And on one recent unseasonably sunny day, we went canoeing on the Genesee River, and with a little gentle coaxing, I sunbathed topless in the park. Me!

The pièce de résistance? He borrowed a car and we drove up to Lake Canandaigua to spend the night in a friend's cabin. We dined on pâté, mustard, and a baguette he'd picked up in a French deli in town, and I allowed myself to go way, way past my one-drink limit on wine. Afterwards we cuddled by the fire for hours, making love all night to the sound of waves crashing on the lake shore.

Hey, I was stuck in a romance novel and loving every minute!

We were an official couple on campus. How could I be this lucky? Pierre was perfect: forceful, highly intelligent, well educated. He opened me up to so many new experiences. Best of all, he had plans and goals and visions for the future, and I could hitch a ride alongside him.

Pierre pushed himself back from the table and cleared his throat. "Lucie? Where has my Lucie gone?"

I snapped out of my reverie and closed *The Ring and the Book*. My stomach was growling anyway. Time soon to get out the ingredients and make a pilaf. "Yes?"

"I have something to tell you." He walked over to the window and looked out on the familiar landscape: grey and drizzly. I held my breath. Finally, he turned to me, cleared his throat and announced, "I've been offered an amazing job. In Mexico. I'll be working at a scientific *instituto* doing research and teaching."

Huh?

"Oh," I managed to say. *So soon for our idyll to end.* My turn to get up from the table and hide my face in the refrigerator. I concentrated on pulling out eggs and milk and frozen blueberries. I decided to hell with pilaf. I'd make my signature whole wheat pancakes for lunch. "When will you leave?"

"In two weeks," he replied. Then he tiptoed behind me and

lifted me off the ground. Ignoring my mock screams, he carried me into our bedroom and threw me on the bed. In the midst of kissing me, he asked, "Why don't you join me?" As if this was the most natural thing in the world.

Yeah, who needs a PhD when you have love?

In the weeks that followed, a Swedish male friend warned me not to go to Mexico with Pierre. "He's too macho for you."

"Not at all," I protested, "he's a feminist."

My father mysteriously weighed in with, "Don't marry a European," and my mother held court from their living room couch, incapacitated with a bad case of sciatica, inquiring, "Why don't you get married?"

She hardly appreciated my answer. "But we don't know each other well enough to get married." *What would she tell the neighbors?*

Colorado had not worked out for me. Could Puebla, Mexico, where we'd be living? On the appointed day I borrowed a car and drove Pierre to the airport, an easy drive, not long enough for me to prepare. We found his gate. No delays. He'd be boarding soon. He slipped off his backpack, set it on the floor, and we sat down to wait. My last chance to say something memorable. "Listen," I said, "you'd better write—"

He directed one of his sexy continental glances my way. "Silly woman!" He dragged me to my feet, embraced me, covered my face with hot wet kisses and danced me around in a circle. Was that a tear I spotted? He didn't care who was watching. Neither did I.

"Rows 25 to 32, please board now."

He quickly composed himself. Gripping my shoulders, his face lit up as he said, "Remember, Lucie, I don't know how busy

I'm going to be, setting up the lab, the classes, lecturing, finding a place to live. . . ."

He was beaming; I was coming apart. I plastered a silly lovesick grin on my face, watching as he shouldered his backpack and strode confidently away, eager for his next adventure.

Pierre left; I stayed behind. The time had come for me to teach a semester of freshman English, an experience I'd been looking forward to for the past two years. No way was I going to miss that opportunity: "my very own Intro to Literature class!" Days before my class started, I got word I'd aced the master's written exam with a "commendable"—the only grad student to do so—probably due to Pierre's tutoring which enabled me to relate the literary works we were studying to the political turmoil of the nineteenth century, the Industrial Revolution, the Napoleonic wars. All that remained was to take the orals the following spring. My dissertation on Beckett or Browning, I could probably write anywhere.

But when I called to tell my father the good news, he said, "Sorry, but in my book, you're a failure."

"How do you mean?" I asked.

"You're not married!"

I flashed back to my sophomore summer internship in a day-care center. A young Hispanic mother had bemoaned her fate: "I'm twenty-five and unmarried." She tried to explain that her life was over, she was finished, aged out of the marriage market. I was incredulous.

Learning of my father's reaction, Pierre sent me a congratu-lations card featuring the staff of the Instituto throwing me a kiss. "We are very proud of you."

Which is not to say I didn't curse Pierre for leaving. I finally met the man of my dreams and was in love for the first time ever.

Why the need to move almost three thousand miles away when everything was going so well? I'd invested quite a bit of time already in getting my degree. If I followed him, and I knew I would, what would happen?

The teaching turned out to be the best job ever, though I missed Pierre like crazy. I could be creative, come up with wacky themes for the weekly compositions, introduce a bunch of semi-literate teenagers to my favorite literary geniuses. I was only a few years older than my students. One planted himself in the front row and stared at me with what I can only call "bedroom eyes." I was flattered; hell, tempted! I was fairly certain a touch, a hand on my shoulder, would send me into paroxysms of desire.

Pierre mailed me reams of poetry: love poems to be sure, but also vivid depictions of the sights and sounds of Puebla where he had rented a two-bedroom apartment and found a roommate to share expenses. Naturally I loved the poems and the photographs he'd taken to illustrate them. I repeatedly requested more information about what he was actually doing, which projects he was working on, who he was spending time with. All I got were more poems and Polaroids, which I pasted dutifully into an album.

During the semester I managed to travel twice to Mexico to be with Pierre and meet his new friends and colleagues. He was managing to publish scientific papers on his research while teaching classes entirely in Spanish. Everyone seemed to love him as much as I did. Each time I rejoined him, I felt I had come "home," and I cried at the airport when I boarded the plane back to school without him. He was so in charge, so sure of himself, so irresistible. *My man!*

When it came time to take the orals in May, I prepared as hard as I could, putting in eight-to-ten-hour days reading and researching, but the two trips to Mexico to visit Pierre, and the lack of a good library there, did me no favors.

The oral exam results came back: the professors failed all of us graduate students save one older gentleman—an unheard-of maneuver—and they rightly got flak from the college administration. Not much help to me. The orals were repeated in one month. Surprise, surprise: This round they passed everyone, all my colleagues.

How much could they have learned in four weeks?

Meanwhile, I was too busy packing to bother sitting for the test again. Done with academia, I headed off to Puebla to start my new life with Pierre. I kept busy tutoring our Mexican friends privately in English and wandering about the *mercados* identifying the exotic fruits and vegetables there, the mangoes, papayas, *calabacitas,* meats, cheeses, chilis, and the incredible chocolate, and picking out provisions for the meals I hoped I had the talent to prepare.

"Que va llevar?" chanted the food vendors. Little by little, I gathered they were asking what I wanted to buy. Understanding the actual words being uttered took me a while longer.

On the weekends, we jumped in the little blue Renault Pierre purchased secondhand and visited the Museo Nacional de Antropologia in Mexico City, climbed the pyramids in Oaxaca, and camped out on the beaches in Veracruz. What a delightful time we were having.

My PhD? Oh well.

In Puebla, we played house. I wandered about, absorbing this new culture, took buses to the Instituto to meet Pierre. At night we sat in the *zócalo,* dining on brain soup, kidneys, goat. I met one Mexican girlfriend, young, fun, and flaky, who happened to be fluent in English: Chita. She showed me how to buy fabric in the market and helped me sew a dress for myself; I taught her how to consult a doctor when her period was late, much too late.

My Spanish was very rudimentary; in high school I'd taken only one semester. The only improvement occurred as I mastered cooking vocabulary, painstakingly translating ingredients. The food was tasty, the mescal with the worm in the bottle less so. I loved the Mexican people, especially their sweet embrace of their children, who were included in all activities at all hours and seemed to thrive without the strict bedtimes so popular in the States.

One weekend our whole group of twenty-year-olds, scientists and families, were lying about on the grass in a park sunning, nibbling on picnic food, tossing balls around. As usual I plastered a phony smile on my face as everyone around me gaily chattered away in Spanish. *Wait! What was happening?* Suddenly I understood what they were talking about, the gist of it anyway. *Magic!*

Though I continued to mix up Spanish and French words, I was emboldened to venture out more. I found a real job teaching English at a high school and continued tutoring students in our apartment. I wrote long letters home to Mom and Dad, detailing all my adventures in this alien culture and assuring them, no matter what, I would not be stranded. "Stop worrying!" I told them. "Pierre's a prince. Believe me, if we break up, he's good for a return airline ticket."

Breaking up? Unlikely. I had my man in my sights and no intention of letting him go.

Dizzy in Love

Spinning in a 360-degree circle, arms raised like a little girl, I viewed impossibly fluffy clouds touching down on the horizon and two magnificent volcanoes, Popocatépetl and Citlaltépetl, their views unobstructed by skyscrapers, highways, power lines, or telephone cables. *So this is what the sky looks like!* I spun and spun, it was all so sublime.

I was the darling *novia*, outfitted in a dazzling white Mexican blouse festooned with brightly colored embroidered flowers and sporting faded blue jeans with two sexy patches I'd sewn on to hide a rip, two fish swimming in the neighborhood of my crotch. I wore my yellow work boots and pinned my signature long hair up, off my neck, as a concession to the blazing sun.

I sat down on the grass in the noonday sun, shunning sunglasses and hat since I never burned—all I ever got were more freckles—watching Pierre play soccer with his scientist colleagues. When the game ended, he sauntered over to me. I studied his advance across the field. He was swinging his arms—so sexy and smiling and seductive and . . . short?

"I never noticed," I confided that afternoon, "but you're rather short." *How could I have missed that?*

"What are you saying, Foolish Talking Bird?" He laughed and reeled me in for a kiss. "I'm at least 170 centimeters."

I pushed him away and looked around; our friends made a

show of turning their heads in the other direction. "No, you're not, Skinny Little Laughing Skeleton," I mocked. "You liar, you!"

By way of answer, he lifted me and swung me around until I was breathless. Taking my hand, he ran with me across the fields to our dusty little car. As we approached, I looked at him questioningly. "No more lessons for you, Lady. You've been a bad girl." During our previous lesson on driving standard shift, I'd jumped out of the car three times, slamming the door each time. He'd done the same. Either I was hopeless, or he was one bad teacher. The latter was unlikely, judging by his popularity with the physics staff and the students. "Oh please, one more chance to strip the gears!" I cried out.

"Don't forget. We're meeting Francisco and Sofia for dinner. We have work to do beforehand," he said, giving me a broad wink.

Ah, Francisco! Another dreamboat, but taller. My pupil as well as my friend. He who leaned in inches from my face as I tried to teach him how to pronounce "enough." All I'd have to do would be to smile, not even bat an eye, and I'd be upside down on my Mexican serape straddled by one hunk of a man. If I were his wife, Sofia, I wouldn't trust him too far. But no worries—he was safe with me. I was in love with my Frenchman.

Dinner? I dreamed of fish, *huachinango* or *dorado*, preceded by *sopa des sesos*, which I learned to love before finding out I was eating cow brains. Too late. The spicy brew was a favorite of mine now. *"Ándale!"* I shouted. I figured I'd have time between lovemaking and leaving for dinner to make more headway with my Spanish grammar book or my story. "Hey, you know what, Pierre? I'm getting *borracha* tonight. I'm drinking not one but two Dos Equis!"

After a short drive home, we entered the apartment which was sparsely furnished as Pierre preferred. The few pieces of furniture were made of wicker. Pierre's roommate, Deepak, was in his room fooling around with Chita. Boy, did they make a lot of whoopee, as in "Whoopee!" We followed suit. Afterwards, I took a shower and stationed myself at my desk, facing the small square sun-drenched courtyard with its flowers, its darting lizards, its colorful pots of cacti. A paperback book, *La Muerte de Artemio Cruz* by Carlos Fuentes, which I'd proudly finished reading in the original Spanish, sat atop the desk. I hadn't yet admitted to people that I'd understood almost nothing; I kept turning the pages, hoping I would get the gist of the story. *Guess what? Never happened.*

I was interrupted by the landlord's two young daughters, tapping at the door. *"Basura?"* Five and six, sporting tiny flowered aprons tied around their waists, they came by once a day to take out our garbage. Another man came to deliver bottles of water, and an older woman showed up once a week to clean the apartment. "Gracias, muchachas," I uttered in my horrible French-inflected Spanish. I handed them the small bag of garbage and gave them each a generous tip. They looked at each other and giggled, then ran down the stairs to knock on the next door.

I returned to my desk and pulled out my thinly disguised short story. Me watching me through the looking glass?

She hungrily took it all in: the dusty road, punctuated by rows of maguey, spiky cactus plants, barren stretches of parched earth, and the undug roadside graves of careless or tired or suicidal animals. . . .

25

Dinner at dusk with our friends in the *zócalo* was fun, if nerve wracking, as Francisco persisted in fondling my knee under the table while lecturing Pierre. "Not a good idea to have your woman roam about the city freely" and "Why don't you two get married?"

Was Francisco insane?

I looked over at Pierre, who hadn't noticed any funny business. If Pierre caught on, what would he do? Challenge Francisco to a duel? *En garde!* And what of poor Sofia? "Oh, c'mon," I protested, trying my best to get back in the conversation while prying Francisco's fat fingers off my thigh. *There!*

Many of the scientists kept their women under lock and key, letting them out only for church or shopping. Sure, men followed me and made those lewd noises, but what of it? Was I a threat to the social order? Liable to infect the other wives with unnatural ideas? *Hoped so!*

I stifled a laugh and shifted my weight, moving out of range of wandering hands.

The dorado fish was wonderful, but I cringed when two peasant women with babies strapped to their backs came begging for the bread in the breadbasket. Older children, seven or eight, gathered in corners till late at night selling chicklets. I was disturbed by this level of poverty and the realization that we, lucky enough to be employed, were considered rich. I started to realize how much waste there was back in the States.

One thing I could not accept was the average Mexican's cavalier attitude toward death. Why bother with lights when out riding your bicycle at night? If you died, you'd be with God, and there'd likely be a parade as your casket made its way to the church. I knew I could not stay in such a country forever. I did not want to raise our children here. Five months, though, had passed quickly.

The next morning Pierre woke me up at dawn to breakfast with him before heading off to work. I spent the morning giving private English lessons to those of my students who deigned to show up, then hung out with Chita for another sewing lesson. I was hopeless—failed sewing in junior high—but sewing filled up the time till Pierre came home. And being with Chita and speaking English was such a relief.

That night I placed an official-looking letter that had arrived from France next to Pierre's dinner plate. He waited until he'd eaten before opening the envelope.

"*Merde!*" He flung the letter to the floor. I quickly stooped to pick it up. "What is it about, Pierre?"

He poured himself another glass of wine before speaking. "I postponed my military service as long as I could. It's compulsory in France, you know. Now either I return home and serve, or I lose my citizenship."

No! I certainly don't want that to happen. I love France! I love him!

By morning he'd decided to return to France. With any luck he believed as a scientist he'd be allowed to do alternate service in a lab.

I'd trotted after him from Rochester to Mexico, hadn't I? Why not Paris?

On Saturday we hopped on the rickety bus to Cholula to see an exhibition at the university library. On the way over Pierre hammered away at me mercilessly. "What are your goals?? Where are you going?"

Are we there yet? Was it my fault he was so driven, such a scientist, so French? I shrugged.

He shook his head sadly. "I've known what I wanted to be since I was eleven."

I rewarded him with a smile. *What a man!*

Goals? Well, let's see. You dragged me here to Mexico. Now life as a college professor, my goal these last few years, is out.

I had no new ideas. I squinted out the dusty window, trying to remember the names of the various cactus plants. Wait! "I . . . I'm going to have a baby in 1976," I finally declared. Well, it was the one thing I knew I wanted, had always wanted, since I was five.

He nodded his approval and waited. He was striking. Simply gorgeous. We'd make beautiful babies together. I imagined a little daughter with thick, curly black hair, ruby lips, his bone structure, definitely his nose, our large brown eyes. My wit.

"But you know what?" I blurted out, my Irish rising. "There's no way I'm going to be your girlfriend when I'm forty-five!"

He rested his slender finger alongside his nose—I called it his Thinker pose—and pondered my meaning for a minute. In previous discussions he'd insisted he was not the marrying kind. But now he said, "You can have the babies, and I will travel around and come to visit!"

Hmm. "You know, Pierre, we can have any type of marriage we want," I whispered, suddenly serious, meaning of course any type he wanted.

The bus stopped to pick up more passengers. I made room on the bench for a Native American Indian woman dressed in a sparkling white artisanal blouse and a long blue skirt. What a classic Mayan nose! She stowed her wire cage holding two live chickens in the overhead rack, sat down—careful not to disturb the sleeping infant on her back—and reached into a deep pocket, drawing out a perfect orange mango. Peeling it, she offered me a slice. I looked to Pierre for advice; he grabbed the slice, bit off half, and gave the rest to me, all the while engaging the young mother, unused to such attention from a gringo, questioning her about her life, the chickens, the baby, charming her with a torrent of fluent Spanish. *He really was something, wasn't he?*

A few months and one ultimatum later, we packed up and flew to New York where we were married by the city clerk. I'd chased him, cornered him, and caught him! My parents paid for a small reception at the Villa Bianca restaurant in Queens, attended by my family and friends, and one tiny little French lady, Mamie, mother of the groom, who hastily flew in.

"Are you sure, Lucie?" Mom asked the night before.

"Look, Mom, if it doesn't work out, we'll get a divorce," I blithely replied. "That's how we do things in 1974."

Mom stuttered, "That's not the way to go into a marriage—"

"You don't get it. This is my fate."

Hand in hand, Monsieur and Madame Bonhomme headed off to France for a lifetime of adventures.

ell

The City of Lights

One night after dinner Pierre led me away from our rental, up and down the twisting streets of Montmartre, to a dimly lit café with pink and orange paper lanterns hanging from the ceiling. We seated ourselves at a banquette half hidden in the corner and signaled to the server. "What should I get, Pierre? I'm not much of a drinker, as you know."

"Just say, *'Un coup de vin blanc, s'il vous plaît.'* I think I'll get the same." The server appeared, very tall and forbidding, dressed all in black, took our order, and disappeared. We were free to spy on the other customers. "This is what French people do in the evenings," Pierre explained. "They meet here to socialize, like those four over there." He tilted his head in their direction. "It's more common than visiting in each other's homes, the way you do in the States."

"Can you tell by looking what kind of people they are, Pierre?" I asked. A game I loved to play.

"You want to test my psychic abilities, eh? Fair enough. I'd peg the women as primary school teachers. My impression is that the men are old friends, perhaps army buddies or—"

The server approached just then with our drinks, which he deposited on a tiny white square napkin. I sipped at my ice-cold wine, but Pierre gently tugged on the waiter's arm to detain him. "Can you tell me who won the soccer match? Ah. How do you like working in this neighborhood? Do you see a lot of tourists? What, you're not a native to Paris? You came here all the way from Le Périgord? You must miss your family." Pierre peppered him with questions, treating him like a person rather than a means to an end, something I often failed to do. It was a gift Pierre had, engaging with everyone, from a server in a café in Paris to a Mayan woman on a Mexican bus. The server lapped up the attention, finally bowing his head to excuse himself, leaving us to enjoy our drinks.

We'd been in Paris for two months, camping out in a one-room apartment with no bath in the posh sixteenth arrondissement while searching for jobs and a more permanent place to live. Pierre was slated to report for military service in one month, and we quickly learned no one would hire him until he satisfied this requirement. In fact, when I interviewed for a job, potential employers questioned me about what I'd do if my husband were assigned to a lab in another region of France. Wouldn't I want to relocate to be closer to him? They were skeptical about my claim that I would stay put, even when I explained we were used to separations.

"Pierre, I know you want to buy us an apartment, and I wish I could contribute. The one we saw on Rue de la Roquette today looked promising—much better than that horrible little room in Barbès you almost moved us into."

"Don't remind me, please."

"Never again will I stay behind to wash my hair while you're out house hunting."

"You are a very funny lady. But honestly, I thought that studio would suit us—"

"How could it? I didn't feel safe there. All I could see were these men everywhere hanging out in the streets. Just one room with a galley kitchen. We'd kill each other there in no time." I reached across the table to touch his hand. "What were you thinking, my love?"

"That Lady and I don't need much space?" He attempted a lascivious wink.

"Sorry, but I couldn't move in there. If only that landlord had believed my story about my father falling ill and our needing to return to the States immediately. I thought it was a pretty good excuse."

"Well, that's over. That greedy little man's got our twenty-five hundred franc deposit." Pierre sighed. He glanced around the room and signaled to the server that we'd take refills. "I'm going to buy the place on La Roquette. We're running out of time."

My head was swimming already. I was such a cheap date. I struggled to focus on the conversation. "Pierre, you do know I need a proper bathroom and shower? That's nonnegotiable."

He reached over and kissed me. "You're so cute when you use big words."

"Hey, I'm a big city girl. I know a slum when I see one. So, what's next?"

"I'll sign the papers and select some workmen. Tomorrow we can pick out new wallpaper and *moquette.*"

"*Moquette* is like industrial carpet back home, right?"

"That's what one uses here. The workmen will tear out the coal chute, build us a proper bathroom—"

"Oh, stop! I'm getting hot!"

"Well, let's go home then. Maybe I can do something about that!"

"Just what kind of woman do you think I am, Monsieur?"

We settled the bill, waved goodbye to the waiter, and walked down the hill to the métro. "We don't need much," he said. "A six-inch foam mattress on the floor, like you had at school, an armoire for our clothes, a small table and chairs."

"We'll need a few more things. A lamp or two, for example?"

"Anything you want, Lady."

We stopped to smooch, like any other French couple, under a streetlamp on rain-slicked streets in the foggy night.

"You're the best," I whispered.

"Hurry," he urged, pulling on my arm. "I have to show you something."

"A new move?"

He stopped dead in the street. "You do realize you are what we call *une femme de tempérament*."

"Meaning?"

"You like *it*. Do you?" He stared into my eyes.

"Let me show you how much."

We giggled and ran off, two kids just starting out. In the flash of an eye, I became the first of my friends to be married and living in the City of Lights, in my own home, drinking *café crème* at all hours of the day and night.

Even my father must have been impressed.

Inside the Walls of La Roquette, 1974

*O*mounted the spiral staircase on the left, the one that reverses direction after the second floor, to get to our two-room railroad flat on the third. Like a typical Parisian, I was working on my sixth cold of the season, but luckily not the Big G (grippe, or flu), and unlike a typical Parisienne, I was going to have to improvise an evening meal. I threw down my handbag, opened the window, and gazed out in wonder at all the movement in the street. Bus 69 thundered by right on schedule (every quarter of an hour), along with motorcycles and those bikes with motors on the front wheel, Renaults, Citroens, and anything else that could add a note to the crazed cacophony of the streets. I watched the throngs of other hungry people, many suffering battle fatigue from the métro, rushing home to get to their dinner. A whiff from the coffee-grinding shop downstairs floated by, an aroma designed to delight the soul. Relatching the window, I remained transfixed. That first year in France, everything amazed me.

Look at all those women, pushing imported English strollers made of plastic and spit, shopping, always shopping for the next meal and the one after, never sure of pleasing enough, and the people of all sorts and in all sizes, from all over the world, who came to La Roquette—to eat, what else? It was *la grande bouffe*, the continuous French food orgy and full-time obsession with food and which wine goes with what.

I spotted movement: a homeless man crouched in the dirty alleyway adjoining the Hungarian bar opposite our building. He was gnawing on the end of a stale baguette. I imagined him dreaming of the open market at nearby Richard Lenoir a few days away: the flowers, the cheeses, the jettisoned food, the kindly vendor who might save a packet of meat scraps to give to him.

Oops. I glanced at my watch and dashed into the bedroom, realizing I'd better change out of my clothes, slip on jeans, and not forget my *pantoufles*. Wasn't that what started our last fight? Can't risk scratching the floors with my heels or catching that which is most feared by the French—a chill that goes straight to the heart—by walking barefoot! Pierre, my dashing French husband, was due home any moment, he with the long, straight black hair parted on one side, the finely sculpted features, and perfect Gallic nose. And don't get me started on that accent!

If it were up to me, I'd simply scramble up eggs, make a quick vinaigrette for the salad greens his mother brought over from her garden, serve cheese and bread and wine, of course, and a little slice of her homemade rhubarb pie. Would that suffice? Unsure, I took eggplant, tomatoes, squash, onions, and garlic out of our mini-fridge and threw together a ratatouille; I set it simmering on the stove and sliced up fresh bread from the Jewish bakery. Wouldn't Pierre be impressed?

Eight o'clock: No Pierre. Had he said anything about a deadline or a special project? If only we had a phone! I poured myself a glass of *vin rouge* before stepping into the tiny living room near the front door where I stretched out on the daybed, our "couch," to leaf through my writer's journal, back to the beginning, the *coup de foudre* of love at first sight.

Après-Sexe

*They were both on the point of tears, both not daring to
show it,
both turned away towards opposite walls.
When heads turned, eyes locked.
For one brief second, souls
leapt out, danced ring-a-round-the-rosy, high jumped in the
air. . . .
The air was so still.
Maybe this is it, she thought, daring, not daring.
Maybe this will be it, he wondered, hoping, loving her
hair, blinking.
They glanced away, held hands, talked softly.
They would never think of this moment in the years to
come.*

*But now I was thinking of that moment, how fine a moment
it was: the overheated room in the upstate university town,
the mountains of snow balanced against the bedroom
window, our nubile young bodies, sleek with sweat,
disentangling with regret.
He had a girlfriend in France: too emotional, a
depressive. I had . . . no one.
The earth opened up, swallowed them whole, held them
gently in its maw like a protective mother cat. What
happened to one would henceforth happen to both.*

Madame Karol

*O*closed the journal and stashed it away to listen to the old woman singing on the other side of the wall while she readied her bed for sleep: hymns in Polish, Ukrainian, and Russian, lilting airs of peasant girls and princes. A thin soprano voice, a little creaky like her bed, but a good voice, a happy voice. Madame Karol. She tapped out a good night. I tapped back. I knew tomorrow she would laugh hysterically when she saw me. "Did you hear when I said, 'Knock knock, *bonne nuit, mes enfants?*'" She'd clap her hands, doubling up at the idea of such a good trick.

The first time I met her, soon after we moved in, she practically assaulted me as I was pulling out bills and letters from our mailbox in the courtyard. In impossibly fractured French she let me know her husband's name was Karol, hence her name, and she'd been a widow for eight years. She'd come to France from Poland via the Ukraine and learned her French in the streets, present tense only, if you please. On first hearing it was incomprehensible, especially to another foreigner like me. That did not slow her down in the least.

That first day, she tugged at my arm to get me to follow her as she darted up the stairs, looking back gleefully every few minutes to make sure I hadn't run off. She insisted on giving me a tour of her tiny apartment. Everywhere, white and flowers—on the curtains, on the cloths covering the furniture, on seat cushions, on the wallpaper. Flowers and plants, fifteen years old, were lined up three deep for the mid-morning sun. I followed her in my boots; she slid along the tile floor on slippers like Pierre's, looking like an overage Sonja Henie. A few slides took her into the bedroom, where I timidly followed: miniature red, yellow, and orange Orthodox Church hand-painted Easter eggs popped up everywhere in groups of three, music boxes with dancing ballerinas, and Karol's strong Slavic face on the wall brandishing his certificate. "Ah, Madame, he was something. Thirty years on the same job. Can you believe that?" Pictures of hunters hunting. "Everybody loved him. When he died, a woman in the street asked me if it were an important person's funeral. There were many, many people and cars. 'No,' I said, 'it's my husband.'"

"Everybody came to tell me how good he was. And I see that woman on Oberkampf Street. Her husband died and she married another! They asked me to remarry too. I said, 'No! What for?' How can women do that? Not me, I couldn't."

I hoped I never had to confront that situation. So far luck had been with us. Pierre's "military service" consisted of one month of basic training outside Paris, followed by assignment to a nearby lab for the remainder of the year. The pay was negligible. Any job I could find would have to support us. While he was gone, I interviewed like crazy. I failed again and again to get an office job due to the fact that the French typewriter has four letters in the "wrong" places. *I can't type for shit, anyway.* But I succeeded in landing a job teaching English (with a New York accent) to Parisians and doing translations on the side. Through contacts at work, once his military service was over, Pierre was promised a permanent job at an observatory outside of Paris.

Tonight, bedtime for my neighbor, but not yet for me. I located my copy of Simone de Beauvoir's *Le Deuxième Sexe* and started to read, but almost immediately I heard Pierre's footsteps coming down the hallway. I jumped up to open the door. "Bonsoir," I said.

"Bonsoir," he answered, kissing me on both cheeks. He headed to the bedroom to throw down his clothes, parading past me buck naked on the way to the shower. "Show-off !" I yelled out as he passed, giving him a light slap on his rear end.

"Help! *Au secours!* I'm being attacked," he cried.

"Oh, go take your shower. I've kept your dinner warm." When he emerged from the bathroom in the long Mexican shirt he liked to sleep in, and with his wet hair slicked back, I smiled. "You're too handsome, you know?" I served him a heaping bowl of ratatouille. After he finished, he pulled me onto his lap for a quick cuddle.

"That's nice," I said. We adjourned to the daybed in the living room, cradling two glasses of cognac. He showed me how to warm it up between my hands. Again.

He stared into space. The apartment was very quiet. I didn't hear the street noise anymore. I managed to filter it out most of the time now.

"You seem preoccupied," I ventured.

"It's a problem we're having, a scientific problem, that's all." He squinted into space for a few seconds longer, slowly returning to the world of the living. "So how were your classes today? Did everyone talk like this: 'Ze rain in Spain falls mainly on ze plain'?"

"Exactly. Who told you?" I sipped my cognac before continuing. "Actually, I had to cover classes for another teacher. I had five classes today, from *faux débutantes* to advanced. Unreal. I was bouncing all over Paris. I'm beat."

When he failed to respond, I realized he wasn't listening. He was far, far away. "You must be tired, working such long hours," I said. "How about we take a trip this weekend?"

"We'll see." He picked up and flipped through the bills that had come in the daily mail.

"Or we could eat at that little vegetarian place in the Marais, the one where those stork-like waiters have rope around their waists instead of belts."

"Yes, I know you like that place. Problem is I told my mother we would stop by for a visit. She's counting on seeing us."

Not losing a beat, I continued, "Not a problem. I bet we could go to Alfortville in the afternoon and return in time—"

"Lucie!" He held up a hand to stop me from going on. He was laughing. "Please. Understand I have obligations."

I willed my tongue to be still. No point in pursuing the topic when we were both tired.

A last burning swig of our drinks and off we headed to bed. Pierre immediately fell into a deep sleep, but I lay in bed, jumpy, unsettled, unsure of what was happening.

Fitting In

So there we were, mere months after our arrival, installed in our very own railroad flat in the eleventh arrondissement, a working class neighborhood amicably shared by Arabs, Jews, Africans, Euros, and the native French people. The shops were thriving, and people thronged the streets. Our location was spectacular, trekking distance to Notre-Dame, Île de la Cité, St. Germain des Prés. Yes, the apartment was tiny, but once we purchased cheap particle board furniture, a mattress to throw on the floor, and a single bed to be used as a daybed, we were set. Fully furnished. Charming in its way.

Our big expense involved papering the ancient walls with a garish design of huge orange and brown flowers. Pierre, my husband who could fix anything, figured we could strip off the layers of old wallpaper ourselves, but underestimated how many layers a century-old building might have. After a few weeks we admitted defeat and called in workmen to finish the job. They removed the coal chute too, installed a heater, and finally, built us a bathroom. There was no way I would use that hole in the ground in the hall water closet nor wash like the French do, as we had to do in our rental, soaping up one section at a time at the kitchen sink. Pierre was forewarned: "Okay, call me an American! No pubic hairs in the kitchen sink for me! If having a toilet and a shower make me a spoiled brat, so be it. I am one."

Before long, Pierre, always outgoing and an organizer, con-structed a social life for us, managing to invite couples over for a big meal almost every week. Lord, I struggled to master the formal order of French meals: entrée (tomatoes in vinaigrette, celery remoulade, artichokes); first dish (quiche lorraine, tomato pie); second dish (boeuf bourguignon, rabbit in mus-tard sauce, mutton chops); side dishes (mashed potatoes, spinach, pasta); salad (because in France you're never too full to have salad), cheese (350 varieties); fruit; and finally, dessert (apple tart); and (whew!) coffee. Can't forget the after-dinner drink, *pousse-café*! I left the intricacies of which wine to serve when entirely to Pierre as well as the timing for before, during, and after drinks.

Once in a while I rebelled, nothing to it, and served Ameri-can pancakes and lardons on a plate. One plate. One course. Naturally, people were shocked to the marrow, but too polite most of the time to mention it. Pierre wagged his finger at me, but I could tell he, too, was amused by the display of French rigidity.

Our social circle expanded gradually: French people who had traveled or were well educated or Jewish like me, other foreign-ers with whom Pierre conversed in fluent Spanish, and various anglophones I picked up here and there. One hundred friends in the end, not one of whom I could converse with as well as I could with a fellow New Yorker standing behind me on a bus line in Flushing. The French do not believe in sharing their innermost thoughts. This is the country where you can know a person thirty years and still address them formally as "*vous*."

Surrounded by people, I yearned for a real friend.

Exiled in Paris

Crottes de chien. Wet dog doodies. Even in the ritzy neighborhood where we spent our initial months, they were everywhere.

I guess *chiens français* did not take to squatting in designated areas, and there certainly were no pooper scooper laws. Not how I pictured Paris would look. Everything seemed to hurt: my knees hurt from the constant rain, my nerves from the grayness, my brain from trying to understand why many Parisians chose to have a fancy dining room rather than a bathroom en suite.

I loved Paris in the springtime. The architecture alone made me swoon. Nevertheless, I longed to sing "Here Comes the Sun."

But once you've lived in New York, you can live anywhere. Right?

Sure, right. But lately, I didn't feel all that good; I wondered if I was happy all the way down at the bottom. A blackhead on my chin disgraced me deeply. The silk-faced ladies of the métro laughed each morning, sharp-eyed and lipless though they were. I munched on croissants, *pains au chocolat, tartes aux pommes* like anyone else except I put on five pounds. I felt unnatural and un-me. I imagined Pierre's mother muttering: *"Is she trying to embarrass my son?"* I decided to exchange my faded student rags for chic Parisian ones and shop for sleek shoes to replace overworked work boots.

One Saturday, I entered a little store around the corner on Boulevard Voltaire—such beautiful clothes in the window. I tried on one orange and brown outfit, boldly Parisian, with its fringed vest and long fringed slit up the side of the straight skirt. Perfect fit, but I wanted to see what else was in the store. However, when I asked to try on another outfit, the saleswoman became quite agitated. Fine. I paid for the Thanksgiving-colored outfit and headed over to a shoe store, hoping to find brown knee-length boots to replace the Fryes I'd left behind. Another misstep as I tried on multiple pairs of boots. The shoe salesman, livid, chased me from the store, shouting, "Madame, you're making fun of me!" A humiliating experience.

That's when I realized it would forever be the destiny of my right big toe to be wedged in sideways, wrinkled and wriggling, in stylish French shoes. I was between sizes! I was stuck. I knew it. I began to suspect why.

I wanted to scream every time I talked to the mother of a French girl I knew in New York City. She rattled on about her daughter: witty, clever, creative.

And me? I shrieked inside, while nodding politely over tea in china teacups. How could she have known she had hit upon two of my small vanities? How could she have suspected that me too, I'm funny. Me too, I'm intuitive. Me too, I'm a person! To know that, she would have had to know me. That might have taken her another six weeks or six years or forever, depending on her astuteness. *Eh bien,* voilà Frustration #1 of my self-imposed exile: *Nobody knew me.*

I had to start from scratch with everyone from the concierge to my mother-in-law, with no allusions to a common past allowed. I couldn't speak my own language. Even my husband had only known me since 1973. I began to doubt I had a past or a personality. A challenge, yes. But how I ached to find another again to whom I could speak swiftly, intimately, who would not judge me on the basis of what I was wearing or even what I was saying, who knew who I was—a person I didn't have to prove anything to. I pitifully called upon a name from my past, my best friend since junior high school—*Oh, Wendy, where are you? I need you. . . .*

More than merely missing her, I missed what she did for me, the subtle ways in which childhood friends flatter each other, fatten each other's egos, fill in the missing lines of our self-esteem. How could I live without this? What could I do to glue myself together in the meantime, assuming that sooner or later raw need succeeded in finding me new friends to replace the old?

I continued walking up toward République, glancing in shoe stores, never daring to enter.

Between classes the next day, I strolled along the Seine, perusing the book stalls. I stumbled upon a copy of Céline's *Voyage au Bout de la Nuit* and made a purchase. Sitting in Tuileries Gardens, I got swallowed up by the text and continued reading that night at home. Céline describes a Midnight Cowboyish visit to my hometown (if New York City is ever a hometown to anyone). Besides the fact that he has no money, no friends, no place to study, and instead is still sick with malarial fever, he identifies other reasons for his physical and mental depression:

> *"It was more a matter of changing old habits—once again I had to learn to recognize new faces in new surroundings, new ways of speaking and of lying. Laziness is almost as strong a force as life. The banality of this new farce you*

*must now play overwhelms you and it actually takes much
more cowardice than courage to begin it all again."*

Though for the moment we were free of malaria symptoms,
Pierre and I started out in Paris with no money, no friends, no
place to stay. I liked Céline right off. I suspected that ill-fitting
shoes weren't totally responsible for my malaise. Laziness, that
made sense. The farce of trying to adapt and assimilate was getting me down, which might explain my mostly acrid comments
on a lovely spot of Earth. I struggled to understand why a fervid
Francophile like me, speaking textbook French since I was thirteen, with countless predilections for things French, leading up
to my marriage to a Frenchman, should reveal myself mostly in
excremental visions and deprecatory remarks on the fairer
French sex. Was it only my naturally sarcastic New York soul that
caused me to snip and snipe at French mores?

I removed my journal from my tote bag and looked at last
weekend's musings:

*I sit in a typical French glass-enclosed sidewalk café and
sneak sidelong glances at the perfectly erect, proper,
haughty-faced patrons seated to either side of me. I, too, sit
stiff-backed, trying not to look too apologetic for my
synthetic garment-district jacket with its cheap fur, and
watch the passersby, poker-faced, occasionally turning to
my partner with a wry observation (eyebrow raised, nose in
air, lip slightly curled) on what-just-went-by. 'Atroce!'*

Now as I read, what I realized was this: that the glass-enclosed
sidewalk café was the perfect metaphor for the French. They were
always inside the café, and you were always outside. They talked to

you through the glass. It was hard to get at what they were saying, what they were meaning, what they actually looked like—because of the glare and distortion of the glass and because of the distance. They liked it that way; they even preferred it. They sat there quite perfect. They'd spent, after all, incredible amounts of money on their get-up. But at night, when no one was around, they went home to a dinner taken in from the window ledge, where to pee one had to venture down the hall or out the back. Pubic hairs in the kitchen sink; Dior in the métro. They lived for that one moment in the café spotlight—for they were the ones who were onstage and being watched, and not us poor beggars passing by.

Being a New Yorker did not help me here. Frustration #2: *I didn't know these games.* I didn't like to play dress-up. In fact, I didn't like to play games and I had no desire to learn how.

And I now identified Frustration #3: *I didn't like what I saw.* I felt excluded and not at all sure I wanted to be included. I inhabited a cultural no-man's-land. Céline says:

"That's what it is, exile, a foreign land: the merciless observation of existence as it really is, during those long lucid hours unique in the experience of human time, when the customs of the preceding country have abandoned you before the other new customs have had the chance to take you over, to desensitize you."

"They" say two things are always true: One, you can't run away from yourself; Two, you can't go home again (of course not, you're already there.) Paris was just the same game, tied up in different-colored ribbons and funny-patterned paper that I had presented myself for Christmas as unique and special. Just life, deprived of the accustomed wrappings. We see inside the box and we don't like it; we see the outside and say it's wrong, it's phony and artificial. We don't want to wrap things up that way. We also don't want to see what's inside really. With the old wrappings, the old habits, our ways of life were okay. They didn't shock, they didn't seem like lying. But now, to give all that up, that's hard, that's asking a lot. And to learn new techniques for disguising? How boring. What a farce indeed! But the alternative, to continue to view the game, without any trimmings, to be alone in this blinding perception and unable to turn to a friend and communicate? How many are courageous enough? Even Beckett had to write to alleviate the pain.

What does the exile do? Assimilates, of course. Despite his initial resistance, which can last weeks, months, or a lifetime. Céline discloses his motivation:

> "Another country, other people around you, moving about in a rather bizarre fashion . . . a few small vanities less, a few vanities dissipated, your pride that suddenly has no foundation, no longer finds a lie, a familiar echo to support it, and you don't need more—your head begins to spin, your doubts make you dizzy, infinity opens just for you—a ridiculous little infinity—and you fall right in."

Frustration #4: *Did I have to give in and become like everybody else?* How did one go about melting into the pot, and did one ever melt all the way down? Why did certain people melt, others blend, and others stick stubbornly to the sides of the pot? Personally, would I assimilate tomorrow or always be "that funny little foreign lady?"

I wanted to be different; I wanted to be like everybody else.

Would I end by conforming, by renouncing my status as exile? Would I stay and call it home?

Worn out with worrying, I taught my final class of the day and walked slowly home with these weighty themes on my brain. I was one lonely soul.

ele

Unhappy Faces

I commuted to my job as the French do, back and forth,
back and forth until Friday night rolled around. What did I
see? Unhappy. Unhappy faces in the métro. Women's faces. I had
little sympathy for them. Most bodies were well put together,
matching. Unruly auburn hair with exactly the same tones and
textures as the long-haired fur coat around the shoulders, same
as the shoulder bag, the shoes, the scarf. Standing by the door,
pointed nails curved around a pole. What did they buy first—the
coat, the scarf, the hair?

Another, a secretary, in dark blue jeans, Cardin shirtwaist,
silver slave bracelets, charms, rings, jewelry dingle-dangling
from legs, arms, neck, ears, nose. She no doubt earned a pittance
and dined on a single hard-boiled egg and expresso for lunch.

An older woman with a bright paint job—sprayed, greased,
and oiled—sat flipping through *Elle*. I imagined her husband to
be a civil servant, perhaps a railway engineer for RATP.

Poorer women, barelegged and unshaven, knitted away like
machines, erect, barely moving their arms. Others were intent
on true love photo mags or crossroad puzzles. I spotted a serious
student engrossed in *Le Monde* sitting next to a bag lady (a uni-
versal constant), who was juggling wine bottles and dirty socks
while carrying on a heady conversation inside her head and out.

Bodies thin and strong. Skin clear like steaming milk poured into a white porcelain bowl. Hair framing the face. And hard looks. Even the young looked hard. Sharp eyes for fellow passengers. Beneath twenty-year-old eyes, yellow puffs—an all-nighter, debauchery, laundry at 2:00 a.m.? Tired masks of faces, lines hardened in place. The worst was the mouth. Even a sexy young thing with a nice body and good skin often sported a tight-ass mouth.

I concentrated on working my lips together silently, like rolling tobacco, puffing them out sensually, all the while visualizing *soft, soft, soft. Look at me,* I cried silently. The girl who looked like she hadn't slept in a month approached. I thought: *I won't yell if you barely brush my elbow.* What I said: "Of course, sit down next to me. Wait, I'll move my bag." *Cause I'm soft and easy.* She opted for another seat!

True, I was obsessed with lips and the way they revealed character. I jumped at the sight of a pair of full-bodied lips belonging to a woman on the seat opposite, in the open for all the lipless wonders to gape at. Did the others regard it as an indecent display? Me, I rejoiced to see lips (and exulted in knowing mine are nice too). I stared at the Black woman two seats over, the Hispanic or Arab man sitting with her, and any other foreigner I could identify. Usually the rest of the body appeared softer, looser, less controlled. I feared Pierre's lips were on the thin side.

I concentrated on being soft and easy as I slid out of my folding seat, letting it slam back against the wall with a bang of rebellion. My stop—Bastille—beckoned. I forced open the doors and jumped out, spun around, and stuck out my tongue at all of them.

I think I'm regressing.

꿈

Mme Karol Visits

Mme Karol tended to tap at our door, and if I wasn't quick enough, she'd turn the knob and sneak up on us. "What are you doing?"

"Nothing much," I answered one night, gathering up my books and signaling Pierre to put his away. "What's new? Come with me into the kitchen, we'll make some tea."

"No, no. I decided to bring you something."

"Would you prefer tea or tisane?" I asked.

She hesitated, held up her index finger, and ran back to her apartment, returning seconds later with a gift plus the usual chocolate, cookies, and lumps of sugar.

As her "children," Pierre and I benefitted from the following: stale matzos on all Jewish holidays, her homemade borscht and fruitcake, fresh flowers every weekend from the country home of her best friends, gifts of plants, and tonight, prewar curtain material, a nubby, creamy Egyptian cotton.

"It's not nice from the street to see only one curtain on each window," she said on that occasion, "and I know you're only starting out."

"The material's lovely!" I kissed her on both wrinkled cheeks and Pierre gave her a hug. I itched to start sewing immediately. I'd give our skimpy red Fiberglass curtains to one less fortunate.

Mme K loved to sit and teach us languages, often six at a time. She rattled off words in the original language and translated for us, hoping to impart some of the original force of what she was recounting. "Is that Polish?" I asked. Pierre leaned forward to hear the answer. "No, what do you think? It's Russian. Polish is ——. And Ukrainian is ——or sometimes——." We learned little, but she had a good time. That night we learned *spitsky, pepinishky, babishky,* and started ranting and rhyming. Of course, she laughed the longest.

She liked to tell dirty jokes too but warned us half-seriously that we could do *that* when we were alone. "When I first arrived in Paris, people did much worse than that, in the métro, right in front of you. It wasn't nice. Why do they do that?" She winked, feeling naughty, outrageous, very proud, and in general thoroughly delighted with herself. She threw us one of her take-me-or-leave-me looks.

Any time she saw her "children" baggy-eyed, she'd pick herself up and trot off down the hall to bed.

She was, hands down, the best neighbor I ever had, the best entertainment, easily beating out any of my friends, roommates, or lovers.

Alfortville

"Why don't we ever travel, Pierre? I have vacation days coming—"

Saturday, we were riding the métro to have lunch with Pierre's mother. He interrupted me, "Yes, you are right. I am working too much. I even made a silly mistake this week in a calculation."

Impossible. I waited for more.

"So shameful," he said, staring at his feet and shaking his head ever so slightly from side to side. "How about I plan a surprise for you? Next weekend."

I jumped up and down like a little (American) kid. The other passengers paid me no mind, except for one Simone de Beauvoir lookalike who let the tiniest smile play upon her lips before turning her attention back to her notebook.

Had I made her proud? *If so, score one for Mme Bonhomme and one for womankind.*

Mamie was a little French lady, four-foot-eight at most, with straight brown hair, rounded body, dowdy clothes. Her claim to fame: a flawless complexion, smooth like a baby's behind. And she was almost fifty years old. How I envied that skin. She was a good soul too. Never breathed a word against me. She reminded me of Edith in the TV show *All in the Family*: sweet but dim.

The three of us spent a rather boring afternoon seated around the table in the dining room—there was no living room. Mamie was a good cook, of course. Lunch was not a trial of any sort. Her rhubarb pie was not only delicious but topped with a nice firm crust. Since French desserts are not as sweet as American ones, I saw no need to deny myself a second slice.

"Let me show you my garden," she suggested after we cleared the lunch dishes.

Pierre and I picked ourselves up and followed her out back. We walked dutifully through the rows and rows of vegetables and flowers, each one overflowing with healthy plants and bursting with reds and greens and whites. How did she manage to take care of this large garden and still have the energy to work as a nurse's aide and clean houses on the side? Tending to the garden must have been backbreaking work. She was definitely amazing in her own way.

We tramped back to the dining room table and politely turned down the offer for more coffee.

I asked Pierre, "On the way back, why don't we take a walk through the town for once?" Each time we'd visited, I'd noticed a semi-lively commercial district with stores of every stripe. "We could use a lampshade to cover the bald bulb in the living room lamp."

He chose not to promise any deviation from his usual trajectory. Instead, we were condemned for the next forty minutes to listen to Mamie's complaints about her upstairs neighbor whose ten cats were stinking up the stairway.

Before we left, Pierre asked about his father. Papi, a one-time alcoholic, had abandoned both of them years before. He'd shacked up with his drunken mistress and fathered two sons.

Poor Mamie had had a breakdown, forcing her to ship Pierre off to live in the mountains of Lorraine with her mother, sisters, brother, uncles, aunts, and cousins. When he turned eight, at the urging of her social worker, she brought him back to live with her in Paris. By then she was a nurse's aide, working nights at the local hospital. Left on his own, he'd admitted to me schoolwork became his only refuge.

Papi had since reformed his ways. He'd taken custody of the younger children and become a leader at the French version of AA. Mamie confirmed what we'd long suspected: Papi was a regular visitor, an overnight guest, often bringing along his young sons whom Mamie pampered. She did their laundry, mended their socks, and baked individual miniature apple pies for each one.

"Don't let them take advantage, Maman," Pierre counselled.

Mamie shrugged. To me she whispered, "He's the father of Pierre." The only man in her life.

ele

Honfleur

The next Saturday morning, on a brilliant June day, we drove to Honfleur for an adventure, as Pierre had promised.

He'd borrowed a car from work. I didn't even know he could do that! Honfleur turned out to be a lovely little town northwest of Paris. We spent the day dreamily watching the fishermen at the Vieux Bassin harbor unload their catches, dining on fresh seafood, snapping pictures of the light at different points of the day. It was easy to see why Monet and the Impressionists favored this spot. I loved the architecture, the sixteenth century buildings. After we walked the length and breadth of the town, we'd pretty much exhausted all there was to do. Our *pension* turned out to be rather basic, clean but not a place we wanted to linger in. At night after dinner, we made our way over to an authentic-looking pub decorated with seafaring paraphernalia inside and out: anchors, fishing nets, scrimshaw.

"Tiens, voilà un marin!" announced a big fellow at the bar as we entered. He'd had a few. Pierre steered me away from the bar to a dark table in the corner.

"What does that mean?" I whispered.

"It's a local greeting. Like, 'Look who's here!'"

"Oh, but—"

The elderly waitress came over and we ordered two beers. Pierre was clenching and unclenching his fists. What now? Why wasn't he following his usual script chatting up the waitress? I couldn't wait to tell my friends and family back home about this overnight trip to a city I hadn't seen before. We hadn't talked to any residents yet. I hoped to have a couple of anecdotes to recount. The waitress deposited the drinks at our table. I sipped my beer. Refreshing after a long day outdoors.

Pierre pulled on my arm and signaled that we should leave. "Already? I haven't finished."

He darted a look at the bar. I did the same and noticed the big fellow and his buddies staring at us. "They don't like tourists here, huh?"

"They don't like kids like us, from the city, with spending money," Pierre explained.

"Oh."

Pierre got to his feet, slapped down a few francs on the table, and headed for the door. "Dammit, Lucie. C'mon!"

As we made our way to the door, the lead drunk climbed off his stool. He was not much taller than Pierre but built like a linebacker, more solid than most French men I'd seen. His arms looked as big as Pierre's whole leg. He planted himself between Pierre and the door. "Not going to buy me a drink?" he asked, punching Pierre on the arm. Two of his buddies rose off their stools and stood behind him. The bartender/owner watched the scene with interest.

Merde!

Pierre smiled at the men, turned to the bartender, and ordered drinks for everyone, meaning us and them. No one else was in the bar.

"What kind of boat do you have? What's the catch like these days? I go sailing once in a while but haven't been fishing since I visited my father on Île de Ré." Pierre bravely kept up the banter. The lead guy slapped him on the back as the punchline to a joke he told. More drinks arrived. I could cut the tension with a knife. What could I do but stand patiently by the door, chewing on my cuticles, too nervous to get any closer? Could Pierre get us out of here alive?

Out of the blue, he had a brilliant inspiration. He started singing the refrain to *"Auprès de ma Blonde,"* the French national drinking song, and within minutes, the guys had their arms around each other's shoulders, swaying back and forth. The words are simple: At the side of my blonde, it feels good to sleep. The refrains went on and on with no indication they would ever stop. I watched as a bead of sweat made its way down the back of Pierre's neck.

As a verse ended, Pierre threw me an apologetic look and I heard him say, "My wife is expecting a little one—"

News to me! I immediately slouched and stuck out my belly.

"—and I have to take her back to rest now."

I smiled weakly, convinced my sundress looked nothing like a maternity outfit. Why hadn't I worn my white Mexican blouse? Or munched on more pastries on the way over? The big fellow gave me the once-over and conferred with his buddies. "When is she due? She's awfully tiny. And what are you having anyway?"

My math skills being what they are, I abstained from responding. Pierre mumbled something that sounded like much too soon. "Yeah, Pierre, what are we having?" I asked. I couldn't resist.

"A little matelot," he responded, and suddenly the temperature in the bar cooled, and the four men sang a refrain from a French children's song I'd heard on the radio: *Ohé, ohé, matelot,* they sang, on and on.

At long last, the big man looked me over, winked, and gave Pierre a friendly shove that almost landed him on the floor. We waved goodbye to our new friends and beat it the hell out of there.

Once outside, Pierre asked, "How do you say, *animosité*? Those guys were bored, out of work probably. Best to humor them and leave." I laced my arm in his, snuggled up against him, and let him guide me back to our pension. "Same word," I answered. "Good thing I have you around to protect me. You played that beautifully." He beamed. *Men are easy to figure out. The sex would be great tonight.*

Sunday we left after lunch. I wanted to stay longer. Of course.

When we came home, I struggled to keep the momentum going. The next weekend I suggested, "Pierre, why don't we see what's playing at the independent movie theatre on Boulevard Richard Lenoir? I'd love to see another Spanish film. There's one starring Geraldine Chaplin. I'll go look it up—"

"Not tonight, Luce. I have some work to do for a presentation I'm giving."

"On a Sunday?"

Pierre shook his head reprovingly. "Listen, why don't you give a friend a call?" He began packing up his attaché case.

Hmm. What an idea! Even if I'd had a friend like that, receptive to last-minute invitations, she'd probably have lined up two *vernissages* to attend at two different galleries, dinner reserved at Le Drugstore, followed by a concert at the Musée de Cluny, a ballet, or an intimate soirée. Who were my friends? Where were my friends? The other teachers at the language school were single and hung out together, never thinking to invite me to their get-togethers.

Pierre proceeded to the front door where he slipped on his shoes. "Why not make another cassette tape for your mother? She'll like that. Say hello for me, okay?" And with that, he was out the door, and I was left facing another day of lackluster house-keeping punctuated by breaks where I'd endeavor to scribble down the titles of books I would never get around to writing.

Greek Night

*P*ierre must have gotten my message because he scheduled a rendezvous with a couple he knew from work. I was psyched to be going to hear Georges Moustaki, a Greek folksinger the French called their own. The concert was all I had hoped, but even better was the reception I got while strolling through the lobby at intermission. Two different men came running over to me, jabbering in Greek. I smiled tolerantly, pantomimed that no, I didn't speak Greek, and yes, I knew I looked Greek. They did not give up easily, and the more they insisted, the more their chatter sounded like sweet talk.

No one ever figured me for an American. Their stereotypical American woman was more or less a California girl: statuesque, blonde, blue-eyed. I didn't come close. Greek, yes. Italian, usually. Portuguese, occasionally. American, never.

Keeping with the Greek theme, we headed over to a Greek restaurant. Greeks were my weakness—the other wife's too! Flirting never hurt anyone, right? We carried on with the two bronze-colored, dark-bearded waiters, daring to flash our eyes, boobs, mini-skirted legs. These guys were broad-shouldered and a bit beefy, a sharp contrast to our slender mates. In moments like these, I almost wished I weren't married.

"You meet us later, okay? We bring more ouzo," whispered my waiter. He dared to reach out and touch my hair.

I playfully pushed him away. "Not allowed, young fellow. You must behave." I licked my lips. The husbands remained oblivious, engrossed in scribbling equations on their dinner napkins. The food was scrumptious, the background music straight out of Zorba the Greek, and all in all, we had quite a titillating evening. At home, I mounted the Moustaki poster Pierre bought me on the door of our closet, the better to stare at. From then on, whenever Pierre and I did what Joni Mitchell calls "the goat dance," I pictured myself surrounded by the young studs in the Greek restaurant. *Naughty! Naughty!*

Métro-Boulot-Dodo

*D*espite our two recent outings, I sensed life grinding to a halt. Just a rough patch? We were twenty-four (me) and twenty-two (him). Perhaps I should have expected a certain degree of immaturity to be built into the marriage.

Pierre was a good husband, I had to admit. He took care of everything, buying an apartment for us, paying the bills, and picking out most of the furniture. I had no idea what things cost or how much money we had.

Our home was in a great location. We both had jobs. The fact that we had people to socialize with was almost entirely due to his efforts.

Unhappy. Unhappier. Unhappiest. Who said I couldn't conjugate?

I stared at him as he picked out his clothes for the workday. He was a bit of a stranger. Our frequent heated "discussions" left me gasping for breath and him clutching his stomach.

"Ce n'est pas un reproche," he claimed, as he itemized my many faults. "You're perfect."

Tell me another! Apparently, I could not cook or clean like his mother, nor manage much of anything on my own. Everything I did was, in his eyes, "half-assed."

We arose in the morning, hopped on the métro to work, came home, ate, argued, then headed for bed. The French have a name for this syndrome: *métro-boulot-dodo* (train, job, beddy-bye). In other words, what we Americans called the rat race or the daily grind. Blah town, I called it. I hadn't changed. Why had he? I thought I was marrying a poet. Instead, a nitpicking, carrot-up-the-ass scientist had moved in. I wondered if our troubles and the constant bickering were partially my fault. . . .

Perhaps the responsibility of being an adult, married with debts, worried him? From the moment we landed in France he'd been preoccupied, overly cautious, unable to relax and have fun. The city of Paris was spread out before us with other European cities at our very doorstep. Yes, we had to earn a living, but I wanted to have fun.

I picked up a copy of Gail Sheehy's *Passages* in a bookstore that stocked English language books and started reading it on the métro. Silly me! I thought I only had to worry about marrying a man like my father—conservative, adventure-adverse, withdrawn, and withholding. Meanwhile I'd married my mother, queen of the double message. Ha! The joke was on me. Who knew that was even possible?

My first class of the day was in a trendy area I hadn't been to before. The students were pleasant middle-aged secretaries and a few male accounting clerks taking advantage of their employer's free English lessons. All beginners with little to no English. They were going to require a ton of energy from me. Forbidden to speak French on penalty of being fired, I became the Marcel Marceau of language teachers. It was like talking to aliens. My only fear, the *faux débutante*, he or she who had picked up a few words and phrases here and there, along with faulty grammar, an atrocious accent, and other bad habits I'd have a helluva time correcting.

From my antics, the class understood they were waiting in

line at a bank. When they paused in their playacting and looked to me, I supplied the proper words enabling them to communicate with the teller. "What do you want to do in the bank?" I asked them. A student stuck out her arm and then pulled it sharply back. "Oh, you want to *withdraw* some money? Repeat after me, class: "I'd like to withdraw some money. And you in the first row, why are you in the bank?" The older woman mimed counting out francs and centimes and handing them to the teller. "Yes, you're making a *deposit*." A joker in the back of the room jumped up, brandishing a toy gun. "Oh no, class, Roger's *robbing* the bank." That was good for a few laughs.

After we acted out our scenario, I wrote the new vocabulary on the blackboard for them to copy. Together we fabricated a little story about our day at the bank, using our new words, and read it aloud. We practiced perfecting our accents. All in all, it was a good effective method for teaching a foreign language, but after eight months of pantomime, I confessed to being rather bored by the whole thing.

With class over, I grabbed a lamb souvlaki from a stand outside, ate my lunch, determined to soak up at least a few rays of the bashful sun, and climbed back on the métro to travel to my two other classes of the day. Before I knew it, it would be time to head home. I almost dreaded spending another evening there alone with Pierre. *Where did my French lover go?* I felt so restless. If I didn't do something quick, depression and desperation would surely follow.

Self-preservation kicked in. "*Hard-hearted Hannah*," played through my mind. I realized I'd better get a baby out of this marriage. Conventional wisdom: Have your first child before you turn thirty. By the time I got to that stage with someone else, I might be too old. I knew a baby wouldn't fix things. But I'd always wanted to be a mother and be extra loving and affectionate to my child; in other words, mother him or her as I had yearned to be mothered.

On my way home, I stepped back into the bookstore and interrupted the conversation of two beautifully color-coordinated clerks. "Do you have a book on raising a baby?" I inquired. The thinner clerk, the one whose platinum-colored hair was swept into a perfect French twist, tossed her gauzy black scarf over her shoulder, and with a huff, led me to a back corner. "Take this," she ordered, laying a book, *How to Parent*, by American psychologist Fitzhugh Dodson, in my arms. I paid, and walked out, content. I had a plan. I just had to work out the finer points.

Bastille Day,
July 14, 1975

*P*ierre and I hung out our windows watching the parade and throwing confetti down to the street. What ringside seats! Every parade or demonstration in Paris passed right under our windows as the crowds marched down Rue de la Roquette all the way from the Bastille to Père Lachaise cemetery. How lucky were we?! Thousands in the streets, celebrating.

We were still young. We should have been down in the streets, demonstrating our solidarity with the labor unions, the political parties, the masses, while singing the French socialist anthem, "L'Internationale," with that phrase that I loved—"*la lutte finale*" (the last fight).

I looked up from my journal the next night to ask, "Pierre, why don't we ever talk?"

"What is it now?" he asked, sliding his bookmark into the magazine he'd been reading at the kitchen table. He then tucked the magazine neatly into his attaché case.

I went into the kitchen and started to dry the supper dishes stacked near the sink. "Well, it's just—"

"Can't you try to relax?" he asked as he positioned himself

behind me. He began to massage my shoulders with those strong fingers of his.

"Me? I relax plenty. But when I come home I'd like to . . . ahh, that feels good. Don't ever stop."

"Sit down and let me work out these tight muscles."

I did as the doctor ordered. "I guess I just feel lonely and alone. Sometimes."

"You're adjusting, that's all. Did I have it easy in the US? At least you speak the language. More or less." He pounded his fists lightly on my back, a signal that the massage was over. He kissed the back of my neck before moving off to the bedroom to get ready for bed. I glanced at the clock: 9:30 p.m.

I followed him into the bedroom. "Yeah, your English was pretty pathetic when I first met you. Luckily you heeded age-old wisdom and took a native to your bed. Does wonders for your accent!"

"Your French is much better than my English was. You worry too much."

"Teaching English all day long and speaking it at home doesn't help."

"Why don't you speak French to me?"

"I dunno. I guess by now it's just a habit to speak English to you."

I watched him taking off his clothes, putting on his Mexican shirt, going to the closet and picking out his outfit for the next day, lining up his shoes, socks, underwear. He trotted off to the bathroom to wash up. I positioned myself outside the bathroom door. "So do you think we should try having a baby soon? For the new year? Remember 1976?!"

No answer. I could hear him brushing his teeth and spitting

into the bowl. Peeing. I stepped aside as he exited the bathroom and trotted after him into the bedroom. "What are you doing exactly?" he asked.

I shrugged and flung off my clothes. I put on my sexy or-ange-and-black nightgown with the spaghetti straps that I once wore outside to a peace march, and climbed into bed right after him. "Let's make a baby!" I said, excitedly running my hands over his body. "In a few days it will be 1976. You promised!"

He grabbed my hands. "Tempting, but I need to be in shape for tomorrow's budget meeting. Hold this thought for the week-end." He kissed me chastely on the cheek and rolled over facing the wall. I listened for the start of his rhythmic breathing.

Foiled again!

If we only had a television. . . .

~ele~

Le Réveillon,
December 31, 1975

*T*he French celebrated New Year's Eve. Guess how? By stuffing their faces with shellfish: *oursins, huitres,* and my favorite dish and Mamie's specialty, *coquilles Saint-Jacques.*

We crowded around our tiny table on Rue de la Roquette with Mamie and Papi and his two sons. Pierre's parents were apparently hanging out together that night. Dating? Pierre, half amused, referred to them as *"les bohémiens."* The boys were quiet and watchful. They shared Pierre's fine features; he took little interest in them. I was pretty sure he uttered not one word to either of them the entire evening.

When they departed, I asked, "Pierre, do you hate your father? You must."

He responded with a quizzical look.

"I mean, he deserted your mother and you—"

"Yes, I know the story, thank you."

"Well?" I persisted.

"I don't let it rule my life."

We cleaned up the kitchen and headed to bed where I turned Pierre's face to me. "Don't close me out. Please." I stroked his arm. "Who took care of you when your mother had her breakdowns? You said a neighbor brought you dinner each night. Social services should have intervened. You were only eight and—"

"Where is this going? I'm tired. I need to sleep."

"I'm trying to understand your relationship. I mean you two don't talk, don't even look at each other. It's sad. He must be proud of how far you've gone: two academic degrees, fluency in Spanish and English—"

Pierre sat up in bed, shaking me off like a dog with fleas. "Look, Little Miss-Has-to-Know-Everything. Can you drop it?" He headed into the kitchen for a glass of water.

"You threw him out of the apartment that time he was drunk. You told me you shoved him—"

"Luce, enough! Spare me your textbook psychology." He climbed back into bed.

"I'm sorry," I whispered in his ear. "So sorry."

I couldn't get a good fix on his father. He was the one person in France whose accent, a kind of Breton brogue, made comprehension for me impossible. I nodded vigorously if he said anything to me. *Eight years of high school and college French down the drain.*

He was big and burly, good looking in a blue-collar way; Pierre did not resemble him in the least. He and Mamie were two country bumpkins come to Paris for opportunity. He knocked her up soon after they met working in a hotel, did the honorable thing by marrying her. A vet of the French war in Indochina, he drank too much and deserted Mamie after a few years. My guess was that there was too big an intellectual gap between them. Pierre definitely got his brains from his father. Even as a child, Pierre caught on quickly, realizing his mother had her limits, intellectual and emotional.

"You had to be the man in the house, and you were only a child," I mouthed, full of pity. Pierre had deep emotional scars from this childhood. I'd always believed I was the one person in the world who could make it all better.

His father certainly never tried to make it up to Pierre. I refused to forgive him. And later, I did not forgive the hand-me-down onesies he brought in a plastic bag for our baby.

I was not too proud to use them, but c'mon, no present for his first grandson?

My Goal for the Year,
1976

*T*omber *enceinte.* To fall pregnant. The French love to fall (*tomber*). For example, you can't simply faint. You have to *fall* into the apples. Such colorful language. A whole picture story. And *enceinte*: within the confines of. Confined? Imprisoned? For a little while anyway.

Back to me. Pregnant. I was incredibly excited but I missed my mother. No one to *kvell* with me. I let a coworker know I was going to have a baby. She asked, "Is that a good thing?" and waited to gauge my reaction.

I was appalled. How could it not be? I was married, healthy, certainly old enough. I wagged my head up and down vigorously until she squeaked out a thin "*Félicitations!*"

No gushing about the baby to come?

The French, I soon gathered, seemed to have a rather unromantic view of the process of giving birth. Strangers, neighbors, other friends looked me over. "*Courage!*" they all said, patting me on the arm. Not all that encouraging. No kissing, no exulting; no fantasizing about the baby and what he or she'd be like, who they'd resemble, what a freaking miracle it all was.

Disappointed but undeterred, I knitted in silence every evening: tiny hats, sweaters, pants, booties.

Pierre surprised me by wholeheartedly embracing what was happening. Before supper one night he took me on his lap and asked, "Do you know how beautiful you are?" He was not in the least put off by my changing body. I was a bit incredulous—I couldn't imagine an American man, not any I had known in New York, Colorado, or Mexico, acting that way. Points for Pierre.

I was dying to tell him what happened that morning. "This guy was following me as I walked back from the Engels' bakery. I stopped and pretended to look in a window, hoping he'd pass, but he circled around me. You know how I 'carry' all in front? He stopped in his tracks when he spotted the bump."

"You do have a cute little tush and those great legs. . . ."

Impatient, I stopped his roving hands. "No, Pierre, listen. What did he do? Was he the least bit embarrassed to *draguer* a pregnant woman? Eight months pregnant?!"

"Let's see." Pierre assumed his Thinker's pose. "He asked you to take a walk with him?"

"Yes! What is that about?"

"It's, how you say, a pick-up line?"

"Huh?"

"The man says, *'Tu veux faire un bout de chemin avec moi?'* If the girl is willing, they walk away together. Quite civilized."

"Really?" I stand up. "Isn't that what you say to a prostitute?" He shrugged.

"In my book he was a . . . creep. A pervert. I could hear him mumbling a few words and it sure wasn't an apology."

"Oh, my poor innocent little American," he said, approaching to give me a hug. I shook him off. He backed off a few paces, looked around the tiny living room and finally back at me. He rubbed his belly, attempting to be comical. "What's for dinner, wifey?" he said in his best imitation American accent I normally found quite funny.

"Is that all you have to say? You are content to let me loose in a world with characters like this prowling around? Why aren't you outraged? Come to think of it, why can you never show any emotion?" I was on a tear now, hormones raging.

Pierre frowned and walked away into the kitchen. He started pulling vegetables out of the fridge. I followed right behind him and slammed my hand down on the counter for added dramatic effect. "Look at me when I'm talking to you!" I shrieked. Pierre whipped around and grabbed my wrists tightly. He was clenching his jaw. "Pierre. . . !" I said his name as a warning. I was a bit scared. What had I done? He looked like he wanted to throttle me. After a few seconds he dropped my wrists and headed for the bathroom, locking the door. My breath was coming in choppy—there was not enough air. I leaned against the wall, waiting.

Pierre eventually emerged from the bathroom with a sour look on his face. Another stomachache? He put on his jacket and walked toward the door. "Where are you going? What about dinner?"

"Leave me alone, Lucie," he said, and headed out.

Now what had I done?

I survived an unprecedented heat wave. My ankles ballooned out. Week after week my students observed my condition, saw me wearing the same three maternity dresses over and over, but never congratulated me. I was embarrassed to acknowledge my pregnancy. *Embarazada* as the Mexicans would have it. I was definitely the elephant in the room—or my baby was. In my free time I read about the stages of fetal development and suffered from every imaginary complication in between doctor visits. An American woman had tipped me off to the best obstetrician in the world, Dr. V, the guy who took over the Lamaze team, and with Pierre's supplementary insurance, we had no problem affording him. Any time I brought up my irrational fears, he'd shut me down with simple phrase: "Madame, I have delivered a gazillion babies."

Mostly, I remained impatient and eager to meet my child. Hey, I knew what I was doing was *"extraordinaire."* Any woman could have a baby? No, what I was doing had never been done before.

All the while I plotted. Got to hold on till baby is born, put up with Pierre until then.

∽ele∼

June 1, 1976

I wrote long letters to Wendy, my one New York friend who truly loved getting mail from me and actually responded.

Chère amie,

Completely unnerved by the drilling going on underneath my window—they're installing telephone wires or something. Anyway Pierre says the city of Paris, on one pretext or another, regularly digs up the streets every six months or so.

The weather is getting to everyone lately, heavy oppressive skies which clear for a few minutes of sun or which drizzle half-heartedly for a half hour.

Oh, for a good energetic New York City downpour!

June 16, 1976

A letter from Wendy arrived:

Luce, my sons and even my husband are excited about Op Sail which is happening in a few weeks. Do you realize how many square riggers will be present in New York Harbor and from how many countries? They'll be a ticker tape parade of course. I know you're a bit removed from everything over here, but you do realize we're celebrating the US Bicentennial? A shame you have to miss it, but in your condition, best to avoid plane travel. Maybe you can watch it on TV. Do any of your neighbors have one? If not, I'll try to send you a few pictures in my next letter.

In the meantime, take it easy. Knitting is fine. Keep off your feet if your ankles are swollen! Just your luck to experience a rare Parisian heat wave when you're nine months pregnant.

I penned a response immediately:

Wendy, please take lots of pictures, especially of the tall ships. They're my absolute favorite. If baby Milou is born before, I intend to tell him the Bicentennial celebration is all about him.

Pierre, who is somewhat of a sailor, you know, would love for me to say, "Why don't you take a little junket to New

York? I can manage fine here by myself." But hey, that is not happening. I'll need all the help I can get to birth this baby the Lamaze way. Papa Pierre has an essential role—spraying Evian water down my dry throat between contractions and capturing all the activity and excitement on his camera. And he better not forget that.

Time for a midmorning nap. Have fun. Hope I don't disgrace the Lamaze team by howling in pain!

Milou O'Clock

(Finally)

Bulletin: Milou heading south. Deep south.
Letmein. Letmein. Let Me In.
First you have to come out.
Oh.

One fine August morning Milou came a-knocking at the door. Only one day late. Not having a phone ("Too expensive," insisted Pierre), at five o'clock we tapped on the common wall we shared with Mme Karol. She let us in to use her telephone. We alerted the clinic that we were on our way.

Milou. Where'd I get this name? Every French kid and grownup kid was a fan of the Belgian Hergé's comic books featuring the intrepid boy-detective, Tintin, and his snow-white doggy, Milou. They were as popular as Mickey Mouse back home.

Yippee, I cried between contractions. The previous night Pierre and I walked halfway across Paris to "bring it on." Once home, we played Scrabble in French and he won by using all seven letters to make the word, *sadique.* I fervently hoped that wasn't an omen.

All night I stayed up timing my pains, in labor the minute my head touched the pillow, but unsure whether the contractions were real enough, often enough. And you know what, they hurt! Hey! What was that about? Pain? Every week my mother had patiently listened and made no comment as I explained that childbirth pain is completely avoidable, the implication being she did it all wrong. Well, that's what the Lamaze team claimed in their group indoctrination sessions: "If you have pain in childbirth, it's your fault. You're not relaxing; not breathing properly; you're tensing your muscles; having bad thoughts. . . ."

Five-thirty in the morning. Decided: we'd go to the clinic but leave my suitcase at home. That way we wouldn't risk looking foolish if it turned out to be a false alarm. We walked the two blocks to Boulevard Voltaire and figured we'd hail a taxi to the Château Belvédère clinic, located on the outskirts of Paris in Boulogne-Billancourt. Living in the heart of Paris, we still had no car. Fortunately, I'd chosen the weekend when Pierre was around to go into labor. *Nice to have a plan in place.* While we waited, we tortured ourselves about whether this trip was even necessary, as contractions had hardly progressed in the previous five hours.

An hour went by—no taxi. "Let's forget it," I said. We headed back across the wide intersection of Boulevard Voltaire and Rue de la Roquette, but halfway across, I got slammed almost to the ground by a monster contraction. "Hell, let's go." We turned around; a taxi stopped.

At Belvédère, one hour later, we were shown to a pleasant blue and white room with a big window facing the garden and I was put to bed. An exam revealed I was dilated only *three* centimeters, but the baby's heartbeat was strong.

The staff predicted I would *accoucher* by the beginning of the afternoon, definitely before lunch. They told Pierre to come back in two hours. He decided to return home to fetch the suitcase.

They were cutting it a bit close, I thought, knowing he was undoubtedly going to ride the métro each way. *Mustn't waste money.*

Unreal. Milou was coming today? I hoped I was up for it. There I was alone in Paris with all my close friends and family far, far away in Queens, New York. I was lonesome in that pretty room, so unlike a typical hospital room. Where were the hoses, the beeping instruments, the medicinal smells? I realized I had to pee and I was very hungry. *Where was everybody?*

At 8:20 a.m. the contractions were still coming. I wasn't humiliated after all. A young doctor popped in, checked me out, and instructed the nurses to give me intravenous calcium and glucose to speed things up. *Oy, have I mentioned my tiny, needle-shy veins?* The nurses finally got the needle in, and I swear, as soon as they did, the contractions started coming every two minutes. All monster size. *Wait, we're not ready!*

I prepared for each contraction, got clobbered nonetheless, rested for a few minutes. Too soon I was snared by another. "Lots of pressure inside," I announced matter-of-factly. Milou baby was at the gate, already pushing at the cervix. Nurses, aides, midwives entered, made note of my anguished face, examined me, and dashed about trying to locate the doctor, my birthing coach, and Pierre. They urged everyone to get a move on.

Milou was on his way! Was Pierre going to get back in time? My doctor was where?

At the center of this hurricane, I remained strangely composed. Not a calm person by nature, more inclined to brood on things gone wrong, medical mishaps, and such, I found I was too preoccupied with controlling my contractions to worry about the staff's problems. Mme Roget, my birthing coach, was the first to show. Usually a comforting presence, very Russian Jewish, kind and relaxed, she seemed a bit off that day. She was talking too much as she positioned herself where I could see her and led me through the various breathing exercises. While we were occupied, Pierre dashed in, stowed the suitcase, and set up his camera. My doctor, the leading French practitioner and advocate of "natural childbirth" materialized next, beaming, at my bedside.

We started right in working—well, I'd been working for a while—and soon I got the word to push, which was difficult since Mme Roget, concerned with triggering preterm labor, never allowed me to practice pushing. But I did my best. Dr. V announced he needed to stretch the cervix, which he declared to be a bit "thick." Once that was done, the baby would pass right through. Now all Milou needed to do was slide out. *Piece of cake, right?*

"*Poussez, Madame.*"

I pushed, pushed, pushed, determined to obey the doctor, the birthing coach, the nurses.

Nothing.

I pushed even harder, tightened my abdominals, scrunched up my face.

Zero effect.

Next, I pulled with arms on the bars, took longer breaths, no longer worrying about bursting the capillaries on my face. Pierre was stationed at his post, squirting Evian water down my throat. He ran back and forth to the camera he'd set up in a corner of the room. How did he deal with my pained and contorted face, my graceless body, and the puddles of blood I imagined pooling on the floor? No idea.

Still Milou budged not.

Dr. V declared that Milou was *bloqué*. *What page was that on?* The baby's head had failed to rotate properly, and the back of his head was presenting first. Guess what? It was too big to clear. (See posterior head birth.) I took this news in stride. Vaguely, I realized that it was too late for a Caesarean; Milou was already in the birth canal. And there was no reverse gear in sight.

La-di-dah, I wondered what would happen now. I was too busy counting breaths and managing my pain, careful only to let out a few discreet "ow-ows," not wanting to disgrace myself or the Lamaze training I'd received in the last nine months. My Type A personality would not allow me to fail or disappoint my mentors. This was me not on drugs. I was in the zone. In the moment. Passively awaiting instructions.

Dr. V cleared his throat. "We must cut." He quickly did an episiotomy and instructed me to "tell your American doctors I did this without anesthesia." He grabbed the forceps off the tray, positioned himself at the foot of the bed, and yanked. Everyone else pushed down hard on my stomach, two nurses were practically lying on top of me, I pushed with all my strength till I must have been beet-red in the face, about to explode. I had no more breath in me until. . . .

Something started to give. Dr. V announced, "*Ça y est. Ça y est. Continuez, continuez. Poussez. Encore. Encore. Encore. Encore.*" Then the simple words Pierre and I had heard in all the training videos: "*Le front. Le nez. La bouche. La tête. Voilà votre enfant!*"

A few more super pushes—Milou was crying when he was only half out of me—and he was born! "A big baby," the doctor declared. "Here, take your son," he said, handing him over to me as Milou was pissing gleefully. Pierre came out of the corner where he'd been taking photos, and announced, "His name is

Alexandre Bonhomme." *Oh, silly me. I thought we were going to discuss naming once we knew the sex of the baby.*

He was still Milou to me, all slippery and bloody and adorable. I could barely believe it. Pierre started laughing hysterically, unable to stop. He retreated to his corner. Wait—was he crying? Just a bit. The doctor placed the baby on my chest while he cut the umbilical cord, bloodying my favorite white Mexican blouse. I massaged Milou's little tush, talked to him. He was relaxed and observant. I let him in on all the good times we were going to have together.

Meanwhile Dr. V "cleaned up," sewing me back together, rushing next door to help out a woman whose doctor couldn't be located. Within minutes, another baby cried. The nurses took possession of Milou, bathed and measured him, dressed him up in the beautiful turquoise hand-knit outfit I'd made for him. I saw Pierre bending over him, talking to him, playing. When it was my turn, I got to hold him again and noted his enormous dark blue eyes, wisps of black hair, tiny little nails. He did not look like anyone I knew. *More like a mongoose.* Pierre came over to us, grinning. He apologized about the photos, "I was shaking so much." He confided that at one point he had almost fainted.

I whispered to the baby, "Remember how you used to kick me all the time, roll around in my tummy like it was party time? I didn't mind one bit." We exchanged visiting cards and promised to see more of each other.

I kissed Mme Roget, an unusual display of affection for me, and she was pleased. Truthfully, she hadn't been much help with the birth.

The next day, I was shocked to learn she had passed away while having dinner in a restaurant with a group of friends. What happened? Apparently she had fallen down the stairs in her home the day before. That lovely woman, I couldn't believe she was gone. What a shock! The nurses informed me her family was sitting *shiva* for her. They gave me the address and I asked Pierre to stop by and offer our condolences. I was grateful and honored that her last act on Earth was to bring my son into this world, making room for one more soul.

I stayed a week at Château Belvédère with other French mothers and their newborns. By watching the staff during the day, I learned the proper way to diaper and bathe my son, care for his skin, nurse. I needed no lessons on how to kiss him or love him. I figured that out by myself. He stayed in a small cot at the side of my bed during the day—I spent hours staring at him, watching him closely as he raised his head and tried to make sense of his surroundings. At night he was taken away to the nursery; I slept like an angel.

Every afternoon the nurses sent me to wander in the garden while my baby napped. I listened to the birds, the chirping of the babies inside the small château-turned-clinic, thrilled to the breezes on my thin frame. Bliss. I had never been happier.

And Pierre, how did he react? He bought me a lovely silver choker necklace to celebrate my having given him a son. He travelled back and forth to the clinic every day, often bringing along one or more of our friends. We laughed about the day our single male friend, Bernard, visited me alone.

"He almost fainted when I pulled out my boob and started nursing. I mean, that's what I'm supposed to do, right?"

"What did he say?" Pierre asked between fits of hysteria.

"He remembered he had left a book in his car! You should have seen him skedaddle. I thought the French were unfazed by nudity?"

"Apparently not in his case."

"Apparently not," I said.

Bliss turned to nightmare. No, too strong a word. How about non-bliss?

The following week back at home, I panicked about my failure to breastfeed, his diarrhea brought on by a staph infection, his colic, and his enormous appetite. Most babies slept fifteen hours; he hardly slept. I was toast. No one warned me I would not be lazing around, sending photos home, reading my books, knitting booties, or just basking in the sun with my darling baby boy. But he grew quickly, acquiring new skills, flipping himself over backward, reaching for my earrings, smiling all the time, seeming to have a sense of humor. He balked at being left alone in a crib or cradle or carriage. He insisted on being where the action was. I quickly learned to hold him with my left arm and wash dishes with my right.

"*C'est un petit coquin*," declared my mother-in-law. A little rogue.

Just my luck.

ele

I'm a Person Too!

O slid the hangers to one side and clambered into the flimsy
pressboard closet, crouching low, like an ogre. Filling my
lungs with the slightly perfumed air, I let loose, "I'M A PERSON
TOO!" With all the noise from the street below and the thick
walls of our hundred-year-old flat, I hoped I was in no danger of
being overheard.

Alexandre screamed in his crib in the grip of another colic
attack. If not colic, hiccups. Or boredom. I wondered whether
the syrup the pediatrician gave me for colic was designed to work
only with 100 percent French-blooded citizens, not the 50 percent hybrid variety. Maybe he wanted to play?

Hey, it was 10:00 a.m. Naptime. Ah, he never got the memo!
Once again he'd awakened at 3:00 a.m., starving, though my little
book for new mothers by Dr. Cohen-Solal claimed babies sleep
through the night after the first month. Ha! Not this one.

Fatigue like a disease cloaked my body and mind. My scalp
was itchy; my nails, broken and jagged. I fretted about Alexandre's poor sleeping habits and whether I might be feeding him
too much. The doctors in France believed in rationing the intake
of milk, but this kid was a regular *khazer*. Yet he never upchucked
and his weight was normal. After two months of bouncing him
around to distract him when he was clearly hungry, I fantasized
about feeding him on demand. Babies were supposed to eat,
sleep, eat every three hours. My baby would wake up after one

hour and howl. Every day I walked him up, back, and around our tiny place. About the time when two, two and a half hours had passed since his last bottle, I would give him another. I scribbled down times of his feedings to help me remember if he'd had six or seven bottles and when. I tried to see a pattern. When was he going to give up and go to five bottles?

I asked myself why the hell I persisted in distracting him when I knew he was hungry. Damn the norms. At the next doctor visit I confessed. "Alexandre's getting rations for a six-month-old baby."

Shocked, the doctor scolded me, "Well, don't go beyond that!" I asked if it were possible to overfeed. And he said, "No."

What a jerk I was. What jerks they were (doctors). Feeding on demand out of one corner of their mouths; feeding not more than every three hours out of the other. Average quantities given which didn't come close to my son's demands. Granted he was a big, vigorous baby, but not a giant. Why listen to them? They weren't spending their days and nights with a starving baby.

Alexandre woke up every night. Ha! Find that in a mothers' manual. "In six weeks, babies distinguish day from night." Bullshit. My neighbors bragged that their babies were *sage* and at four, five, six weeks, sleeping through the night. They mentioned that they let the six- or seven-pound helpless, clench-fisted, lost little things cry and cry and cry all night. Training. "You have to train a child while it's young," they explained.

Fitzhugh Dodson says going to a child when it calls is the best way to instill optimism and self-worth and self-confidence. Therefore, I ran when my baby cried, and I often cried with him at three in the morning while Pierre slept, back turned to us.

Postpartums: Why didn't a woman write about them? A

sensation of emptiness, *un vide*, as if a woman's womb had always to be filled? I spent twenty plus years with a "sensation of emptiness" and went back to it after nine months of fullness without any problem, Doc! It was the fullness outside that got you—every second, twenty-four hours a day—especially after two lazy prepartum months at home knitting, dreaming, walking in the sun. "I'm a person too, you know. Believe it or not!" became my battle cry when I was exploding; the closet, my go-to place. I roared three or four times daily and worried the neighbors on the whole block had heard me. "ENOUGH!" I continued to scream at the top of my lungs, feeling crazy.

I fantasized late at night. "Boy, you should only be left in the desert, without any water. You'd see what it means to be thirsty, starving!" Ungrateful kid, he didn't know or appreciate how good I was to him. I was killing myself, goddammit—I couldn't do it anymore. I wasn't a person anymore.

Plus, Pierre would scream at me in the middle of the night, without moving from his bed: "How can you go on waking at night?" He was far from understanding the supremacy (for me) of the baby's wishes. You can't reason with a two-month-old baby.

I couldn't just stay in bed, could I?

Hunger: a half-hour wait for a baby is equivalent to an adult's going without food for two or three days. I could not believe this position I'd been put into vis-à-vis my baby. Doing my utmost left me totally wrecked. Suddenly, I had a visceral understanding of every woman who'd ever shaken her baby. Or worse. Deprive a person of sleep and get out of her way. I would never have hurt my baby—was it only because I was educated, intelligent, because I knew better?

I worked on calming my breathing. Pierre was not due back

from the physics lab for another four or five hours. Not that he would rescue me. Instead, he'd gaze sullenly at the pile of dusty shoes by the front door, the laundry half done, the windows that needed washing and, lo, the evening's entertainment would begin.

Where was my time?

I huddled in the closet a few minutes longer.

Alexandre continued to wake up screaming every single night at 3:00 a.m. Delaying the final feeding until midnight had no effect. While I tended to him, Pierre shouted orders in my other ear, "Don't pick him up. Let him cry. You are spoiling him." The amount of noise the two of them made was unreal. "He's starving," I explained as I fed, changed, comforted my baby. "You could help, you know."

"I have to get up in the morning. I have a job. You made a choice to stay home." He'd roll over to face the wall.

Dr. Fitzhugh Dodson says in his book that you cannot spoil a child under two years of age.

Last night both male Bonhommes started in again. I couldn't bear it. Bleary-eyed, I made my way to the kitchen, pulled out a bottle of formula, and popped it in the bottle warmer, but not before stubbing my toe on a kitchen chair. I sank to the floor, holding my foot and trying not to scream as tears leaked down my face. "Aieee."

Pierre called from the bedroom, "What is it now? Why are you up? You're going to make yourself sick!"

Rubbing my foot eased the pain. The baby was emitting ever-more-frantic cries. I rose to my feet, a bit wobbly, grabbed hold of the bottle, then paused to let the blood return to my head. Pierre managed to creep up behind me soundlessly and pry the bottle from my hands. "Listen, you are spoiling this kid. He can't be hungry. He ate a few hours ago. Now stop it! I have to get up for work in two hours."

He spit when he talked.

I covered my ears. The baby was screaming louder and louder; Pierre was competing to reach the same decibel level. Sound was bouncing off the walls. I spotted Alexandre's wooden baby rattle lying on the kitchen table. With a piercing shriek, I launched it at the farthest wall with all my might, hoping to get them both to shut up.

Of course I threw like a girl.

"What have you done?" Pierre yelled, as he tut-tutted over the small dent in the wall. "What's wrong with you?" He wisely took his pillow, pushed past me, and headed off to sleep in the living room.

I fetched the bottle, gathered up the baby in my arms, and whispered, "It's a good thing you're so good looking, or you'd be in the garbage by now!" As I fed him I gazed into enormous eyes, no longer blue but deep brown, eyes that seemed to take up half his face; I cuddled his miniature, compact sweet-smelling human body with all the appropriate baby bulges and creases—and the hidden nuclear capacity to one day blow my entire world to smithereens.

I nodded off for a moment. His fussing revived me. He'd drained the bottle dry. I cleaned and powdered him, put on a fresh diaper. Start to finish: one hour. Once back in his crib, his hand darted out like an adder's tongue to catch the swinging mobile above his crib. "No kiddo!" I told him. "I'm the boss here. Playtime is over." I passed out on the mattress for an hour until 5:00 a.m. when he was up for good.

And here we found ourselves. I'd fed him at five o'clock, again at eight. He was still crying out. My back was killing me. How I craved sleep!

Venting was not helping. Earlier that morning I'd penned these immortal words in my journal: *The birth of a baby is the death of its mother.* Metaphorically speaking. Harsh words but I stood by them. *Get a grip, Lucie.*

I stumbled out of the pressboard closet. I looked around our bedroom and saw: our foam mattress on the floor, the crib on the wall opposite, the tattered rug, the Egyptian cotton drapes I'd sewn covering the windows, the changing table my mother had "invented" when she flew in last month to meet her first grandson. Resourceful Depression baby herself, she'd simply turned a small dresser upside down and plunked a big pillow down on it. "Voilà," she'd said. "Otherwise, you're going to wreck your back if you keep bending to change him on that . . . mattress." She was never one to hide her disdain for the way other people lived. She had limited use for empathy; she and Pierre absconded one afternoon to drift down the Seine in a bâteau mouche. Why had Pierre and I never done that? Meanwhile I was stuck with baby.

Mom must have picked up on the weird vibes in our household. She flew home after a week's visit, admonishing me over our last breakfast together to "pull myself together—or else."

I narrowed my eyes and asked, "Are you kidding? I haven't had a good night's sleep since Alexandre was born; I weigh less than I did before I got pregnant; my hair is falling out."

"You have a handsome young husband. You don't want him looking around, do you?"

"Okay," I said. I took a deep cleansing breath. "You do realize I'm trying my best to be a perfect mother?"

Mom reached across the table to take my hands. "The baby will be fine. It's your husband I'm worried about."

Then stop flirting with him.

"Mom, let me add 'dress better' to my to-do list."

This morning it was down to me and the little one again. I picked up my red-faced son and comforted him as best as I could. "See, here I am." Without warning the sun emerged: He smiled that beautiful smile of his, as in *Tricked you again!* A little laugh escaped me. Rascal! What were Mom's parting words? "You're going to have your hands full with that one."

Alexandre glanced about gleefully, his eyes feeding hungrily on all the colors in the room. He didn't look a bit tired. I picked him up and walked into our galley kitchen. An acrobat by necessity, I attempted to wash the breakfast dishes with one hand while balancing him on my hip with the other.

Welcome to my life.

I carried my baby back to the bedroom, laid him down in the crib. "Play with your mobile, kiddo," I instructed. "Papa made it for you." I gave it a tug to set it in motion, grabbed clean clothes, and made a dash for the bathroom.

All the while in the shower I was on alert, picturing the little fellow thrashing about in his crib, crying inconsolably, maybe even tangled up in the stupid mobile. After five minutes I ran out, towel wrapped around soapy waist, wet hair leaving puddles on the floor only to discover he was cooing happily to himself and holding on to the monkey's tail. "Hey, you're not supposed to be able to do that yet." I gently detached his hand; he squealed, and sure enough, palmed it again. He let it drop, reached for the giraffe, the octopus, the gorilla.

"Good boy. You're a good boy." I collected my favorite outfit:

pink hip-hugger jeans and black flowered blouse, backed out of the room, dressed, slapped store-bought color on my cheeks, and tied back my hair with a paisley scarf. Still dying for a nap, but I refused to let myself dwell on that. The noises from the bedroom began to get louder and more plaintive.

I grabbed a pen.

Sick Yokes

The birth of a baby is the death of its mother, the mother's actual dying in childbirth at one extreme, and at the other, the aged mother whose son trips over her body after he has cut out her heart. "Did you hurt yourself, my boy?"

Excuse me, I shouldn't have told you. But you knew it all along. Make room for the next generation! Is it a wonder we're jealous when it cries at three in the morning? Who wouldn't want to be it—hugged, rocked, squeezed, sung to, hot mama lava streaming out of warm nipples pressed firmly into our little birdmouths?

As I reread it, I came to the realization: I needed to get out more. Ecole Ducon, where I'd worked steadily for two years, had stopped sending me translations to do. No word from my old boss or any of my teaching colleagues. Not one congratulations card! Truthfully, I had no desire to go back and teach. I'd learned all I set out to learn from my ESL students. By this time I could have been a university professor, teaching and publishing academic papers on the side. I had been a contender, meant for great things. Here it was 1976, the bicentennial year. Women were in the middle of a revolution back home. And me? I was losing myself.

All I managed to do in those days was to read a few pages of a novel in the afternoons or make a few hurried entries in my journal while munching on sumptuous pastries from the Rue des Rosiers in the Jewish quarter. Being a stay-at-home mom, which I'd lobbied for strenuously, was not the baby-mom lovefest I thought it would be. Where was all the time I was supposed to have—while baby napped—to do my writing? I was forced instead to live on a two-month-old's schedule. What was I supposed to do for adult human contact?

As if answering my prayers, two older neighbors dropped by in the afternoon with baby presents. But over café and *petits gâteaux*, they could not refrain from offering unwanted advice: "Don't pick him up. He's 'making his lungs.' Let him cry." And on this gloomy Paris day: "Don't put on a light. It's only two o'clock. I never *allumer* until six."

Hey, this is my baby, I wanted to cry out. *I am going to pick him up every time he whimpers and blaze all the lights in the house when I do. So butt out, ladies!*

My baby was calm and curious and adorable. He liked to be in the center of things.

When the ladies left, I supposed it was time for a bit of fresh air. I placed him on the changing table, rubbed his little belly, dressed him in the cute blue-striped cotton tee shirt and undie ensemble favored by the French, topped with a little sailor onesie and hat. I ran up and down the three flights of stairs, first with his baby carriage, finally with him, and took off in the direction of the little park on Rue Parmentier. I spotted it one day when I was charging up and down the streets around Boulevard Voltaire, doing a few minor errands, but mostly putting off the moment when it was time to close myself and baby back into our tiny dollhouse apartment.

As the park came into view, it started to rain and thunder; z's of lightning lit up the sky. *Merde!* I swung the carriage around and headed for home. Up the spiral staircase first with the baby, down to fetch the carriage and lug it back up. I fed him a bottle and he mercifully went down for a two-hour nap. I started washing and peeling veggies for a leek and potato soup and put a low flame under the pot. In the living room I opened my journal to a clean page, sat down with a cup of strong, freshly ground Arabica from the coffee grinder next door and a half-stale *pain au chocolat* I'd stashed where Pierre would never find it. I might put on weight, but that was my concern. How I hated when he chased me around the apartment snatching cookies out of my hands.

Ah, momentary bliss.

Forty-five minutes passed. The petit monsieur woke up, hungry again. I was smack in the middle of a great scene. I wanted to kill him.

Some Things Resist Being Ground

"*Give* me ten minutes," Pierre said angrily, pushing his way in the door after accepting a peck on the cheek from me and giving one to the baby. He emerged from the bathroom, after several minutes, stopped in the kitchen to taste the soup. "Ah, Lucie, more salt please!" After sprinkling in a teaspoon or so on his way to the bedroom, he said, "And this tile floor is rather sticky."

I ignored his accusatory looks. We sat down to a light meal of fresh vegetable soup, salad from his mother's garden, cheese from La Laiterie, bread from the Engels' bakery, and fruit from the Arab market.

Shopping was a complicated affair there. Forget the one *supermarché*. Buying canned or frozen food in one store when you could be patronizing several small stores that knew where their fresh produce, meat, and bread came from? Unthinkable!

When we both were working, if Pierre got home first and prepared dinner, he used to joke, "Look, I cooked you a salad." Now that I was home with the baby, there were no jokes.

I admit I'd become a little bit of a caricature, ready to pounce on hubby, with one horror story after another, dramatizing to the hilt, as soon as he walked in the door. I could hardly complain about the washing machine or the dishwasher breaking down—are you kidding?—our refrigerator, the size of a bar refrigerator back home, did not even have a freezer compartment, which ne-

cessitated my going shopping every day but freed me from worrying about food additives. I guess I was lucky not to be putting
our milk and cheese out the kitchen window ledge. I couldn't
claim I was having problems cleaning. How long did it take to
clean a dollhouse? We had the indoor plumbing and bathtub I
had insisted on, when we first trudged up the three-storied spiral
staircase to the coal-smeared walls of the bathroom-less flat—
with good light—that was now ours. The toilet posed a problem at
times, as it ground whatever was put into it into little pieces, enabling them to float through the tiny hundreds-year-old pipes
that ran under the city of Paris. Well, let's say certain things resist
being ground—to mention one mentionable, cotton balls. What
exactly did I complain about on this occasion? Does it matter?

In the middle of my tirade, I said, "Let's stop this, Pierre.
Don't you hear the baby is yelling, and his voice is louder than
ours? He can tell we're arguing."

"Okay, but I'm tired of your *soupe à la grimace*. Be happy,
dammit!"

I frowned. How was my unhappiness my fault? Why wouldn't
he take his share of blame?

I spooned out more soup for us both. "Pierre, let's go out tomorrow night. Why not? Madeleine Renaud is at the Théâtre d'Orsay
doing a Beckett play. You know how I'm dying to see that."

"Dying?" He frowned into his soup bowl. "Why must you
always exaggerate?"

"We can hop the métro and go eat Chinese food at Empire
Celeste. Have a fun evening."

"Wait a minute, Luce. We've already discussed this. If we go
to the theatre, we don't need to eat out too."

"You've discussed it! You've decided!" I shouted.

"Lucie!" We both turned to the baby, whose chirping had gotten rather high-pitched in the last few minutes. Were we fighting or "discussing?" Let's ask the baby!

Pierre picked the baby out of his crib and carried him to the living room to play with him. I got stuck doing the dishes and cleanup. In the old days, before baby, at least once in a while, with a great show of altruism, Pierre would don a little white apron his mother had sewn together out of two Lin des Vosges dishtowels, pull closed the curtains, and set to work. First, he would fill the basin with hot water and add an infinitesimal drop of detergent. For quite a while he would appear to be busy, soaking and scrubbing the dishes, glasses, utensils, and frying pan. At a certain point he would decide it was all clean enough, drain the basin of soapy water, and in a thin trickle of clean cold water, rinse the dishes and set them in the drainer to dry. What a ritual! He would beam with pride afterwards and assure me that not many French husbands would be caught dead doing such a thing.

Tonight, Pierre quickly returned to the kitchen. "Oh Mama, this little fellow wants to be changed." He handed me Alexandre, and at the same time, reached over and shut off the Niagara-like flow of steaming hot water I used to wash the dishes.

He gently pushed me out of the way, donned an apron, and rolled up his sleeves. And at that most inopportune moment, Mme Karol, who was practically family, and took liberties as such, sneaked up on us in the kitchen. Pierre was at the sink! They both let out godawful shrieks. She doubled up, convulsed in laughter, holding a handkerchief to her tearing eyes. He turned a sickly white. I patted her on the back and motioned for him to disappear. He obliged. It could not have been more scandalous had she walked in and caught us fornicating.

When she quieted, Alexandre and I accompanied her to the front door. I put a finger to my lips, as in, *This is our little secret.* She wisely decided to forego the little nightly chocolate ritual we had, kissed the baby, and tiptoed out of our apartment, down the hall to her place.

If I hadn't seen it with my own eyes. . . .

When I reentered the kitchen I saw that Pierre had his coat on. "Oh, no."

"Remember, Lucie, I told you this morning I had to go back to the lab tonight to finish work on a project I'm doing with Bernard."

"How nice."

"I wish, Luce, you would be more supportive of my work."

His work. I had retyped a couple of physics papers for him back in Rochester at midnight, trying to correct his English but understanding even less than what I gleaned from *La Muerte de Artemio Cruz.* Conclusion: Scientific journal English was not my English. How did he thank me? He said, "Lady, I think you missed a typo."

I spent the evening, my only time for adult companionship, curled up on the living room daybed, writing letters.

That night, at 3:00 a.m., right on schedule, the baby screeched awake. Again. Pierre scolded, "You're wearing yourself out."

I was already up and running, noise on all sides of me, ricocheting off the walls. I heated up the milk, scooped up one ugly red, almost evil-looking, little monster from his crib. He looked exactly like his daddy.

"Kiddo," I said, "You're too much." I repeated my mantra: "It's a good thing you're so good looking or you would've been in the trash by now."

And I tried hard to hug away his anger.

Don't get me wrong. Fact #1: I loved my son. We both did. I spent hours making funny faces at him, waiting for a reaction. I watched him staring pensively at the little stuffed doggie in his crib, the colorful Mexican serape hanging on the wall, trying to figure things out. He was having great thoughts already. Anyone could see that. Fact #2: He started to babble in two languages and I could confidently say, he was basically a happy boy.

His mother, on the other hand. . . .

What's beautiful is a baby's potential for happiness. He wants to smile and laugh and touch and taste. He looks at you, listens, and one day old, he already seems happy. A few weeks later he smiles to let you know it. The world is his. He claims his place in it.

What's sad to imagine are all the babies not permitted their happiness from the start. Beaten, starved, or simply neglected. No wonder there are such frustrated, warped, and unhappy human beings in this world.

Consider the immensity of a baby's urge to grasp at life. When it's denied, look what we get: hatred and violence, world wars, atrocities. If only women ruled the world . . . we wouldn't be so quick to throw our babies into the fire.

A baby is love.

Cuisine Franco-Américaine

*M*ost days I spent in the apartment, alone and stir-crazy. Feeding, diapering, washing, laundering, playing with baby, and stressing over what to prepare for the evening meal. One day I had a bright idea: *I'd learn how to cook.*

Living in Paris with a mini-fridge and no freezer, the emphasis was on fresh. All of us Parisians walked down our street towards Voltaire with our little string bags to purchase fresh butter and cheese and eggs in one shop, poultry in another, red meat in the shop that had wild boars hung upside down from hooks at its entrance. We stopped at the *brûlerie*, inhaled deeply, chose the exotic coffee beans of the week, and watched as the owner ground them up.

I stocked up on ingredients. Wouldn't Pierre be surprised? I told myself anyone could cook. All one had to do was follow a recipe. And I had one (of sorts) from his mother: *tarte aux pommes*. I peeled and cut up the apples, cooked them down into a mush, then added cinnamon, sugar, and a scoop of her preserves for extra taste as she had instructed. The process took a little longer than I expected, the result being that I was rushing to make the pie crust and get our dessert in the oven before Pierre walked in the door.

A knock. Already? "Pierre, I can't open the door. Use your key."

"What do you mean? Enough of your games. I've got pack-ages in my hands."

"I know. Sorry. Please, come in. You'll see immediately what the problem is."

I heard him juggling packages around. Finally, he put the key in the lock and opened up. His face cracked open in a wide smile. "Oh, my poor Lucie. My poor little American cook. What have you got there?"

He dropped his dry cleaning on the daybed, taking me by the elbow and escorting me into the kitchen.

"What did I do wrong?" I held out my two hands covered to the wrist in dough, cold sticky dough. A bit like Play-Doh actually. Pierre turned on the cold water tap and dribbled water on each hand.

"Now mash your hands together and knead the dough. Here, let me add more water."

Finally, I got the stuff off my hands and shaped it into a ball. Pierre washed up and finished making the pie he doubtless had watched his mother make a thousand times. We ate the pie for dessert. I thought it was pretty good, but Pierre said, "I don't want you to make anything complicated, little woman, because I might not get home in time to rescue you." He was almost gleeful, covering his mouth every few minutes to indulge in more snig-gering at my expense.

"Ha ha. Right you are. Why do I bother? Look, why don't you clean up and I'll give him a bath."

"No, I'd rather do the bath."

"Afraid of Mme Karol seeing you?" I teased and enjoyed watching the red flush creep up his neck.

"Don't be ridiculous, Lucie." He scooped Alexandre up and

disappeared into the bathroom with him while I dealt with the patches of cold hard dough stuck here, there, and everywhere on the floor and counters.

On a rainy afternoon a few weeks later, I decided to give cooking another try: I unearthed a French cookbook, *Tante Marie*, a wedding present, and leafed through it. Whatever persuaded me to try Recette #226, Boeuf Bourguignon? The recipe called for an entire bottle of red wine. Naturally, I complied. The dish simmered for hours, imbuing the curtains, the bed linens, even our thin carpet with its rich, smoky odors. I peeked inside the pot, satisfied that it looked like a stew should.

Aiming for elegance, I carefully set the table with colorful cloth napkins atop our blue and yellow Mexican tablecloth and wine glasses that matched, no vulgar containers or bottles in evidence. Pierre walked in, grinned, and served himself a heaping portion.

"Pas mal. Pas mal."

Victory? One for Lucie? *Oui!* And a bonus: a stress-free evening.

Sadly, the dish was poorly received by my American stomach: Noxious reflux and indigestion kept me up all night. Pierre was fine and wanted to know when I'd be making the dish again.

I realized I was not in the habit of eating much meat. I tended toward cookbooks featuring plants: *The Grub Bag, Diet for a Small Planet, The Vegetarian Epicure*. How I missed all three of my cooking companions left behind in the US. They were simple and clear to follow, featured ingredients I could relate to, and they also served the dual purpose of tasting good and preparing readers for the Revolution! (A number of recipes were actually calibrated to feed an army.)

In Mexico I mastered enough Spanish to make recipes out of a simple cookbook designed for *recién casados* (newlyweds). We loved the cream of carrot soup and even the kidneys. I learned to peel tomatoes by holding them over the fire until the outer layer flaked off. I failed to recall a single culinary disaster. Not one. But here. . . . I spent the evening and most of the night in the bathroom, and actually welcomed Alexandre's 3:00 a.m. feeding which at least provided a little distraction.

Pierre resumed his prebaby habit of inviting guests over to dinner during the week as well as on weekends. "Since you're interested in becoming a better cook, you can practice on the Lafontaines. They'll be coming over for dinner tomorrow night."

Thursday? After a full day alone with baby?

Luckily, I had never been shy about trying out new recipes on unsuspecting guests. I prepared a pasta dish that called for a peanut butter sauce. An unwise choice as the only place French people or transplants like me could get their hands on peanut butter was the American commissary. I realized too late French children did not grow up with taste buds specially adapted to sticky peanut butter and were unlikely to be seeking it out in strange places.

Thursday night, Pierre ate more of the exotic dish than I did. He may have been the only one of us eating. I observed Pierre's colleague and his wife. They chewed in small, tight movements, leaving more on the plate than I'd spooned out. They smiled and explained more than once, "We're not in the habit of eating a big dinner."

"Atroce!" I was sure they were saying to each other as soon as they were down the stairs, out of the building, and heading toward their car. We closed the door, took one look at each other, and laughed so hard we were choking.

"Not nice, Lucie—" Pierre sputtered.

"Did you see their faces?" I spit out. I loved a good show.

Pierre screwed up his face in imitation of theirs. He tried to be serious. *"Mon dieu*, what a fiasco!"

"Tough on them. They needed to be shaken up. Out of their complacency."

"Still, not nice," he said, as I spooned more pasta from the pot into his mouth. Pierre and I will always have the peanut butter fiasco to laugh about. . . .

For my next experiment, my ambitions were more modest. I was roasting a chicken in the oven, but all was not well. Pierre arrived home, took one whiff, and dumped it in the garbage.

"Hey!" I protested.

He ran down the stairs and headed to the poultry butcher's shop. Fifteen minutes ticked by. He returned and let me know he'd bawled the butcher man out good for daring to sell me a spoiled chicken. Whew. Not my fault for once. The butcher in question subsequently closed up shop. It made no sense, but we both felt guilty.

Never the type to give up, I next attempted the classic French dish, *canard à l'orange*. What could go wrong? We both loved duck, and the recipe did not appear to be beyond my capabilities. We invited the Lafontaines back to share in this meal. What troopers! All went well until an hour after they'd left for home.

Pierre commandeered the toilet; I positioned myself on the lip of the bathtub. Joined in gross intestinal misery, we threw up for what seemed like hours.

Petrified that I'd poisoned our guests, we called them up the next day. Nope. They were fine. That night on the radio we learned a particularly virulent stomach virus was making its way through Paris. Whatever. I vowed never again in my life to eat duck in orange sauce because I knew it didn't taste nearly as good coming up as it did going down.

Eventually I imagined I'd dare to make a rabbit in mustard sauce, sauté mutton chops, or even cook a goose. But apple pies, bottles of wine, peanuts, smelly chickens, and duck were knocked permanently off the menu.

Pierre could be counted on to prepare tasty fish dishes about once every two weeks, ensuring we did not starve. And the baby was getting plenty of wholesome food because I heeded the doctor's prescriptions, preparing fresh vegetable soup every morning for him and blending it with whatever meat we were having. He was a hearty eater, gobbling it all up without complaint.

And me? I still needed to find an outlet.

ele

Promenading Through Paris

O pushed the baby carriage to the park most afternoons, arriving before the other mothers, hoping for peace and a little sun.

But my baby cried in the park, the only baby in the world who cried in a park. He was not happy in the carriage. I had no choice but to take him out, hold him tight against the late October cold. And all too soon he was thirsty or wet and we had to go back.

When was my time to cry?

Pierre typically started in on me over breakfast. "You're impossible! Are you never satisfied? This American malady!"

I didn't even know what he was referring to, storming around the apartment in his slippers with that *serioso* look of his. My sending the laundry out?

"Stop that laughter!" he commanded, and I obeyed, afraid as always to push him too far.

Bulletin

January 1977

Alexandre Bonhomme at five months old slept through the night. For the first time ever!!!

Deliverance?

Who Was More Fragile?

*P*ierre and I sat side by side on a bench late one Sunday morning in Tuileries Gardens with our son napping peacefully in his stroller. Parisian women were out in full array, displaying their colors, their purples and reds, their feathers and lightweight knit shawls, and clinking silver bracelets. I could not fail to notice Pierre's eyes tracking a tall, slim girl in a roaring twenties felt cloche hat and red lipstick as she passed in front of us with her model's walk, making her way toward the gates. He was captivated, and, as I turned toward him, he did not try to hide his fascination.

Men! I opted for humor. "Do you realize gazing openly at such a woman can substantially shorten your lifespan? Particularly if you happen to be in the company of your wife. And baby!"

"Oh, poor Lady," he crooned, slipping an arm around me and squeezing. "Anyway, I don't expect to live that long."

"Huh? What do you mean?" I asked, stiffening. "Are you sick? Because if you are, you should tell me. I'm your wife, you know." I tapped my foot. *Why must I always be prying information out of him?*

He removed his arm from around my shoulders, bent forward, and gazed at the ground, preparing his response. By then he knew when I needed more information, needed to be appeased. He shrugged his shoulders, glanced up at me briefly. "I don't believe I'll make it to thirty-five." He was dead serious.

"Well, nice time to let me know! Anything else to share?"

"Sure. Did I ever tell you my biggest fear? That I'll wind up a homeless person?"

"That's ridiculous. How could that happen? Why—" I stopped as I flashed on his brutal childhood. I reached out and gently stroked his face. It was up to me to erase his childhood trauma and replace it with happy new memories of the three of us together. I could not fail. I studied his face, the face I fell in love with. What a handsome profile! And the little Bonhomme was going to look just like him when he grew up.

Pierre slapped his hands down on his knees and stood. "Time to get back home," he said.

Once home, we left Alexandre in his stroller in the living room, still asleep. I pulled Pierre into the bedroom for some quick diversionary action, or as the French call it, *divertissement*. Afterwards, as we lay in each other's arms, he said, "Sorry. Sometimes I'm fragile."

"Me too!" I happily confessed.

He smiled. "As long as we take turns being fragile."

"Agreed. Can I ask what brought this on, these morbid thoughts?"

He turned to the wall. I put my arms around him and spooned.

"My mother. I'll tell you later."

We both heard fussing and Alexandre emitting little cries of distress. *"J'arrive,"* I called out to him and jumped up to dress. Pierre carried him into the kitchen. "How's my bouncing baby boy?" I crooned, as I prepared his bottle, took him from Pierre's arms, and laid him back down in his crib. He managed the bottle alone now. Soon he'd be able to sit up by himself. We went back into the kitchen and I reheated some coffee. I returned to our discussion. "What's the matter with your mother?"

"She's very upset at the moment. She's convinced someone has broken into her house even though there's no evidence of that. She insisted on making a police report. I had to change the locks."

"Well, if it makes her feel better. . . ."

"You don't understand. I tell her, "No, Maman, you are imagining this!" He sat straight-backed at the table, staring into his coffee.

"And?" I asked.

He gulped.

"This happened when you went to visit her last week?"

He nodded.

"Does she need a doctor? Or . . . a hospital?"

"No. No. No. It will pass." He closed his eyes for a moment before going into the living room and sitting down at the small pulldown desk. He started opening the day's mail.

"So, what should we do for her?" I persisted.

"Look, she gets like this every year about the time my father left her. I can handle it."

"But—"

"No more talk about it, okay?"

He shut me out. Again. Even he must realize what he's doing. "Look, after I'm done with these bills, why don't we go out again? It's such a lovely afternoon. We can go treat ourselves to a late lunch of *croque monsieurs* at that little corner place on Île de la Cité."

"What a lovely idea!" I said.

"By the way, what bills are you paying?" I asked, leaning over his shoulder. "Are we in any trouble?"

"I thought you'd never ask. No trouble. But you realize you are not working. As for me, after a year of earning only a small stipend as a military man, I am still making only entry-level pay. And I need to make sure my mother's expenses are covered."

"Oh . . . don't let me distract you then. You're doing a great job."

Once he finished with the bills, we left. He commandeered the stroller and I skipped to catch up with him. Fearing I was pushing the envelope, but unable to stop myself, I said, "We can get passion fruit *glaces* at Berthillon after our meal."

A mock frown from Pierre. "You'll never change, will you?" He looked deep into my eyes for a long minute.

"Well?"

"We'll see," he said, as we crossed the Seine for the third time that day.

Explorations

I awakened to semidarkness and near silence. Pierre had departed earlier that morning on a three-day assignment to another lab farther north. How would I manage on my own? To ward off any anxious thoughts, I readied Alexandre and we headed for the street in observer mode.

Skinny girls with long legs and short skirts were already mounted on ladders or stooping, cleaning the glass windows of the bakeries; the smell of fresh bread overwhelmed my senses every time a customer opened the door; a few early birds made conversation inside. I parked the carriage and entered, my son on my hip.

"Bonjour, Mesdames, Messieurs," I said.

"Bonjour. What would you like today?"

I purchased a *pithivier*, one of my favorites, with its rum-scented almond cream inside, puff pastry crust outside. I resisted the urge to eat it on the spot and stowed it away in the carriage.

Back to my assignment. The woman who ran the salad and ready-made hors d'oeuvres place proudly chalked up the menu on the windows and door: *celeri remoulade*, the bargain of the day. All along the street, merchants opened shop, cranking up the metal gates, sweeping, sponging, cleaning, and displaying their day's offerings. They stopped to salute the first passersby beginning to trickle toward the métro.

In the butcher shop a redhead perched on a stool, filing her nails. Her husband was already hard at work, hacking at recalcitrant slabs of meat. At his young age, his shoulders stooped over the butcher block from morning till night, he was well on his way towards having a hump on the back of his neck.

The fruit store on the next corner added light and color on this street without trees, vibrant nonetheless with its reds, yellows, greens, and oranges. As I pushed the baby carriage, the sky began to lighten. Workers in blue uniforms, smoking a cigarette or waiting for someone, saluted us as we passed with a "Bonjour Madame" or "*Bonne journée.*" When I was still working I would see the same people hurrying to work. We'd approach each other and push past. We never acknowledged the part we played in each other's lives.

Today I required a long walk in my wondrous working-class neighborhood to wake up my writer's senses. As the morning wore on, the sun came up, and the merchants prepared to go into action for those whose lives were in the street. By ten, modest chickens sat all tucked in, without their heads, in pinkish-yellow rows tilted toward the street; wild pheasants fixed in flight stared down at us from the walls; and yellowish ducks, plump and greasy, waiting for an orange sauce (blech!), tried to show off their best side. Rabbits stretched long, skinny, and red, on ceiling hooks to snare us, and the special, wild boar, its huge black bristles stuck together with blood and yellow dust, threatened to pull down the house. As if that weren't enough, next door, unmentionable innards stewed in their juices, tempting only the finest and poorest palates.

My boy was cooperating today. For once. Propped up in his carriage, he stared wide-eyed at the streets' attractions. He was transfixed by the wild boar, clearly his favorite.

We walked up, down, and around the neighborhood, ending

up in a beautiful park, the Père Lachaise Cemetery. If it was good enough for Oscar Wilde and Jim Morrison, it was good enough for us. I sat down on a bench and gave the little monsieur a bottle. He dozed off, allowing me to snack on the insanely delicious pastry I had chosen for my lunch.

Within a half-hour, Alexandre was up and getting fussy so we headed back home a little after noon. The smell of roasted chickens filled the air, and a plump rosy-cheeked matron manned her station, preparing couscous to go. The cafés had affixed their fifteen-franc menus, with their tables blocking the street. By two o'clock, the shopkeepers usually gave up and gave in to the fatigue of countless merci, au revoir Madame et Monsieur; by four they were at it again, readying for the dinner crew at six.

In between two and four in the afternoon, the street laughed at an occasional forgetful soul, a foreigner, often me, who promenaded about with empty hands and a light head, forgetting that French storekeepers close up shop then and treat themselves to a long, leisurely lunch.

We headed upstairs, he to a nap, and me to my writing desk. I planned to write a story about that enigmatic redhead perched on her stool. Here was what came out instead:

La Roquette is not only a relic from the past but a sort of second-hand Delancey Street for disenfranchised New Yorkers like me. Yesterday, French citizens started the revolution with the storming of the Bastille up the street a bit on the corner. Today, the Angel of Liberty is still trying to lift off. Yesterday another prison, this one for women, stood at the other end of the street. Today, the walls still stand, occasioning funny comments when we give our address. No one ever asks us to spell the name of our street; every

Parisian has at least heard of it. Every union strike in Paris starts at Bastille and works its way down the narrow streets to Place de la République. All we have to do is lean out our third-floor windows. It's a non-stop performance. Unfortunately, the soundtrack's a bit shrill.

How did I get so lucky to live here?

Go Round the Playground

*W*e were not alike. Unless you counted that we all had vaginas out of which had once popped a raw, slippery little red fishie. Or that a man, one penis in each case, had laid siege to that vagina, owning it, moating it off from the world, locking the rest of the bastards out. This wasn't much for common interests—or was it?

Marooned in Paris with my rather demanding husband and baby, desperate for companionship, I had thus far failed to make one friend while out pushing the baby carriage up and down Boulevard Voltaire or when dropping in at the various neighborhood playgrounds.

Marooned in Paris? Must be an oxymoron.

On a clear, slightly breezy day, I decided there would be no more fooling around. This would be the day I would meet someone. I plopped myself down next to a young French mother wearing heels and a smart outfit like most of her clan. She took no notice; she was too busy wiping her daughter's fingers with a wet washcloth she kept tucked into a corner of her top-of-the-line baby carriage. I was a bit self-conscious knowing what shape I was in: a foreign-looking woman, a little older, thin, hollow-cheeked, no color on my face though I spent part of every day in the sun, slopped together in food-stained jeans and shirt, hair hanging long, frizzed, wooly, shapeless.

Had she spotted me before? I hoped not. On good days when

my son napped in the sun, I often climbed up on the back of a bench in my ripped jeans, acting like a rebel, eating a cherry flan and reading my book. I would close my eyes and be truly happy. Most days though, as soon as I pushed the big carriage into the park, he would start squawking. He'd continue as I scouted out a position or a view to interest him. Finally, I'd remove him from his carriage, carry him close to a tree, and show him the sky and the birds. I'd rock, tickle, and sing to him. Despite my valiant efforts, we'd be forced to leave after a short time. I yearned to stay longer, unwilling to go back to my cramped apartment to sterilize seven dirty bottles, wash clothes in the bathtub, or make the daily batch of fresh vegetable soup all new French mothers were required to feed their babies.

I searched for an opening line. Although desperately lonely, I was a little leery of playground friendships. I'd had brief conversations before and not sought out more. Why? The teething crisis stories, the charming little tidbits, the scoldings, the complaints, the last big cold with fever. God, I longed for a way out of that bottle-feeding, tooth-cutting, and ass-washing universe!

But I needed a friend. I'd always had female friends. I needed help. It was a question of survival.

"What a handsome son you have," the woman, Camille, said.

"Thank you."

"Oh, you're American!" She clapped her hands. She was visibly proud to be chatting with an American. "I've been to Chicago. On a visit with my father when I was fifteen. He's a neurosurgeon. My parents are divorced, you know. My mother is Jewish, and she wasn't comfortable in France. . . ."

"I'm Jewish too, but my husband isn't," I confided. Our instant rapport thus explained itself. "What about your husband?"

She confided she was not even married yet though her Chloé was six months old; she and her boyfriend planned to get married in a month. To get medical benefits through *la sécurité sociale*. "Otherwise, why would you bother?"

She couldn't be bad, this young girl, a *fille-mère* (single mother). As we talked, at several reprises, I noticed her sniffing the air nervously, narrowing her eyes at approaching drafts, wondering whether little Chloé was getting chilled. "We should be going," she said several times. She hinted and hinted for us to leave, clutching her blazer tighter and tighter over her spare shoulders. It was a sunny, cloudless day, which I no longer took for granted. Compared to New York, Paris was rather stingy when it came to sunshiny days.

Oh well. We walked out together and agreed to meet at the end of the week. I grinned to myself: *Mission accomplished.*

Though conversation was what drew me to Camille, after a few weeks, we fell into a pattern of chitchatting about nothing much. I was not up to swinging both ends of a conversation. On warm days when Chloé wasn't sniffling or campaigning to get into the sandbox, Camille picked at herself: straightening or flattening her clothes, glancing at her heels, worrying aloud.

"This morning I was afraid to look *débraillée* (sloppily dressed). I ran back to the apartment to get a blazer to go with my jeans and boots."

"You look quite nice, Camille," I reassured her.

"I've lost a few more kilos. I must say I'm not unhappy about it. Did I show you what I bought this morning?" She pulled a long, brightly colored wraparound peasant skirt out of her bag.

I fingered the rich material. "It's lovely."

∽◯

But the following day, she was upset. "My boyfriend disliked it intensely. It hangs in the closet, never to be worn. He said, '*Que c'est vilain!*'"

"Too bad," I said carefully and noted she seemed close to crying. "Camille, you must be thrilled to see Chloé's growing and changing day by day."

She brightened up. "Do you know my boyfriend Jacky and I take Chloé into bed with us to look at her? You never saw a baby with such a total lack of privacy." She giggled. "We turn her this way and that, and we're beaming. We made her!"

When I'd see Camille coming with the polished chrome of her carriage flashing in the sun, she often looked a little worn under the eyes, but never ever slopped together.

I met her boyfriend, Jacky, when she invited me up to her apartment off Boulevard Voltaire. *Now that's a real macho*, I said to myself. Swaggering, shirt unbuttoned halfway down to his navel, crinkly cropped hair. He was of Italian descent, she proudly informed me. He hardly glanced my way, played with his daughter, dusted off his pants. Basically closed off the unit of two. I sensed I should be moving on—it seemed almost indecent to intrude on their space. If I read Camille correctly, she telegraphed a simple message: *I'm with my boyfriend today. You understand.* I left as soon as I could manage it. The happy couple. It wouldn't last. It wasn't a curse or a wish. Intuition? Of course, I could have been projecting. . . .

The next day I asked, "Is your boyfriend macho at all? You know those Italians. . . ."

"Oh, no. We're both free. We have lots of friends. . . . Well, he is jealous. He doesn't want me to go to work, afraid I'll meet men at work, fall in love with them. How silly! We're deeply in love. I never look at anyone else."

At this point after two years married to a Frenchman, I had to admit things were not going as well as I'd hoped. All my resentment, anger, and intimations of oppression boiled over. The more feminist literature I read, the more I put a name to those vague paranoid dreams I'd had ever since we met three years before. *That terrifying dream of his drowning a friend of mine in the bathtub as I looked on . . . or was that me he was drowning?*

By turns I was frightened, sad, nervous, preoccupied, disillusioned, pessimistic, depressed. I worried I was not trying hard enough. I questioned his disregard for me and the baby. My cruel fate: forced to listen to Camille rave about her upcoming wedding. "He didn't want a baby. But I decided to make one anyway. And now you should see him—he's crazy about her." She was beaming when she glanced in my direction. "Are you okay?" she asked. "You're pale."

I tried to shrug it off, finally confessing, "Pierre and I . . . we're having difficulties."

"Oh, how awful for you. What a shame," she responded, packing up her baby rattles, water bottles, extra diapers, quickly rising to her feet.

Another afternoon I dropped in at Camille's with Alexandre in my arms. She hadn't come to the park the last few days. "I'm sick," she explained, ushering me into a crowded living room where her mother, a friend with her two-year-old daughter, and

Jacky sat. "Have coffee with us," she said, hardly meaning it, content with the guests she already had.

"No, I won't stay long. I wanted to see how you were."

"Oh, I vomited all night. The flu. . . ."

Without warning, Jacky started in beating their dog, Nikita, a beauty, whipping her viciously with the leash. "STOP BARKING. ARE YOU GOING TO STOP? I'M WARNING YOU."

I hadn't noticed the dog or the barking, but now I, we, were all transfixed.

Camille screamed at him, "Jacky, what are you doing?! Leave her alone. Please leave her. She always does that."

Trying not to look too condemning, I slid out. "See you tomorrow. I've got to get back for Alexandre's nap."

"Time to go, big boy," I said in a whisper as I pushed his stroller out the door.

Camille brought the incident up the next time we got together, how mortified she felt. "I really let him have it. He acted terribly. He's too nervous. He's working two jobs now, the old one and the new one he had to start immediately. He gets in at 2:00 a.m., sleeps three or four hours, and leaves. What a life!" *Trouble in paradise?*

Camille loved staying home, spending all day admiring Chloé from a distance and up close and personal. She wasn't much more concerned with a clean house than me, but claimed she was never bored. She had many friends who stopped in for lunch or to keep her company during the long afternoons: a French girl, married to a macho Chinese guy, who liked to escape to her house during the day; a childhood friend up from Nîmes, wanting to divorce her husband and marry her lover; a voluptuous English-French girl; two homosexual guys; and her mother.

They all kept her busy. And if they weren't available, she could always meet me.

Once she and Jacky married, she seemed content with her lot, showing me the photos taken at City Hall on the corner. We both agreed our kids were more *éveillés* (alert) than those deposited at the crèche from two months on. "I'll forever stay home, and we'll move to a larger apartment, a house. We'll need a car for the weekends."

I nodded.

"And I'd like a new washing machine, and God, I hope we can go on vacation this summer."

I piped up, "Pierre and I are thinking of going to La Rochelle one weekend and taking Alexandre along. I've never been there. I hear—"

She bristled with jealousy. "We're going away for a weekend too. Next month." *She was such a child.*

One day soon afterward I stopped by. Jacky was home. I squirmed, ill at ease with him. Hadn't he been upset about my passing Camille my feminist books? "Camille's not here," he said. "She's gone back to work. For a month."

"We needed the money," she confessed when we finally met up. One-two-three she'd managed to find a sitter, no longer concerned about Chloé's degree of sensory stimulation.

After that, we lost contact for a while.

I realized I should look for a job. I'd always worked. When Alexandre came along, I loved the idea of staying home for the first year to tend to him myself. Pierre had never wanted me to stay home with the baby. I'd insisted, and he was still punishing me for my decision.

Back to square one with no other young mother to talk to.

Stalked

*O*ne cloudless spring afternoon, my son slept in the sun while I sat benumbed and content in the shade of a big tree at the Place des Vosges, watching older children on the jungle gym and in the sand, and taking notes on the perversities of French mothers.

I could hardly believe that this incredible seventeenth-century square had become my neighborhood playground. I was transfixed by the red brick buildings with steeply pitched roofs, the arcades running under them filled with stores selling stationery, antiques, ceramics, artwork, and jewelry; the fountains; the sandboxes; the statue of Louis XIII. In one corner was the Victor Hugo Museum, which I vowed one day to visit.

The ceramic shop featured a mustache cup in its window. What a great Father's Day gift for my father. It promised to keep his mustache dry when he drank his morning coffee. Of course, he'd think it was crazy and a total waste of money. As I debated whether to buy it or not, I spotted *her*.

That woman was following me about again. Tall and solidly built, she had thick dark hair in a ponytail and a deep resonant voice that commanded the attention of all the other Frenchwomen.

I figured her to be of Spanish descent or Portuguese, or perhaps an Arab. I'd often caught her staring at me in an almost provocative way. I'd watched her talking to other women at the park, noticed how her flabby upper arms shook whenever she filled in a word in her crossword puzzle book, and her mock-alarmed face lifting to locate the whereabouts of her daughter. Why was she stalking me? Whether I came to this gateway to the Marais, the old Jewish quarter of Paris, thus perilously close to the supplier of my private 4:00 p.m. cheese strudel orgies, or set off in the opposite direction, to a small unpretentious playground off Boulevard Voltaire, or even trekked to an oddly bucolic court-yard playground, surrounded on all sides by high rise buildings, this insolent-looking dame always stationed herself a short dis-tance away, glaring in my direction. What was her problem? Her little girl seemed to be about fifteen months old with beautiful blonde ringlets down to her shoulders, amazing blue eyes like the Côte d'Azur, and a pale angelic expression on her face.

The woman interrupted her inspection of me and the book I was reading, raised her mighty self, looked fiercely around the park, and called, "Jo-Hann . . . JO-HANN!" Once she'd spotted her, she galloped off to collect her child, then walked her into the bushes for a quick wee-wee! Johann was a boy?! She zipped him up, sent him off to play some more, and then pushed her bulk onto the bench next to me. Whatever did she want with me? My unease quickly vanished as she tried out her halting English phrases learned in high school. What a beautiful smile she had.

"You're an American, aren't you?" she asked. At my hesitant nod, she added, "I thought so!" Carefully screwing up her face and moving her lips in almost a parody of a French person speaking English, she asked, "What-iz-your-name?"

Won over by her efforts, I smiled. "Lucie."

"My name is Valentine. Lucie, your baby is intelligent and, of course, *très adorable*."

"How can you tell?"

Before she had a chance to reply, he awoke, happy and alert, signaling his desire to be picked up. I kissed his sweet face, smoothed his hair down, then with the help of some pillows, propped him up in a sitting position.

"See how he looks at the children with those big eyes," Valentine continued. "He's eating everything with those eyes."

"No, but your son's eyes are amazing. I've never seen eyes that round and that blue," I protested.

"Yes," she agreed proudly. "Like mine." She removed her sunglasses to reveal eyes that, except for their brown color, were indeed the eyes her son had inherited. "Where-do-you-stay?" she asked.

I told her: Rue de la Roquette.

"Will you teach me English? What does your husband do? Do you like French cheese?" She rattled off questions like bullets from a machine gun.

"Hold on a minute, please," I said, laughing. *That's it? She wanted to strike up a conversation with a carefully camouflaged, but still discernible, foreign-looking lady? Me?*

Alexandre started fussing, so Valentine and son walked back from the playground with us. She lived only three blocks from me on Rue Godefroy Cavaignac—and quickly I saw how wrong I'd been about her. She recited her history: an abused foster child who survived a catastrophic car accident, a high school dropout who got knocked up by an older guy from Yugoslavia, a common-law wife, a mother. But the equation improbably added up to sweetness and light with a sprinkling of feistiness, a streak of rebellion not unlike my own.

I no longer viewed her as a behemoth but rather a sparkling

twinkle-toes dancing besides me. She was curious about the world and would not let her enthusiasm be dampened. I listened carefully—surprise! Her fancies skimmed the eccentric. Beneath the heavy frame, I discerned a finesse of perception, a wit, an intelligence. All my other "friends" in Paris were college educated, multilingual, well-travelled. Only working-class Valentine would stick by me till the end.

Camille, needless to say, was momentarily forgotten.

I left the park that day and by 4:00 p.m. was home, observing my ritual, which consisted of brewing myself a pot of freshly ground coffee and sitting on the couch with a large porcelain bowlful, a cheese strudel from Rue des Rosiers, and a good book, and thoroughly enjoying myself in the best way I knew how. I celebrated the fact that my boy had embarked upon his afternoon nap for a good two hours. Oh, the freedom of it all. It was a sensuous delight, and ranked most days, after strolling through the quarter pushing the baby carriage into every way-out corner to see what I could see, as the only other highlight of my day. But now I had my stalker! What crazy adventures might we have together?

Having a baby, I was completely his. I knew I must find things in life that were mine, adult pleasures. Perhaps I could manage to persuade Pierre to go out tonight? I brushed crumbs off my lap and called the Vietnamese girl who usually sat for us. Yay! She was available if we needed her.

I showered, tended to the baby, recorded his whimpers and gurglings on a cassette for the New York branch of the family, and tried to adopt a positive outlook.

Pierre returned earlier than usual and headed for the shower.

"I have a lot to tell you tonight. . . ." I yelled after him.

"Can you give me a few minutes?"

Freshly scrubbed, he stationed himself at the table and pulled out *Le Monde* to read.

I dared to interrupt. "How about we go to the Cartoucherie tonight? I hear the music is great."

He shook his head. "Too tired."

Pierre was pulling one of his "tired" routines. It worked like this: if Pierre was tired, or simply not in the mood to go out, subject closed. The same applied to lovemaking. I was so incorporated into the French way of life that I hesitated for a long time to push either issue.

I cancelled the babysitter. After a light dinner, I bathed the baby and put him to sleep. Pierre and I retreated to our respective corners. With no TV—"too expensive," declared Pierre—I worked on a bright green one-piece baby outfit I'd been knitting for a while. Pierre polished his black shoes, aired out his suit for the next day, and retired early.

Catch More Flies, How?

"My husband, Eric, is a Yugoslav," Valentine confided next time I saw her. "And so terribly jealous!" She consented to his constraints though she tended to harp on her pre-seventeen liberties, when she frequented the Quartier Latin and went out dancing with her girlfriends. She loved dancing. She showed me a photo of herself on the beach at seventeen: she was terrific looking! It was sad to realize that six years had sufficed to turn her into a massive matron whose heart-shaped face and perfectly oval brown eyes might easily be overlooked.

Her husband allowed her to take Johann to the park and to pick up groceries at Prisunic. She was also in the habit of stopping off at her aunt's and her sister's against his will. Otherwise, she'd sit up in their apartment in the atelier half, which she admitted stunk of leather, sewing on buttons—forty on an haute couture suede coat for Ted Lapidus. Eric, a master craftsman, spent his time bent over his worktable, cutting the leather with his long-tapered fingers.

When we were caught in a sudden rain shower, Valentine invited me up to their apartment. They lived in a real hole. Worse than mine. Mine was a palace.

She introduced me to Eric, a tall, thin reed of a man with a black leather apron tied around his waist. He grunted a hello and told her to get him a beer. She seemed more than happy to fetch a can from the refrigerator and bring it to him. He guzzled it down in one huge gulp. I looked from one to the other. There was a nice sexual current in the air. Time for me to leave.

A day or two later, I stopped by their place and suggested we go to the Place des Vosges.

"What for?" asked Eric, putting down his leather working tools and coming out into the hallway. "What's there? Nothing."

"No, you're wrong," I dared to disagree, albeit timidly. "I've been there hundreds of times, went every day when I was pregnant. There's a sandbox for kids, and it's interesting to walk around the Marais."

He frowned and directed his attention to his wife. "Go to Parmentier, I'm telling you." Yes, Parmentier was closer but not much of a walk on this beautiful afternoon.

Humiliated by this scene as much as by the incident with Jacky and his dog, I kept quiet while repeating over and over to myself, "*Fuck you, Eric!*"

Once outside on the street, Valentine took charge. "Let's go to the Place des Vosges. I'll say we went to Parmentier." She winked. This is what she called *révolution douce* (gentle revolution), the sort of resistance she favored. "Eric knows I'm going to go," she insisted. "The problem is he can't believe we sit in the playground—he's sure we're closing out the department stores."

"Doesn't he see you spend no money?" I inquired.

"No matter. He still suspects us. And he's convinced we are out canvassing for men!"

"What? How absurd!"

"*Ah, bien sûr, avec les gosses!* [Of course, with the kids!] I tell him Johann and Alexandre are real magnets for the guys and have been sworn to secrecy."

"Did I tell you my aunt used to beat me?" Valentine asked another day as we were pushing the baby carriages toward the enormous Buttes-Chaumont park in Belleville, north of where we lived.

The park was a lovely green expanse, a little far away, that was dotted with streams, a lake, hills, and even a waterfall. I stopped cold in the street. "What aunt?" I asked. *Hadn't she claimed to be an orphan?*

"Well, she wasn't related. My mother had to give up the farm in the Berry. She was sick. I got taken up by the system and sent to an orphanage, and eventually, this aunt. She would whip me with a cat-o-nine-tails."

"Yikes. You ran away?"

"In time. I met Eric in a café. He'd arrived from Yugoslavia and could hardly speak French. He'd been apprenticing in a leather shop in Belgrade before moving to Paris to work directly with the stores and couturiers."

"You got married," I prompted. I stopped to wrap the baby blanket more securely around Alexandre and resumed walking.

Valentine let loose her hearty laugh. "No, never. One day I showed up on his doorstep a teeny bit pregnant with Johann." She struck a pose. "Ta-da!"

"*Tiens, voila un marin!*" I quipped.

Valentine's turn to stop in her tracks. "How did you learn such a good expression?"

"Pierre, who else?" I admitted reluctantly. She'd met Pierre once. Neither was exactly bowled over by the other.

"Sure. That makes sense, his father being from Brittany, probably a fisherman in his youth." We continued on our walk.

"I met Pierre at a grad school party. He was dashing. His English was awful though—the one subject he consistently failed in school. He followed me around everywhere, asking, 'How do you say this? How do you say that?' A little annoying but he did learn fast. I bought him a dictionary—"

"Lucie." She pulled on my arm to get my full attention. "Teach me more words. Listen to what I already know: 'I am a *typique* French mother.'"

"Hardly!" I muttered as we reached the entrance to the park.

When Camille resurfaced, she was openly suspicious and envious as Valentine and I talked of books, travel, husbands, and laughed together at the antics of the other French mommies. Camille complained she had lost too much weight working, and come down with bronchitis, and Chloé had been sick too. "I can't do this anymore." Once again she was a stay-at-home mom, with ample time to do nothing but look at her amazing daughter.

Poor little Chloé, still in a carriage at thirteen months, still lying back and being fed her bottle, though she was beginning to push her mother away and rage a little. "I'll never work again," Camille vowed.

She and I failed to pick up our old friendship. In any case she was always busy with her real friends. So, I stuck with Valentine who was a lot more fun.

Mamie's Visit

I wistfully looked around my kitchen as I sipped my morning coffee. Wouldn't it be great to have a nice clean house? Would I enjoy my surroundings more? My mother always claimed I would. Sparkles instead of smudges, no greasy fingerprints on the fridge, no bits of dried egg or gruyere, glue on the highchair, and no rusty can openers nor mayonnaise smears on the tablecloth testifying to my refusal to give up a lifetime of revolting (i.e., American) eating habits. Imagine: a white dishrag with sharp creases hanging near the sink. Or bleached sheets, freshly ironed, on the made-up bed.

But what if it was clean? Aha! Wendy, back in New York, would certainly find it so. Everything was in its place . . . more or less. The dust wasn't ten inches thick, *quand même*.

Pierre would vomit and scream and tear his hair out when he got home.

I should have tackled the mess. But I was too tired. Dr. V had ordered triweekly intravenous shots of Vitamin K, whatever that was, to stop my hair loss. Every time I changed Alexandre, I found his diaper littered with my long black hair. It was quite alarming. Bad enough that I had streaks of white in the front, had them since I turned nineteen. I could live with that but not with bald spots!

With impeccable timing (for once), Pierre's mother, Mamie, tapped at the door and I went to open it. "Bonjour, Lucie," she said after giving me the three-in-one French greeting kiss. She looked around the place but said nothing. I caught her pursing her lips a little. Putting on an apron she'd brought with her, she announced that she'd cook lunch for us: fresh vegetables from the Aligre market, veal scallops in lemon cream sauce, steamed spinach, dandelion salad, goat cheese, and homemade apple tart served with strong coffee. What a feast for a weekday!

She started in, I grabbed my book and retreated to the living room. For the next four hours straight, she worked her magic. The result was a spotlessness (and a meal) I'd never succeed in reproducing. True, she rinsed dishes in cold, soapless water and left green creatures clinging to our salad leaves, but that was the price I had to pay.

After lunch she stretched out on our bed, immediately conked out, and woke refreshed exactly fifteen minutes later. She informed me she typically woke at dawn and went to bed about eight thirty. In between, what a mini-powerhouse—hyper, hyper, hyper. She poured herself another cup of coffee before finishing up.

I pretended to read my book while she worked; I felt guilty and awkward in my own home. Why did she come anyway, all the way from the suburbs? Who told her to come? I resented the intrusion; I hated housework. I suffered silently as she bustled around me. One day I intended to tell her—nicely—to stop. But right now, I rationalized, she probably needed to keep her demons at bay by staying busy.

She'd been known to small talk me to death, but today she asked, "Has Pierre been *méchant*?" (mean)

"Well . . ."

"Ah, men! They're all like that." *Are men really all the same? And how would she know?*

She asked if Pierre was stingy. Let's see. I spent one hundred francs a week, mostly on diapers and baby stuff, and he gave me an awful time about it. The answer was yes. I must have nodded because she started telling me how I could fix that. "You should write checks but enter a different, smaller amount in the check-book register."

She gave me one of her twinkling smiles meant to convey how smart she was. She wasn't, though she was kind of adorable in her way. Unbelievable that she was coaching me in ways to deceive her son! These Frenchwomen were sure subversive. Valentine, Camille, and now Mamie. Aren't relationships sup-posed to be built on trust? Not according to my French "sisters."

Alexandre awoke and Mamie turned her attention his way, squeezing, screeching at, strangling her grandson in kisses while claiming, "Pierre doesn't count any more for me. Only this guy counts now." She meant it. She was a woman too simple for ruse. What was her opinion of me? Of my marriage? My housekeeping? She was awfully discreet. In her eyes I was probably a horrible slob, for she was absolutely one of those cleanliness-next-to-godliness people. Didn't she wonder why her poor son picked an American to marry?

As she prepared to leave, she smiled sweetly and said, "One day you'll be able to afford a *femme de ménage* (cleaning lady)." *Was that a slur?*

ﾟﾟﾟ

Not My Type?

*P*ierre agreed at last to go see the Beckett play *Oh Happy Days* starring Madeleine Renaud and her husband, Jean-Louis Barrault, France's most famous theatrical couple!

Pierre knocked on the door at 6:40 p.m., and when I opened it, thrust two filets of merlin into my hands, saying, "I'm going down to get more fruit."

I yelled down the hall after him, "But we have fruit!" Two apples, three oranges, and a small cluster of grapes nestled in a crystal bowl on top of the kitchen table. I gave it up quickly, quietly closing the door. Pierre was particular about his food and partial to fruit. I should have taken careful note. He was thin and taut like a violin string. His was a musical walk. He was a young Apollo, a Greek statue, a perfection of limb and line. I persisted in teasing him about his slight boyish look, his doll-like arms, especially when he paraded about the apartment nude, beseeching my admiration, demanding that I comment on his manly physique.

This was difficult indeed; he suspected that he was not my type in the way that I was his. Aside from those drawings of his dream girl, Sarah, who he insisted looked just like me, he had also written poems about a small girlish woman with long, thick black hair halfway down her back.

My bad luck: I was more drawn to meat. Not red meat, mind you, but a powerful spread of shoulders, thick thighs, thin calves, full buttocks. A beard would be nice too. I supposed I had in mind men like the men in my family: warm, furry, and cuddly with a human tendency towards chubby. All in all, a bigger man would have suited me better.

"I found delicious grapes," he said, reentering moments later, a bit breathless.

"What took you?" I asked. *You fruit!*

"Oh, I met that Russian guy. He wants me to distribute copies of *L'Humanité* Sunday on the corner of Rues Basfroi and Roquette." Ah, the call of the French Communists.

"There goes Sunday," I muttered, and before he could respond, "Pierre, if we're going out tonight, we'd better get started, no?" I was in a hurry to change into my favorite outfit, the one I'd bought on boulevard Voltaire but had little occasion to wear: the orange and brown tasseled skirt, slit up the side, the short tasseled vest. I'd followed the organic recipe I'd discovered back in Rochester, substituting egg yolk and rum for shampoo and rinsing with vinegar. My hair cascaded down my shoulders: shiny, black, and wavy. My best feature.

Pierre glowered at me for an instant in his dark Gallic way, but with admirable restraint, changed out of his work clothes—blue shirt and tie, blue suit jacket, khaki slacks—washed his hands and face, and deftly started preparation of the meal: mincing cloves of garlic, sprigs of parsley, rondelles of carrots, scraping them gently off the cutting board onto the filets of fish frying in the pan.

The apartment smelled good enough to eat!

"Open the windows, please," he ordered. "Close the bedroom door."

We finished eating by seven thirty. I rushed through the clean-up, changed, and barely had time to comb my hair on the way to the front door. Our Vietnamese babysitter was tapping meekly, and when I opened, I spied Madame Karol behind her, grinning mischievously.

"Oh, I see you're going out. I was going to have tea with you and bring this cake I baked this morning."

"Yes, we're going to see a play."

"Very good. No matter. Have a good time. You're young. Hello, young lady," she greeted the babysitter. "Have a piece of cake."

I retreated into the apartment to grab my red woolen Mexican poncho, then pushed past them both, stepped out into the hall, and ran for my life. The baby had started to howl. I sprinted down the stairs and waited for Pierre in the cobblestone courtyard. I was taking no chances. I was not going to believe this evening until I had lived it.

As soon as Pierre was in my line of vision, I started speed walking towards the Bastille.

"Where's the fire?" he asked, looking amused, but grabbing for my hand to slow me down.

The evening turned out to be fun. Fun, not in the sense of light-hearted, but of sharing a deeply moving, artistic, cathartic experience in the presence of a man culturally evolved enough to appreciate all the subtleties and feel them in the core of his being. And wanting to, more than anything else, rush back home and make passionate love to celebrate.

Pleased with ourselves, we lay on the daybed and talked.

"Amazing. All that moved on stage were her lips. Yet we were riveted to them, to her head jutting out," I enthused.

"So well done. Ah, Madeleine Renaud. What a fine job of acting. A classic," he agreed.

"Wasn't it a shock to see a man appear out of nowhere, crawling?"

"Oh, yes!"

"I loved the way she kept taking all those things out of her bag, in the beginning, and sorting through them—like all the meaningless things we do in our lives, the little routines and rituals."

"So well done," Pierre managed to mutter as he drifted off to sleep, positioning my head on his shoulder first.

For a while, I stayed awake, reliving the performance, jabbering to myself excitedly. My blood was zigzagging through my body like an electric current. I had never been less sleepy.

Hey, he never even noticed my outfit!

Discord

We'd connected in the theatre; we usually connected in bed. Still, we continued to bicker over matters great and small: how much salt to put in the soup, how often to clean our matchbox of an apartment, whether it made sense to buy American-style diapers which were more expensive than French pads you tied up with a thin sheet of plastic and which always leaked.

I tried not to listen to the litany of mistakes I supposedly made on a daily basis. I "insulted" the garlic by not slicing it fine enough; I specialized in affronts to good taste and the proper way to do things. I'd been observed putting a container of milk on the table instead of pouring it into a creamer; taking the baby's shirt off in the blistering heat while having lunch with Mamie; sneaking pastries between meals; and more, so much more.

Every few days Pierre relented, hugging me, assuring me, "You're perfect. Don't listen to me."

Back home, Wendy, who had a master's in psychology, wrote me to say children of alcoholics often turn out to be hypercritical control freaks.

Now she tells me!

"You spend too much money. I give you one hundred francs every week."

"For diapers, food for us, necessities. Do you notice me waltzing around in Dior gowns, spending my weekends on the Côte d'Azur, being chauffeured around the—?"

"Now you are saying *n'importe quoi!*"

"Well, I'm trying to give you the whole picture. May I point out that before our son was born, I earned money too?"

He sniffed. This sparring made us both more than a little sick. Often I fantasized about falling ill and being forced to return to the States to have my parents nurse me back to health. I would not have trusted Pierre to be up to that task. I used to think he would always take care of me, but now I had my doubts. Last month before he left on a weekend business trip, I told him I felt like I was getting sick. My throat was tight, and I was getting seriously alarmed.

"Please, Lucie! Stop with the theatrics!" He glared at me for a second before picking up his backpack. "Take care of the little *bonhomme* [fellow]," he said before opening the door and bolting down the stairs.

How could I feel safe with a man like that? How could I get him to change back?

Sex, Anyone?

*O*ur wacky Mexican friend, Chita, had followed us to Paris to study French, she said, at the Alliance Française. To have an adventure, more likely. Still, she was the only one of all our friends thoughtful enough to give us babysitting as a present, the best present. Pierre had returned from his latest trip, and she volunteered to take Alexandre out for a walk so Pierre and I could have (another) "date."

Finally, fun!

As soon as the front door closed, I disappeared into the multiuse pressboard closet. Pierre went to take another shower. When he emerged, I emerged, clad in nothing but a long red-and-silver scarf, wrapped once around my breasts and disappearing between my legs to emerge as a kind of tail in the back.

"You're too much, my Lady," Pierre mouthed as he moved towards me, eyes already at half-mast, with that fuzzy turned-on look men get.

"Wait. You haven't seen everything yet." I reached back into the closet and drew out a pair of Mexican maracas and started shaking them above my head, and swaying suggestively, which naturally caused the rest of me to wiggle, wobble, and watusi.

"If that's how you're going to be, we need wine." Pierre ducked into the kitchen, returning with two glasses of red table wine left over from dinner the night before. He handed me a goblet, and we entwined our hands to take a delicate sip from each other's glass. "*À ta santé.*" Before long we were sipping and slurping and sucking at every available orifice and source.

I lay awake on the daybed, and slowly sat up and rubbed my eyes. I was still in my ridiculous costume, but Pierre was newly dressed, leafing through one of his textbooks at the table in the kitchen and taking notes. "Wow," I said, coming up to him, putting my arms around his chest and kissing his neck. I spotted the empty wine bottle. "I guess I was wiped out. Not like me to take a nap."

Pierre held up his hand and continued writing. I kissed his cheek and moved into the bedroom to remove my "costume."

"Lucie, you should get dressed now. Chita will be back any minute."

"I know. I know. What do you want to do today?"

"We can go to Place des Vosges, walk around."

"Great." My everyday routine. The baby knew the way already, holding up his pointer finger to get me back on track if I strayed from the usual path. Like his father.

Pierre lifted his head from his book in time to see my frown. "Why are you never satisfied?"

Ah, the big question.

"Pierre," I continued, "why don't we sign up to take a class together? We could learn a new language. How's Russian? Or Japanese? Italian would be easy for you."

"I don't think so."

"But why? That would be so great, learning something new together. We'd meet new friends and—"

"Lucie, not now. Please. I have enough on my plate. And you know that's not how I learn. I have to be immersed in the culture, like in South America and Mexico. Even the US. I'm no good at studying verb tenses and conjugations."

"So maybe a gourmet cooking class?"

An exaggerated sigh issued from his lips. "Are you ready yet?"

"Yes, hubby, ready to go."

When was the last time we did things my way?

Remedial Sex

Same time as last week, I cracked open the closet door and stuck a leg out, a leg sheathed in a black fishnet stocking crowned with a red lace garter. I commenced my imitation Moulin Rouge routine and managed to kick open the other half of the closet door.

"What's going on in there?" Pierre asked as he put down his newspaper and walked toward the bedroom, stopping to turn down the volume on Edith Piaf's "Padam, Padam." Coming abreast of his wife (me), he repeated, "What's this all about?" He was actually cracking a smile. "Am I in a cabaret?"

I stepped out of the closet and slowly unfurled the multicolored scarves looped around my breasts, unleashing full frontal nudity on the world. With my darkest shade of blood-red lipstick, I'd drawn an arrow that travelled all the way down my body from stem to perky little stern. I pivoted to show off the pink-and-blue cotton ball tail pasted on my rear end.

"Come here, my silly," Pierre whispered huskily. But I backed up and circled the room, climbing over our mattress on the floor, jumping over baby toys, finally letting myself get caught in the far corner of the bedroom.

"Oh, Monsieur, that is not for kissing," I murmured as he bent down to flick his tongue over my breasts. I let him push me gently backwards onto the bed. "But Monsieur, I am not this kind of girl," I protested, batting my impossibly long store-bought lashes while pretending passive resistance. *Ridiculous, yes? But it always did the trick. A powerful reminder to Pierre that he had a nubile young wife.*

Pierre pulled me into the living room where we rocked and rolled and romped like the good old days in Mexico. I smartly did not ask for more than I was going to get. In the past, he'd responded, "More?" with a damning look, the implication being I was a nympho if I wasn't "done" yet. *Fine, I'd read about vibrators in the States—next trip definitely!*

Our interlude concluded, I put a head of lettuce into a bowl of vinegar and water, something I detested doing. True to form, all the little slugs slunk out, flattened and very dead—the price to pay for greens straight from Mamie's garden. When I was pregnant, this task fell to Pierre—my stomach was too queasy. Now I just rinsed the lettuce and left it to dry on the kitchen counter.

Pierre emerged from the bedroom, buckling his pants and tucking in his shirt. "Where is that money I gave you at the beginning of the week?"

Here we go. "One hundred francs is only twenty dollars, you know."

"You are in France now. We don't spend money like American chickens without their feet."

"Heads."

"What?" He screwed up his eyes. "Are you making fun of me?"

"No. Take it easy. Look, I still have fifteen francs left."

"Humpf." Pierre sat down to sulk at the kitchen table.

"What are we going to do this weekend?" I asked, hoping to change the subject.

"First I've decided we will go to the photo lab I rented near Bastille and develop some pictures I took."

"Can I come?"

"Of course. I will teach you how to use developer. But now it is time perhaps to go fetch our little man. We've interfered enough with Chita's time."

"She doesn't mind—"

"Ho! Of course she has other things to do with her time. She's a beautiful, young, single woman in Paris. She needs to be going out, dancing and singing and drinking."

"Don't worry about Chita. She does plenty of that, all of the above," I murmured as we straightened up the apartment. Though Chita had moved out of our apartment where she'd camped out for months on the daybed, she invited herself to dinner every week, each time with a new boyfriend trailing along.

That weekend we did what Pierre wanted and spent Saturday afternoon in the photo lab. On the walk there, Pierre made sure to point out every attractive woman we passed in the streets. "See how they look in all their finery."

"Yes. I admire how they get everything to match: their hair, their fur wrap, their purse."

"So beautiful."

I turned to look at him. "You do know that to create that degree of perfection costs money?"

"*Oh là là*. I don't like what I am hearing," he said, but with a smile and a sigh. "Buy yourself a new dress." *Hmm. Can I record that?*

꒰ꆤꆤ꒱

Party Time

We spent Sunday afternoon and evening partying with colleagues of Pierre's from the lab. His closest work friend, Bernard, was preparing his first formal meal in his new homestead, throwing a housewarming party after months of sanding, gluing, sweeping, washing, hanging drapes, stacking records, hammering, nailing, and positioning pictures.

"Look at that spread, Pierre." Being a French party, we chowed down on: chorizo, sausage, olives, pickled onions, corn, tomatoes, salads, eggs, apples with fresh cream, strawberries, cucumbers, fruit pies, and coffee. *And Bernard's a bachelor!*

"Would you like my special cocktail?" Bernard asked as he offered me a glass filled with gin and whatnot and grated nutmeg on top. Amazing! I wandered away from Pierre and Bernard and circled around the room, trying to fit in somewhere. Scientists composed most of the guest list with an artist sprinkled in here and there. I searched for someone normal.

Am I back in college? I couldn't help but notice quite a bit of showing off, flirting, adolescent and bizarre behavior. One man streaked across the apartment, bare-chested and barefoot, wearing nothing but a skirt. People pointed and laughed. Another was engaged in a drinking contest in the kitchen. Judging by the empty bottles on the counter around him, he would soon be a candidate for alcohol poisoning. *What a cleanup poor Bernard will have to endure.*

Pierre signaled me from across the room where he was entertaining a small group. Relieved, I started making my way over when I noticed he was gesturing and pantomiming. *I'm to dance with Bernard?* Ugh. I was not a dancer in the best of times, and these French threw their arms and legs all over the place in a herky-jerky way. I had no idea what they were doing. I faked it as best as I could. Bernard thanked me and released me to go back to my wandering. I needed to find a corner to wait out the end of this party. *How long do these things last?*

I wondered if Alexandre was giving Chita a hard time.

Thankfully, Mme Lafontaine ran into me as she was walking by and invited me into her group. I didn't have much to contribute and contented myself with following their rapid French and picking up some new idioms. From afar I watched Pierre and his group cracking jokes and laughing and presumably having lots of fun.

Pierre acted in a surprisingly lighthearted way with his colleagues. I hadn't seen him that way in a long time. Since Mexico. In Mexico he patiently mentored his students and the more junior staff, and they loved him for it. He laughed a lot. He was the golden boy. I was the golden boy's mistress.

Quite unexpectedly, I caught one of the older secretaries with a nasty smirk on her face as soon as Pierre turned his back to her. Strange. *What was that about?*

Finally, time to go. We walked out with the Lafontaines, and they dropped us at the nearest métro station. During the ride Pierre fell asleep with his head on my shoulder. Nice. But I could not quite forget his one whispered remark to me as we gathered up our coats and possessions: "You make too much noise when you chew."

Fresh Air vs. Clean Apartment

Well, Luce, decision time's at hand. Did I dare cross the Rubicon, meet Camille and baby Chloé again so we could push our baby carriages all the way up the hill to the Buttes-Chaumont? I'd postponed our trip once already. And the sun was shining brightly over Paris today. Or should I respect the wishes, the complexes, the manias of my *tendre et cher* and shop for groceries, plan the week's meals, cook, clean, and do the wash? Possibly Mamie might show up, freeing me to accompany my pals on their expedition. But who knew if or when? *What a drag to live up to others' expectations!*

I knew what Wendy would do. It'd be easy for her. I actually knew what I would do too. I'd give my mother-in-law twenty more minutes to waltz in like the white tornado—though I despised her for cleaning my house and wished she wouldn't and wished I knew how to stop her without killing our already touch-and-go relationship. I really wished she'd understand, but I knew she couldn't possibly. Out we'd go, Alexandre and I, for a joyous carefree promenade all afternoon, as if we had nothing else in the world to do, gossiping with my playground pal, hopefully about all things unbabyish under the sun.

And I'd feel guilty.

And Pierre'd feel exploited.

And we'd joke. "Remember when we split, the Mexican tablecloth is mine!"

"I get the Talavera pitcher," I'd counter.

We'd stored a whole set of Mexican dishes in my parents' garage. They'd been an impulsive pre-engagement present from Pierre to me. We were waiting for the right moment to unpack them—when we had room for them, were more stable, were "established." Did the dishes make the same eerie clinking noises the pitcher did? "Must be an up-to-the-minute report of weather conditions in Puebla," I'd quip.

A tapping at the door. *Saved by Mamie! What Lucie wants for once carries the day!*

The Significance of a Smirk

O rested my best string bag on the kitchen counter and pulled out a hunk of gruyère the cheese man had graciously wrapped up for me in a sheet of newspaper. *Le Figaro*, it turned out. Was *Le Monde* reserved for the elegant matrons of the sixteenth arrondissement? I'd been in Paris long enough not to ponder the effects of newsprint on my taste buds or my longevity. I refrigerated the cheese and next deposited a whole grain bread fresh from the bakery on a wooden board I kept on a lower shelf. Amazing to me still that I'd never seen a fly, ant, roach, or mosquito in this ancient building. What was the secret? As an owner I'd know if the building summoned exterminators. They didn't. Another unsolved mystery. I quickly emptied my bag, brewed a cup of java, and sat down to strategize about the evening. I left Alexandre sleeping in his stroller. He wasn't due to wake up for another half hour.

"That secretary, the one you said was dating Bernard?" I asked that evening before Pierre was halfway in the door.

"What about her?"

"What's her name again?"

Pierre frowned as he took off his shoes and slid into his house slippers. Okay, I should have given him a minute to walk in the door, put down his attaché case, and go through his usual routine, but I was anxious to have my questions answered.

"I think you're talking about Fernande."

"Yes, that's her. At Bernard's party she gave you a very funny look."

"I didn't notice. Why would she? Are you sure you're not making up—"

I followed him into the bathroom. "I know what I saw. Why would she do that? Have you had a disagreement? Is she over-worked? Maybe you should bring her flowers."

Pierre sighed deeply, rolled his eyes—he learned that from me—and said, "My poor little wife, so full of creative ideas and theories. Come here and give your husband a hug." He wrapped me in his arms. *So comforting. So silencing.*

"Pierre, it's hard to be with the baby all the time."

He unhooked a frying pan from the kitchen wall and poured in a generous amount of oil. "Look, when the oil is like this, you throw in the garlic."

He sprinkled cold water in the frying pan and we listened to it sizzle in the silence.

"Is that rice pilaf you're making?" I inquired.

He gave a slight nod.

After the meal, he put on his jacket. "Do not give me an argument. I have to finish up at the lab. I shouldn't be back too late."

"Again?"

"If you understood what a captivating project it is. . . ."

I walked with him to the front door, trying to stall. "Is it true . . . about *cinq à sept*?"

"What is it now?" He turned around to face me, ashen.

"You know, that businessmen pick up prostitutes in the Bois de Boulogne for a quickie? On the way home from work?"

"What kind of nonsense is this?" he barked.

I touched his arm to keep him from fleeing out the door. "Well, is it?"

He glanced around the room, as if searching for the correct response. "Might be. I've heard of that, of course. Are we finished here? Lucie? I need to be going."

"Would you ever?" I held onto his sleeve.

"Enough nonsense. Let me go. I'm going to be late."

"I wouldn't want you to—"

"Yes, I know that. But I don't think men ask for permission. Or need it."

Ouch. Not the answer to put fears at bay. He was halfway down the hall when I called out, "Pierre, I thought I'd go to bed early. Could you give Alexandre his last bottle?"

"No. I wouldn't count on that if I were you."

Such a fucking Virgo! How to get through to him? He was like a stampeding horse with his blinders on about to crash into a fence. Why wouldn't he ever listen? He was an only child, but so what? Couldn't he learn to compromise on anything? Always his way or the highway. *How about my way?*

Camille, Jacky, Baby Chloé

*V*alentine was sure she would not spend her entire life with Eric. If not for her son, she would have left by now. That was Monday. On Wednesday, she confided, "I have to say we could never live without each other. I can really speak to him." On Friday she continued, "He's changing. At first he wouldn't let me see my family. Now he knows I go there. He actually agreed to take me out. We're going for a promenade on *les grands boulevards*!" She beamed and did a spontaneous little dance for me.

She and Eric appeared to be working things out. Good for them. We nevertheless continued our cynical snipes at men and pretentious French women.

Camille disappeared once again. "This time she's dumped us for good," declared Valentine.

"No. She must have better things to do," I countered. I was pissed too but decided to wait her out until one day when I was forced to call for a book of mine.

"No, no, I have only this Dodson book you gave me," she said. We stood talking by her front door. Despite the darkening sky above signaling a coming storm, she did not invite me in. After a few awkward moments, she asked, "And how are you?"

"Oh, *ça va*." My face doubtless told a different story.

"You know, Lucie, it's a bad time for couples now. Everyone I know is having trouble."

"And you too?" I probed gently.

"Oh yes. Oh, dear Lucie, if you only knew. . . . Well, I'll stop by one morning."

Camille never showed up. I was angry and resentful. How dare she screw with my head?

She resurfaced in a few weeks, pale, thin shoulders stooping, but stylishly dressed with new boots to show off. "My husband, Jacky, wants to leave me. I'm incredibly nasty, he says. He hurts me terribly. And he's become impotent with me. One hundred percent! He told me he never considered me his wife. He's looking for an apartment."

"Could be he needs a few weeks by himself."

"Yes, I told him to go. He says I'd better find a smaller, cheaper apartment for Chloé and me. Oh my God . . . I can't sleep or eat! What'll I do?" She turned her stricken face to me.

"But Camille, you're only twenty-three. Look, nothing's decided yet. Even if he moves out, who's to say he won't come back?"

"Right. He says he can't stand it but spends all weekend at home. We have a lovely time. And why doesn't he sleep in the living room? No, he has to come and sleep by me."

"Camille, maybe he's overworked. Try to take it easy,"

"No, I'm going straight for legal advice. He's such a spendthrift. I'm not sure I can depend on him for money. He says it's all his childhood that marked him and he can never be happy. . . ." Camille stopped talking to wipe her tears. "I'm afraid of finding myself alone. I know what it is. My mother raised me alone, and I suffered horribly. After all those awful things he said and did to me, it's terrible to care about him the way I do."

Camille was in full melodramatic mode. I tried to console her with misery-loves-company talk, with talk of woman-strength, confidence, responsibility for oneself. With talk of me.

I was talking to the deaf and getting more and more frustrated. When she mumbled, "I have black thoughts," I was too busy planning that night's dinner menu in my head to react. Later, I blamed myself.

The next week she missed a weekday rendezvous with me. She called but I had already left. I planned to call her that evening when I had the time, but she beat me to it.

"Lucie, *ça y est.* That's it. *Abandon du domicile.* This morning he took a studio in the eighteenth. I'm okay for the moment. I have friends who are with me. Come by one morning, but I'll be running around, going to legal services and all."

I did not call all week, though I was uneasy. I even confided in Pierre, "I suppose I should call Camille. It's her first week without her husband."

"I see," he responded.

Monday, I relented. Too late. The quivery voice on the phone was not her voice, but her mother's. "Camille is out of town at the moment," she said.

"For how long?" I asked, but the line went dead.

Valentine came running over to me in the park that afternoon. "Oh, Luce, you don't know, do you? Poor Camille is in the hospital!"

I flashed on a vision of Jacky beating the hell out of their pooch. My heart skipped a beat. "Did he—"

"No, nothing like that. Much worse."

"Val, for heaven's sake, tell me what happened."

"Yes, okay." She took a deep breath and continued, "Camille tried to poison herself last Friday."

"No," I stuttered, "that can't be right." Delicate Camille, who lived in fear of taking a chill, of *courants d'air*? Of disheveled hair and mismatched clothes? Hadn't she gone to the country?

I deposited Alexandre in the sandbox next to Johann. "What did she do?" I forced myself to ask. Valentine paced back and forth in front of me, shaking her head side to side, her face telegraphing distress.

She mumbled, "It must be the beginning of a nervous breakdown. But she's not seventeen or eighteen. She has her daughter to think of."

"Valentine, come sit down next to me."

"I can't keep still."

"Yes, you can. Come—"

"Johann," she bellowed. "Come to your mother." She startled the other mothers, but once they located the source, they returned to their conversations.

Johann trotted over and resigned himself to being covered with kisses and tightly hugged. After a minute, she pushed him gently toward the sandbox. "Now go play with the other kids." She turned to me and whispered the story into my ear.

No! What could possibly impel Camille to hurriedly mash dog tranquillizers between her teeth?! My stomach turned over at the thought. I stared at Valentine, transfixed by the impalpable, unknowable quality of this act. Why the hell didn't I call her?

She could not have meant to kill herself, to succeed, to die. Such an act sounded inconceivable to me. As Valentine said, what about Chloé? How could Camille bear to leave behind her beloved baby daughter?

Could I too arrive at such a juncture?

Lately I'd been ruminating on writing a story of three women whose lives inexplicably forked at the same place. Women, who, while not really influencing each other, decided for the same and for different reasons to leave their men. I never imagined the leave-taking could involve violence to oneself or others or could be fatal. I regularly entertained all sorts of thoughts. No harm in lurid scenarios of the mind. Fantasies were permitted; reality must reign. What Camille did to herself, her daughter, and Jacky though, was not a normal part of any world Valentine and I inhabited.

Back in New York, ten years ago, I had played with a different scenario, also a story about three women, all from the same New York City Jewish background, college grads who seemed to be spiraling out in different directions, making opposite life decisions. Scholar. Homemaker. Hippie. I'd insisted on a happy ending to that novel.

If only, I thought at the time, I could whiz ahead ten years and see what became of the three women. Nasty was this desire to foretell the future. It plagued me. Life would be much easier to live if you could lean back and enjoy it, knowing the hero and heroine were going to kiss in the last lingering frame of the movie.

Which story would I wind up telling?

"What about Chloé? Was she ready to leave her behind? Motherless?" I asked.

"Never could I do such a thing," Valentine declared. She stopped pacing back and forth in front of the bench. I pulled on her arm and got her to sit. She quieted down though occasionally smacked the bench with her open palm. Side by side we sat in silence, watching kids build forts in the sandbox until it was time to leave. As we parted at the corner of Voltaire and Roquette, Valentine repeated, "She broke with reality. I understand that. But still, her daughter. How could she?" She shook her head in disapproval. Before we separated, she enveloped me in an unexpected hug. "*À demain.* See you tomorrow," she whispered hoarsely before taking off down the street.

Once home I gave Alexandre dinner, bathed him, and when his bedtime rolled around, I put him down and crawled into my bed too. Hours later Pierre arrived home and woke me up. I told him I had a headache and pulled the covers over my head. The very next morning I called Wendy in New York to get perspective.

"Look," she explained, "every suicide is meant both to scare and to succeed. You can't separate these things. It's irrational."

If only Camille had spelled out what she had planned . . . I might have been able to stop her. *To do that for a man!* If Wendy was trying to assuage my guilt, she failed. I called up Valentine that night at dinnertime, knowing it was a bad time. I heard Eric in the background asking her whom she was talking to, turning the volume up on the TV, yelling at Johann to put away his toys and come to dinner.

"Do you have a minute?" I asked, not waiting for a response. "In adolescence I started wondering about my friends and me, where we would be going in life, if we would still have anything in common in ten years. Where in the world would we wind up? I resolved there would be a happy ending to that story: I would find a husband."

"And you did!"

"Yes, but listen. I was desperate to foretell the future, the outcome, the hero snatching me up and riding away with me into the sunset."

"What's wrong with that?" Valentine asked. "I've seen lots of movies like that."

I heard Johann whimpering. Yet I continued at breakneck speed. "But now, ten years have passed. I know with certainty—this story of mine is going to require a different ending. Three different women who will all leave their husbands for different reasons."

A crash in the background.

"Ah Lucie, *je m'excuse*. Can we talk about this another time? I should be at Parmentier on Thursday—"

I took a breath. "Sorry, Valentine. Of course. Say hello to Eric and kiss Johann goodnight for me."

I obsessed about Camille for the next few weeks. I vowed I would never be that selfish, never put my suffering ahead of my son's welfare. I tried to discuss Camille's case with Pierre, but clearly, he was not that interested, having only glimpsed her once or twice. He did manage to share the news that his college girlfriend attempted suicide when they first broke up. *Was this a French thing?*

Interesting tidbit of his past he had heretofore neglected to share with me. I waited to hear more, but he had other important issues on his mind.

Escape to New York

"I want to go home. Alone. To visit my family," I said. We strolled under the huge trees in the Jardin du Luxembourg, me pushing the stroller, he with his hand on the back of my neck.

"Now's not a good time."

"I mean I'll take Alexandre, of course—"

"Listen—" Through the drizzle, a young man approached, waving a bunch of flowers in our faces, exhorting us to "come to Jesus."

"Are you selling those for Reverend Moon?" Pierre asked point-blank.

"I know you are good, you believe in God. I want you to join us." He launched into his poorly memorized schtick about salvation. We interrupted and, to our surprise, he circled back to the beginning of his script. "I know you are good."

Pierre whispered to me that the time had come for magic. "I am a communist," he proclaimed. "Do you still want me to join?"

The young man's bright face dimmed. Temporary power outage? He blinked and said, "You'll change. I know you'll come back to Jesus." But he turned his head sharply, located another potential convert, and trotted off in that direction.

"Geez! These guys are everywhere now," I said.

"Luce, look, I know I am hard to live with. I told you that back at school. I pick on things. I criticize you. Don't take it seriously. I love you. You're perfect." He put a long arm around my shoulders and drew me in for a tight hug against his side. But I was too far inside myself by then, like a polar bear with only its nose outside the cave, sniffing the air.

"I can't let myself be hurt by your words. I can't pay attention to what you say," I mumbled, half to myself, wondering how I could stop believing the words when words were everything to me.

"The rain's getting worse. Let's go back," I suggested.

"Okay. Come this way, Luce," he said, pulling my arm as I tried to get him to walk on a path we had never before taken. Resigned, I followed him out of the garden.

He sensed a change in me. I realized I'd better watch myself. Not the time to reveal my hand.

It had been more than two years since my last visit to New York. I needed to get home to get my head straight. We heard nothing more about Camille and assumed she'd been whisked away, perhaps to live with her mother in Neuilly. Valentine got all weepy when I announced my trip. "You'll never come back." I did my best to reassure her.

Once I'd convinced Pierre that I was serious about my six-week mini-vacation, he arranged to pay me back. In advance. He signed up for an extended sailing trip. Where? I had no idea. For how long? Six weeks! *Quelle coincidence.*

In shock, stranded without resources (no car, no help), I was forced to leave Alexandre alone to circle down the stairs and do the food shopping. I trembled each time at the thought of having an accident in the street, being rushed to the hospital, and no one realizing my poor baby was starving to death in his crib.

When Mme Karol was around, I asked her to mind him for a half hour, but most days she was out visiting her friends or stopping by the cemetery to fill her husband in on all the latest news. During Pierre's absence, Mamie came by twice, cleaned up a bit, and left without disclosing her take on the matter.

Our son chose this very moment to suffer his first ear infection. I spent my days running him back and forth to the doctor's. I waited impatiently for Pierre to return. The day finally arrived. After a quick peck on the cheek, he stood before me, tanned and muscular, but he was not alone.

"Gretchen is new to Paris. Maybe you can show her around?" At his side stood a cheery, athletic-looking, beautifully bronzed blonde whom he'd invited to stay to dinner. *What the hell?*

Dinner? Did I mention I was thoroughly exhausted? Haggard-looking? Seething? The blonde got the picture, even if my husband did not, and excused herself. "I just remembered I have to be somewhere."

The moment the door closed behind her, I picked up a plate and smashed it in the sink. I reached for another, which he easily wrenched out of my hands. "What's wrong with you?" I shouted, not caring who heard me.

"Control yourself," he said. "You'll wake the baby. What exactly is your problem?"

"My problem? You bring a strange woman home to your wife and baby? You think that's normal?" I reached for another plate, but he intercepted me again. "What am I to think?" I screeched.

He pushed me aside and busied himself picking pieces of china out of the sink. I planted myself by his side, waiting for an explanation. I wasn't fussy; any half-hearted explanation would do. He gave me . . . nothing.

The blood in my veins turned to ice. Chilled to the bone, I headed for bed, leaving the greasy dishes, the scorched pots and pans, the garbage scattered around the kitchen. I did not know who he was anymore, only that I had to get away from this man.

Alexandre and I landed in New York after a noisy flight, Alexandre being the official noisemaker. Half the passengers stopped by to rattle keys at him, make funny faces, and tickle him, none of which cut short his shrieks of discomfort. An Italian woman congratulated me on my new pregnancy. What? Wait. Could I have been eating too many *mille feuilles*, *pithiviers*, flans?! Or was it the strudel from the Jewish bakery?

Mom and Dad reluctantly showed up at the airport, a ten-minute ride, to ferry us to their house. They let me know I'd inconvenienced them. During our stay though, Mom bonded with her first grandson, bathing him in the kitchen sink, singing to him, taking him for walks to downtown Flushing. Dad ignored him except for the times Alexandre fretted during a favorite TV show. Dad would yell, "Get him downstairs! Take him outta here!"

Once Mom exclaimed, "Alexandre is adorable," and Dad countered with, "What about me?" *Was he for real?*

I escaped to have lunch at the corner diner with Wendy. I ordered a massive burger deluxe, something I really missed in Paris. And fries. No wonder we call them French fries—so superior to the American version. In France, no need to add ketchup; they taste just fine without.

"So, what's it like living in Paris, Luce?" Wendy asked, cutting short my culinary musing.

"Oh, you know, Paris! The walks along the river quais, the Opera, the organ recitals in the Latin Quarter."

Wendy waited, poker-faced, poking at her cobb salad.

I devoted attention to my lunch, savoring meat that tasted like meat. "It's fabulous, to tell the truth."

Small nod from Wendy.

"Did I tell you I learned how to cook mutton and lamb, duck and goose, and once a rabbit in mustard sauce?"

I stopped waving my arms around and looked Wendy in the eye. I could tell her the truth. I'd tried hinting at it to my parents, but they got belligerent.

"Tell me."

"Wendy, I am not sure I want to stay in this marriage."

Wendy closed her eyes for a moment. "Do you remember what I told you when I met Pierre for the first time?"

"I remember what bad timing you had. We had just gotten married at City Hall."

She ignored me. "I said, 'Pierre is a taker and you're a giver.'"

"Right. When Alexandre had a bad cough a few weekends ago, Pierre packed his gear and left for the day to go swimming at the indoor pool in his old neighborhood. He was back in time for dinner, declaring, 'Well, it's stupid for us both to suffer.'"

Wendy continued, "I said I didn't know if you were enough of a giver."

I sighed and closed my eyes. "Apparently not, Wendy. Apparently not."

During my New York stay, I reconnected with friends I'd known since junior high school. We'd been through our teenage crushes and crises together, yet for them I vowed to keep up the act. We decided to meet in a famous pub in lower Manhattan. After all, I was a tourist now. To our horror and concern, the maître d' refused to seat us.

"No women without male escorts."

"What?" We couldn't believe they were still doing this despite a court order to allow women in. We tried to stand our ground; we raged a bit, but we were not disposed to stage a sit-in. We had too much to talk about. Instead, we let drop a few vague threats, then hightailed it to a more congenial spot a few blocks away.

"And I thought the US was so far ahead of France," I muttered. "Can't anyone cut women a break? What's their problem with—"

"So you speak fluent French now?" interrupted my oldest friend. "How I envy you! Surrounded by all those continental types! Well, you've already snared the pick of the litter. That Pierre!"

"Lucie, you always were strong. And sure of yourself. I always knew you'd have an adventure. No ordinary life for you. Look at me: married to a Jewish boy from New Jersey, two kids, substitute schoolteacher. Boring! You actually had a job in Paris? Kid, you're living the dream!"

"But you're happy," I pointed out. She'd always been the domestic nesting type.

Another broke in, "Lucie, one of my friends is a single mother and she's doing great."

Was that a funny look in her eyes?

"Uh-huh." I tried not to blush and changed the subject. "What's been going on here? What am I missing?"

I made an effort to catch up on the news at home, but beyond smiling at jokes about Jimmy Carter, the peanut farmer, and Gerald Ford, who couldn't chew gum and talk at the same time, I was too far out of the loop. Dad and I bonded over *All in the Family*, though Dad failed to recognize how much like Archie he was. I wondered what was going on in France and realized there was little to no international coverage on American TV. What's more, I was stunned to see the news channels now had commercial breaks. My parents and I watched Channel 5 and listened to the sweet-faced anchor each night as he asked, "Do you know where your children are?" Happily, I did.

I went shopping for a warmer coat for Alexandre—a tiny blue snowsuit—even though he was too little just yet to play in the snowdrifts surrounding the house. The weather dropped to zero degrees one morning and my father had to call on AAA to start his car. I had to admit to myself that the weather in Paris caused fewer headaches for its residents.

The night before departure, I sat my parents down to tell them what was running through my mind. Dad interrupted, red-faced. "Does he beat you? Cheat on you? No? He makes a living, doesn't he?"

Cheat on me? He would never. "He . . . we aren't compatible. I'm not sure I even like him anymore."

"Nonsense," said my father, turning away to light up one of his smelly cigars. "Excuse me." He retreated to the den to watch his bowling matches, adding, "Those aren't reasons."

Mom frowned. "Lucie, have you thought what it would be like to be a single parent? Your baby's too young. You won't be able to manage everything alone. Hang in there. Stick with it. Every marriage has its ups and downs." *Translation: What would she tell her friends? She'd be ashamed. The truth was they couldn't care less about my unhappiness.*

Dad popped back in to add, "Remember? I told you not to marry a European!"

Wendy offered to drive us back to the airport, saving Dad the trip. Her final parting words to me were these: "I'll help you." The funny thing was that being in New York around old friends felt empowering; I began to regain my confidence and remember who I was.

Back Home

$\mathcal{B}$ ack in France, Pierre seemed a little more attentive than he had been. During my absence, he hung out with Chita, went to a concert with her at Musée Cluny, even had tea with Madame Karol once or twice. He had plenty of time for his special projects, such as developing beautiful pictures of Paris and of us three. There was one I had taken of him that I especially liked. He was holding Alexandre, dressed in a bright red outfit; in front of him, Alexandre was turning to look out the window, inquisitive as always. Pierre was beaming down at his son, secure in his arms, and the look in his eyes was unmistakable: *I made this and I am proud*.

I had no choice but to give the marriage another chance. For my son's sake. Alexandre was changing daily. Six teeth were sprouting at once. He never stopped "talking." I was amazed at how exceptionally well-coordinated he was. His arms were so muscular. He crawled like a pro and walked a bit when we held his arms. His favorite thing was working out how to sit up in the bath for a few seconds without falling over. Of course, he liked to throw tantrums if he didn't get his way. I loved being his mommy, as long as I could do it part time.

I started exploring what kind of new job I could get, but doubted I'd find anything challenging. Then while doing research I discovered an interpreter's course given one night a week.

I shared my discovery with Pierre after dinner. "Pierre, if I were to take the course at night and get certified, I could have an actual career. In three years time, I could be working for the UN."

"Hmm." He rubbed his chin in that old-man way I used to find adorable. "I hope you're not counting on me to watch Alexandre one night per week."

"Why not?" I countered.

"I don't like your tone," he said, before storming out of the room. "I already have a job."

In that moment I hated him. The whole pregnancy I'd repeated to myself, *hang on sister, you've got to at least get a baby out of this marriage.* The only goal I could come up with. What a loser I was.

I turned to my journal for relief.

The Rising of the Sun

She was lying face down in the muddy depths below the ocean. Her ears were filled with seaweed, little fishes swam in and out of her mouth and nose. She started to cough and out came emerald-shaded water, seashells, and strings of coral.

How long had she lain like this? Minutes, no, more like centuries. Was she going to stay like this forever? Hell, no! It was time to take a risk. With a mighty effort she rolled onto her back and floated up. Through the silver-tinted water, she could glimpse the sun breaking over the horizon. Surely a sunrise was a good omen.

She sat up, mighty colossus that she was, and spit out oceans onto her lap. Next step—tomorrow—would be to get up on her knees and sing.

I needed to figure out how to sing. Out the window, the sky over Paris was, as usual, gray and wet. What else was new? Funny how no one sings about Paris in the deluge. The weather overall is more temperate than New York. My lightweight purple trench coat usually got me through the winter.

I dreaded being alone today. I phoned Valentine and she seemed to intuit my mood. "Come over. I'll teach you how to make real Moroccan couscous."

I stationed myself behind Valentine and surveyed her cramped kitchen: spoons and cups tumbled out of drawers, aprons were caught in a cabinet door, last night's dirty, unscraped dishes waited patiently in the sink. Valentine caught my eye. "One good thing about Eric—he doesn't care how I keep the house, as long as he eats on time. He knows I'm no housekeeper."

Amazing. But then I remembered: he wasn't French.

"I want to get a job too," she added wistfully as she kneaded the couscous between her fingers. "But Eric does not like the idea. He wants me by his side all the time to sew the buttons on the leather coats he cuts out."

Glancing around her shabby apartment/atelier, I had trouble imagining how three people lived in it. In one room they conducted daily life; in the other Eric worked; the three of them slept in a tiny alcove. Scraps of leather, fur, thread, buttons, and patterns were the only decorations. The toilet was one landing down. I could find no shower or tub.

I perched on a stool in a corner and watched her prepare the vegetables and harissa sauce, add in chorizo, chicken, and seafood. "I know I'd like to go back to work," I said. "The days are endless, especially in the cold weather. The baby's sick all the time. In fact, this is the first time I've been out of the house in two weeks." I slid off the stool and went to check on Johann and Alexandre in the other room. They were playing with a fire truck on the floor while Tino Rossi's "Papa Noel" played over and over again on the stereo. Last time they were this quiet, a few weeks ago, we found Alexandre pulling on Johann's hair and making him whimper.

Back in the kitchen, I asked Valentine about Camille. "I haven't heard anything," she said. "And the apartment—I went over there twice while you were gone—it's sealed up."

"I have no contact information for her. She can't disappear like this."

Valentine patted me on the arm. "She can and she has. It happens." Abruptly changing the subject, she asked, "Luce, what did you do before the little Bonnehomme came along?"

I had to accept that I would never see Camille again.

"I taught English for a private language school. To executives, secretaries, factory workers. You know, *formation permanente*?"

"Of course. You know, don't you, companies must use 10 percent of their profits to educate the staff. Another victory the socialists have brought us French." She beamed with pride.

"Anyway," I continued as I carried out Prisunic cutlery and plates to the table in the main room, "I had to run around Paris and the suburbs: morning class in Charenton, back to Paris to teach at Sèvres-Babylone, train to La Défense for a third course. . . ."

"Did you like it?" Valentine stopped stirring the big pot to give me her full attention.

"When you're a teacher, you're always on stage, *une comedienne* [an actress]. You have to crawl around, do pantomime to make the students understand. French is forbidden. It was fun. I learned all about French society from my students, about the Christmas Réveillon meal, *le trou normande*. . . . Yet I used to wish for a desk job where you can push papers around and be a little dull for a few hours and no one notices."

"I would love to be a teacher—" Valentine interrupted herself to yell, "Johann, you stop or I tell Papa!" Johann had snuck into the kitchen without our noticing and was pulling on his mother's dress. He stared mournfully up at his mother with those immensely soulful blue eyes of his. "Go play now. But pom-pom on your derrière if I have to speak to you again."

Johann wrinkled up his face to cry as he backed out of the kitchen. "Don't worry, kid," I whispered, "we're going to eat soon." We sped up preparations for the meal, and the career conversation was dropped for the moment.

As we were carrying out the food, we heard a godawful cry. We dropped everything and rushed into the main room where we found Johann with a bright red mark on his forehead. Was it possible? Alexandre bit him?

"He wanted my toy. Papa gave it to me." Johann sobbed. Valentine gathered him up in her arms.

We all looked over at Alexandre sitting on the sheet Valentine had draped on the floor. He was engaged in sucking on his shoe. "Must be teething," she said.

"*Pas dans la bouche!*" I said reflexively.

"Not in your mouth," Valentine chimed in.

As I removed his shoe from his mouth, I wondered how to discipline a baby. Fitzhugh Dodson says you can't discipline a child under two. I opted for, "No biting!" *Is the rising tension in our house getting to him too?*

The couscous was superb.

Back home, I put Alexandre down for his nap and returned to brooding.

I'd done everything Pierre wanted. I learned to cook like Mamie and clean (well, almost), put milk in a creamer, apologize to the garlic, and forego the taste of ketchup in my fries; I now slept with my head on his shoulder instead of sleeping on my stomach where I'd always been more comfortable; I hosted needlessly complicated dinner parties for his scientist buddies and their families. All these people ever talked about was the same boring stuff you hear on the radio: how to "accommodate" a boeuf bourguignon; when the French communists will realize they are taking orders from Russia; why Truffaut is perceptive and Almodovar incredible; and finally, what makes French cuisine that much superior to all others that a dying Frenchman crawling about in the desert will forego food and water unless they come from La Belle France (a joke circulating widely at the moment).

At one point—Rochester days—Pierre seemed to want me to have a career. He didn't appear opposed to the idea of my taking off five years to be with a baby. Back then he liked that I had a direction (sort of) until he went about smashing it!

I'd gone along, played along, followed his lead. My grad school friends, that guy from Sweden, warned me that Pierre was no feminist, that it made no sense for me to abandon my doctoral studies.

Truth: I was sick of school, sick of being poor, sick of not being able to afford new boots. I'd had it with studying for hours and hours, of discouraging come-ons from faculty and married fellow students, of watching my youth drain away. Let me come clean: I had gone to graduate school to meet a husband. Nothing was happening on that score in New York City. I reasoned the grass might be greener on some upstate pasture.

I remembered how after our months-long separations—me in New York, he in Mexico—when I was finally in his arms again in the small Puebla apartment he had rented—I felt I had come home. *Mi casa es su casa.* I felt it in my marrow: I belonged with Pierre wherever he might go.

And now?

꧁

New Job, New Life

$\mathcal{V}$alentine was right. We should have been working. On impulse I posted an ad in the International Herald Tribune: PhD Dropout; Bilingual; Seeking PT work.

Un, deux, trois, I was summoned for an interview. The boss, a Czech dissident, needed an assistant to clip articles from the five French dailies and put together a monthly digest in English and French of activities by Soviet bloc dissidents. All I had to do was jump on the bus, which stopped outside our building, cruise through the Marais for ten minutes or so, cross the magnificent Pont Neuf, and walk a few steps to the office.

"Pierre," I shouted, as soon as he walked in the door that night, "I'm in!" I jumped up and down with excitement.

He looked confused. Understandably.

"I've got a new job." I described the ad I'd placed, the warm reception, how pleased the boss and his wife were with my background, the smiles all around.

"How do you know?" Pierre asked, shaking his head. "Jumping to conclusions as usual."

"No, not at all, Mr. Bonhomme," I said, dancing around the apartment to the tune of the Carole King tape Wendy had sent me. Swooping up my smiling son in my arms, I cried, "C'mon, boys, sing with me: 'I feel the earth move under my feet.'"

"Enough now. Give me my son." Pierre pried him from my

arms, and they disappeared into the bedroom. I prepared Alexandre's bottle and his meal of pureed meat and vegetables. Why couldn't Pierre let me be happy?

When I finished in the kitchen, I peeked into the bedroom. Both male members of our little family had fallen asleep on the mattress. I said, more to myself than to them, "You watch—I've got the job. No doubt in my mind at all."

The offer came in at 10:00 a.m. the following morning. That evening I proudly announced to Pierre, "I start next Monday. Eight thirty to one."

"How much?"

"About 2,000 francs a month."

"You need to pay for a nanny to watch Alexandre out of your salary unless you're going to bring him with you."

I paused a moment to digest that. "Sure," I mumbled. It was definitely worth it to me.

"And I suppose you found a nanny already?"

Oops. "Silly man, I have that covered."

"Make sure you do."

"Can you believe it? I've got a bunch of candidates lined up to interview—"

"Believe it of you? *Oui, certainement!*"

I swung into action the moment Pierre left for work the next morning. In a frenzy, I interviewed two dozen people for the job over the course of two days, everyone from a mean old concierge who slapped the hands of another kid she was watching every time he reached out to touch one of the doodads on her shelves to a shy eighteen-year-old French girl, Mimi, who lived around the corner with her husband. Mimi had no experience whatsoever. I hired her on the spot.

"I'm glad you're satisfied," Pierre responded. "Now, no more complaining, eh?"

I yearned for a hug or kiss. Congratulations would have been welcome. Pierre instead excused himself for a half hour to have a drink with a friend at the corner café.

The new job entailed unlocking the door of a small apartment in St. Germain des Prés, composing a monthly digest of articles on Anatoly Shcharansky, Václav Havel, Andrei Sakharov and the like while indulging in a second cup of coffee and a bar of Belgian dark chocolate. Peaceful. I'd return home to find Alexandre finishing up his lunch. Mimi would kiss him goodbye but not before confessing to me that she liked to pretend he was her baby. She loved him already! After changing my clothes, I'd whisk him off to the park for the afternoon. Life was good once again until. . . .

The Bomb

*J*ust as I was settling into our new routine, coming to terms with my day-to-day existence. . . .

"You what?" I put a hand up to my face. Burning hot. Pierre and I faced off in the kitchen of our tiny claustrophobic flat.

He finished soaping up the dinner dishes, drained the water from the basin, and let cool water dribble over them a few seconds, laying the half-sudsy plates on a clean dish towel he'd placed on the counter. Without looking up, he continued, "Shall I repeat myself, Lucie? Surely you heard me the first time? I accepted the job."

I looked around the kitchen for a projectile, picked up my one of the baby's shoes, and launched it with all my force against the kitchen wall. I still threw like a girl. I stomped my foot. I shouted, "Dammit!" How could I make him hear me?

"What are you doing, Lucie, you silly girl?" Pierre said through clenched teeth, moving over to examine the wall. He pivoted, and in three steps, he had my wrists tightly in his grasp, his face peering into mine. "Have you gone *ga-ga*?!"

"Pierre, you're using force. Let go," I said. "I told you before. Jewish women don't put up with violence. I'll be out of here so fast and back to America—"

He reluctantly let his hands drop and moved away, standing by the kitchen window, staring back at me. "Why must you be so difficult?"

"Me? I came all the way over here to your country. I had your baby. I'm difficult? How about the fact that I abandoned my studies to join you in Mexico? I was almost home free—"

Lifting his head, he muttered, "Please. You were sick of that place. You said it yourself. I told you to finish."

"Right, and how exactly was I supposed to do that? You were already in Mexico waiting for me to join you. There wasn't even a decent library. You could have accepted a different job in the States, you know. You had other offers."

"You still do not understand. The job in Puebla was an amazing opportunity: to participate in research, get my name on academic papers, to teach classes in Spanish, to absorb the culture. Don't tell me you didn't enjoy—"

"Always an amazing opportunity. Like this one, I suppose." I failed to keep the sneer out of my voice.

"Don't mock me! Once again, I will explain it to you. Listen to me and don't speak! This job is in *Hawaii*—do I really have to sell it? How many women would jump with joy to know they'd be living in Hawaii? Anyway, I'll be part of a tri-country effort to erect a new telescope, more powerful than any other. I will be responsible for the optics. At twenty-three, working with much older scientists."

He went back to the sink, untied the dish rag from around his waist, and began drying the dishes, stacking them on the small shelf above the fridge and making more noise than usual.

I took a deep breath, striving to regain my calm. He had never mentioned this job opportunity to me. Now I was supposed to jump on the bandwagon?

"Pierre, we discussed our next move. We said we would go back to the States to be near my family. If we moved at all. I thought we'd probably stick it out in Paris for a few more years. We have this apartment in the heart of Paris, our friends, our jobs—"

"Hawaii *is* the States," he said through clenched teeth.

"Not exactly a stone's throw from Queens, New York. Don't you get it? I want our son to know his grandparents, his uncles, my friends. Here we have only your mother—your father's not involved—and she's quite . . . limited." I saw him wince. Had I succeeded in getting through to him?

"Lucie, enough of this. You never listen." He dried his hands, went into the bathroom to wash up, and then into the bedroom to change his shirt. He picked up his attaché case.

"Now what? Where are you going now? Let me guess."

"I'm . . . going back to the lab to work."

"Nine at night? Let's finish here first."

"With you there is no finishing. Always the same complaints," he said, putting down the attaché case.

"We have to finish," I pleaded. My life was spiraling out of control. My control.

"Understand this: A wife follows her husband. That's all you have to know, Lucie."

"You have to be kidding me."

"A . . . Wife . . . Follows . . . Her . . . Husband. Period," he bellowed.

That's fucking insane.

"Let me go," I whispered, more to myself than to him. I squirmed away from him. I didn't need his cold lips on my cheek.

He bolted. Out of sight. I ran to open the door but all I could see was the barely lit hallway. I closed the door and almost tripped on his attaché case. "Ow!" Just then Alexandre called to me. I could hear him climbing out of his crib. "Coming," I yelled. *Or maybe not.*

When I awakened the next morning, I found a note on the kitchen table:

"Let me go," you said. What does that mean?

You two can join me . . . later. I'm due to leave on my birthday in September. More than a year from now. You have lots of time to prepare.

Don't be such a baby, I keep telling you. Be a little logical.

You'll see. It will all work out.

I tore the paper into tiny little squares and flushed them down the toilet, remembering how he used to write me poetry.

But I Love Paris (in a Way)

For the next month I lived in crisis mode. Every day I changed my mind—only once but decisively. Either I'd follow Pierre to his new job building a telescope in Hawaii or I'd go home to mother.

How could he not discuss the job offer with me before accepting it? He never even mentioned the possibility. I could not fathom his reasoning.

"Why don't you stay in Paris?" asked a few expatriate American friends.

No, that option was not even on the table. I'd always thought I would never be here if it weren't for my French husband. I disliked the French too much. I missed my mother too much? Well, I suspected she'd go ballistic and make me pay for my decision. But surely, she'd enjoy being part of her grandson's life?

I missed the intimacy of longtime friendships. I missed Wendy and my friends from seventh grade.

I continued going through hell. Pierre opted out of any discussion by saying, "You're too complicated for me" or "It's your problem" or "Tell me what you've decided."

The bastard. I hated his refusal to see gray. I retorted, "You'll see that it's your problem too, when you have to cross ten thousand miles to see your son."

"Oh no," he said, wagging his finger at me. "You can't take a son away from his father."

Another convenient aphorism!

What should I do? I worried about all the shit: broken homes, divorced mothers with kids, my son not having a male figure to identify with. And especially guilt over doing what I wanted to do, for once daring to accommodate myself. *Did I know what I wanted?* I asked myself that as my parents and my boyfriends had always asked, as Pierre asked now. Why did they always have to belittle me?

All I knew, what my intuition told me, was that this marriage, this relationship was not worth chasing after, not worth going to another country for. What I wanted was . . . out?!

"I'm staying in Paris." I tried that out for size, for a week. I felt lighter. How could this be? This possibility I had never seriously considered seemed right all of a sudden.

Pierre would leave mid-September. I needed to focus. Could I find happiness with my new job? Explore new avenues for myself? Could I be both mother and father? *If I could only stop pacing, up and back, in our teeny-tiny rathole apartment.*

What's a Lesbian Anyway?

*C*hita called me out of the blue. "Luce, I'm at the Alliance Française. I have a class in a few minutes. Listen, I spotted an ad here for a feminist group. Open meeting tonight at 7:00 p.m., métro Louvre. Want to try it?"

"Oh God . . . I don't know."

"C'mon Luce. You said we should keep on trying."

"Remember last time?" I said, flashing on our doomed attempt pre-Alexandre to crash the French feminist scene. We'd gone to a feminist bookstore/food cooperative/café/hangout. The women gathered in groups of three and four, greeted each other with kisses and hugs, whispers and laughter, but Chita and I entered alone and remained that way. They might as well have posted: *You Are Not Wanted* on the walls. "What's special about this group?"

"Luce, I got to go now. See if Pierre will watch the baby." *Fat chance!*

I thought about it during the day. Mothering an infant is an incredibly hectic job, and I was blessed with an extremely active, assertive, and alert baby. However, I seemed to have time to mull things over in my head, time for reading and for letter writing and journal entries. By 1976, our bicentennial, the French women's movement had barely begun. *Féministe* was a dirty word, to men and women alike, and the movement, an object of derision. Yet I'd read a book by a French woman writer recently about the symbolic treatment of women in the media, and another about the differences in the rearing of boy and girl babies. Books by women about women. Did this make me a woman's libber?

Pierre surprised me by agreeing to watch the baby.

Chita and I walked into a large, cavernous hall with a few hundred women milling around, many foreign born, come to Paris no doubt to corrupt the complacent and overly compliant *françaises*. Our motives? Curiosity about these women who dared to question convention. I didn't know about Chita, but I was looking forward to new friends and influences, being, of late, landlocked on the plains of babyhood and wifedom.

At this particular general meeting, the lesbians and the drama club gave presentations. We were seated on folding chairs far from the podium and could barely make out the speakers. We learned from a girl with stringy hair and a tee shirt over bare titties that she'd turned to love with the same sex following one harrowing experience after another with different boyfriends. She looked to be about nineteen years old. Another lesbian confessed that women often put her through the same changes as men. She'd recently caught her woman lover cheating on her.

I was fascinated as I had never heard lesbianism discussed out loud before, and amazed that they were not afraid to reveal themselves in this way. I also stupidly worried that one of them would pounce on me in the ladies' room, misconstruing my attendance at this meeting. But I had to go. Badly.

I took care of my business and was in the midst of washing my hands when I heard, "Well, hello," from the large-boned woman standing next to me at the sink.

"Hi," I responded, aware that I was talking to a lesbian and quite nervous about it. I started twisting my wedding ring around and around. The woman, noting my nervousness, turned back to the mirrors and said, "Don't worry—I don't turn into a vampire until half past twelve."

Ashamed of my reaction but anxious to be out of close range, I squirreled back to my seat. Chita was nowhere in sight. Instead, a woman I had not seen before had plopped herself down next to me. Before she opened her mouth, I said, "I bet you're from New York!"

"How can you tell?" she asked in the flat tones of a Brooklyn native. She looked like a sister.

"I was born in Brooklyn too," I said.

"Flatbush Avenue, right?" The woman continued, "What brings you here tonight? I haven't seen you before."

"Well, I have a baby, and I'm looking for a way to keep my sanity."

"Yeah, babies. Well, I'm a lesbian myself," she added, looking to me for a reaction.

To my credit, I kept a straight face even though this interaction constituted the first actual lesbian, not counting the one in the bathroom, I had ever seen up close. I marveled at how normal the woman looked—and acted. I started out a little nervous around her, but the nervousness soon faded. The woman looked and acted like everyone I knew back home.

Yet another speaker at the dais lamented the fact that lesbians often treat each other as shabbily as men do. My new friend nodded her head in agreement and started to recount the histories of her various relationships and their dire conclusions. *I guess I'm never going to become a lesbian. No hope there.*

After an hour and a half, the main speakers finished discussing the significance of the bra burnings and such that were going on in the States—I gave up wearing bras for the most part before I even came to France. Why do people always reduce everything to sensationalism? France, I estimated, was at least fifty years behind the States in terms of the sexual revolution. I was repeatedly bowled over by the submissiveness of the French women I knew, coupled with their unbridled resentment that boiled over whenever they were gathered together out of earshot of their husbands. Bottom line: They supported the status quo, had never heard of consciousness-raising groups, and could not fathom why American women wanted to change anything.

The drama club spokeswoman testified to the huge success of their last feminist play, written, produced, and performed by local talent. My ears perked up. She ceded the podium to a well-dressed Englishwoman who made an electrifying announcement, "Anyone wishing to help us form an English-speaking women writers' group, please come to the meeting next Wednesday."

The air stopped circulating around my head. The address was a few blocks away. Chita came running over. "Go to the front of the room, Lucie, and get your name on the list!"

I could hardly believe it. I'd been scribbling in my journal since I came to France. I knew I had the makings of a few good stories in that little book. Paris is all about writing, *n'est-ce pas?* No way was I going to miss this meeting. I rushed up to the dais and added my name to the list.

As the meeting ended, I bid farewell to my seatmate. "Bye. It was great meeting you." *And great learning that you are like everyone else. Normal.*

Chita and I walked the few blocks to the métro together, chattering nonstop. She was so thrilled for me.

Feminist Writer's Unite!

Wednesday rolled around, not the best of days. I was forced to call in sick to work.

I sniffled and coughed and choked and tried to carry on as usual with a cotton kerchief draped over nose and mouth. The baby was spared contact with my germs, but the trouble was I couldn't breathe. And the apartment was hot and airless. Not in the best of moods, I nevertheless managed to get him dressed and out for a walk.

That evening I dragged myself to the meeting in the Marais, mainly because it was close to home and Pierre agreed to meet me afterwards and walk me back in the dark. Mme Karol agreed to sit in our living room in case Alexandre woke up.

The meeting, which drew fifteen women—Australians, Canadians, English, Americans—frightened me. Did I know what I was getting myself into?

Soon I sensed the same apprehension in others. I emerged from my silence with suggestions on how to structure our meetings. Why not write on a theme to start with, such as our shared experience of living as foreign women in Paris? The others seemed to latch on to this idea. From the outset, I did not have the purest of motives. I knew I had several good pieces written about my quartier. *The Village Voice* hadn't been the least interested when I queried. Would these women be?

We all crowded together into the small space. Women started reading from their works. Luckily, I had the foresight to bring a prose poem I had written. Aware that I tended to read aloud too fast and did not always enunciate clearly, it came as no shock when the group asked me to read the piece over. Then they wanted to hear it again and then again. I was flattered; I was hooked. Here at last was my chance to take myself seriously.

Fifteen Turns into Five

*O*crept into a small studio in the seventh arrondissement
not far from Boul' Mich. The first to arrive, practically
shaking from nerves, I followed the hostess around as she readied her apartment for the evening ahead.

"So you're a New Yorker too, Ernestine?"

"Call me Ernie. Please. Would you help me put the cheese
and bread on the table?"

I did as instructed. I heard knocking at the door and asked,
"Should I get it?"

"No, I'll do it." Ernie let in an older woman, elegantly
dressed but slightly stooped, clutching a stack of issues of *Dispatch*, the English language weekly.

"You must have stock in that paper," I said.

The woman, Ava, looked me up and down. "I am the editor."

"Great," I said, "wanna see my manuscript?" I was joking—
kinda—she obviously was not in the mood. *Oy, off to a bad start!*

Huge pillows—blood red, shocking pink, blazing yellow—
were arranged in a circle around an old trunk covered in an Indian
print that doubled as a cocktail table. I chowed down on cheese
while wondering how to connect to these women when in
strolled Suzanna, a Brit, rather mousy and nondescript, followed
by Gabriella, absolutely spectacular looking, moving like a thor-
oughbred or a queen. Tall, model-thin, with a mass of black curls
framing a perfect pale Pre-Raphaelite face. *Holy!*

Once everyone was seated, Ernie took charge. "Might as well introduce ourselves, what we're doing in Paris, blah blah blah."

Hesitation on all sides. Gabriella got to her feet and moved over to the bookcase to examine the figurines on a shelf. Breathless, we all waited to see what she'd do. After a few minutes she turned and said, "Here's what you need to know about me: I've had five husbands, a baby when I was nineteen, and more adventures in more countries than you can shake a stick at. Oh, and I'm from Toronto."

I glanced at the others seated around me and looked back at Gabriella. Apparently, she had hardly begun. "I'm an artist primarily. When I have a place to live, other than my car, I construct these dioramas of apartment buildings. I furnish each apartment with little figures and their possessions, and we watch them eating a meal or fighting and throwing furniture at each other or fucking or—" *Holy Moly!*

"What are you doing in a writers' group?" I dared to ask, aghast at my nerve.

"Same thing you are." She smiled, warming up the room. "I'm also a photographer. Take a look." She handed me a black-and-white coffee table book featuring rather bleak scenes of life in Nova Scotia. I dutifully passed the book around to the others.

"Impressive," croaked Ernestine.

Gabriella smirked, though clearly basking in our admiration.

"What about you, Ava?" I asked.

"I have nothing to add," she protested, smoothing down the skin on her neck. "Writing should be judged on its own merits, not biographical knowledge." *Oops.*

"Let's do a warm-up exercise," I suggested, hoping to relieve the tension. "I'll call out a word and we'll write for five minutes."

"That is known as a prompt," advised Ava. The rest eagerly adopted my suggestion. Ernie scrambled for paper and pens.

"Dislocated."

When five minutes were up, we each read our pieces aloud and the others commented on them. We didn't say anything useful in our critiques of each other's works, but we were gentle and accepting, even Ava.

Ernie asked, "More wine?" and walked around the room refilling our glasses.

Suzanna straightened her back and announced, "Ernie and I and Lucie didn't get a chance to talk about ourselves so . . . I was trained as a nurse in London, and I'm on a second marriage. Ernie?" Suzanna neglected to mention until much later that she was the type of woman who could give up her two kids and never see them again because she didn't want them to have "divided loyalties." She'd abandoned her kids, left them in England with their father, who used to abuse her. Why wouldn't he abuse her little girl when she got older? But none of us asked questions like that of a person destined to be a writer.

Ernie revealed her New Jersey roots and that she was busy writing verses for her boyfriend's operetta. Her trouble, we soon learned, was that she was only able to crank out one verse a week, that's how constipated the task of writing was for her. Did she dare to eat? She easily could have been mistaken as an understudy for Olive Oyl.

Everyone turned in my direction. "What to say?" I stalled. My life felt too complicated to reduce to a few sentences. "I'm just a Jewish girl from New York who thinks, perhaps, she can write."

All ohhed and aahed appropriately. After two hours we thanked our hostess and decided to meet at a neighborhood café in a month. From fifteen women initially interested, we were now five, fully committed.

I held tight to this lifeline. I wanted never to give it up.

Gogo Gigot

*G*abriella, an excellent cook, presented me with a gift quite precious and close to her heart—a recipe for gigot, roast leg of lamb. Fitting from the lady of legs. I wanted to impress my guests. I was hosting next.

I made it in a hurry on Tuesday afternoon, steaming up the windows. The bathroom, the bedroom, two flights down, all smelled of coriander, garlic, lemon, and pizza spices. I rushed, taking it out of the oven, covering it with a linen napkin, storing it in a remote corner of the fridge. I made sure to quickly air out the rooms.

Sure enough Chita and her newest boyfriend dropped in. Master moochers. Would they find me out? He slumped into the closest chair and remained inanimate and inarticulate for the next four hours. Chita, after five minutes, casually inquired, "Are you going to dine here tonight?"

I said, "How about scrambled eggs?"

She gave me a funny look and reluctantly agreed. In the kitchen she cornered me. "How are things with you and Pierre?"

"The usual boxing match. Not much sex anymore."

"Would you care if he slept with another woman?" she asked.

Funny question. "Probably not," I admitted and turned back to scrambling the eggs.

When Chita and friend left, I congratulated myself. A whole leg of lamb—for me. For my writers. I served it to them the very next night and they exclaimed over my generosity.

ele

My Writers

ithin a couple of months, I knew that nothing would ever again be as great as the five of us roaming through Paris, on the lookout for miniature people, furniture, pots and pans for one of Gabriella's dioramas. I allowed myself to hope I might make it as a writer, with these women pushing me every step of the way. All my life, I realized, all I ever wanted was a little encouragement.

One month, Ava invited us to meet at her country home outside of Paris. By that time we'd learned that Ava was divorced from a Frenchman and had a second estranged husband lurking about, along with a few English girlfriends. Her stories, like "Black Widow Lady," were polished, and like her, really cold and mean.

On the train to Garches, who slid into the seat next to me but Gabriella! She still scared me. But as the scenery rolled by and we talked, we warmed up to each other. Gabriella was in confessional mode. "I have this little habit," she said with a big toothy smile. "I like to appropriate things."

"Huh?"

Seeing my puzzlement, she explained, "Imagine this. I go to a house and see a letter open on the table by the door."

"You read it?" I ventured.

"No, I take it." She laughed and laughed. "I see I've shocked you."

"Yes. . . ."

She failed to hide her delight. "But why? The owners have already read it. It's open. And I need it."

"For—?"

"Just like you, Lucie. I bet you collect conversations eavesdropping on other mothers in the park or at a café. You steal whole characters for your fiction, violate their privacy, mock them, don't you?"

I squirmed. "I guess you could look at it like that."

"Such great fun, isn't it?" She tossed her dark mane and fixed me with her best impish grin.

"But that's hardly the same thing as—"

"Oh, dearie, you're right, you know I am a terrible person." Gabriella winked while removing a small mirror from her purse and playing with her curls for a minute. By the end of the ride, we'd become friends and she'd admitted, "You remind me of myself."

Yeah, right. "How?" I asked.

"The way I might have been. A middle-class Jewish girl. We look alike, don't we?" We squeezed our faces together and looked in her pocket mirror. *Not one iota.*

"Did I tell you how I married my first husband just to get my baby out of the clutches of the home for unwed mothers? They refused to even let me see him."

"Was he the baby's father?"

"Who the hell knows? I had no idea. All I knew was they weren't going to keep my baby. As soon as I got hold of Berty, I dumped the guy and took the kid to live on a commune in California where the others took care of him—thank goodness—and fed him if they noticed him eating out of the cat bowls." *Cat bowls?*

"Where were you?" I asked.

"Me? Ha! I was out dancing, smoking, hopping around from bed to bed, gathering notes, photos, and inspiration."

"And where is Berty now?"

"My father, who is wealthy by the way, agreed to pay for Berty's tuition at a boarding school in England. We see each other once or twice a year. Better for all of us. You see, Berty's quite shocked by me. He's square as can be. Can you believe it?"

Back home at the end of the long day, I snuggled with my baby. "Never will I let you go."

ﮮﻞﻞ

Fertile Fanny

ate one afternoon in the midst of keeping an eye on onion
soup simmering on the stove, bathing Alexandre, and hoist-
ing him onto the makeshift dressing table Pierre had ingeniously
rigged up in the bathroom, I stopped cold. *Danger, danger!*

I blinked, the feeling passed, and I enveloped my son in a
thick terrycloth towel. And wonder of wonders, when I hugged
him, he put his tiny arms around me and hugged me back! Finally.
To be loved back.

But a thought kept distracting me. I deposited him in his
playpen for a few minutes, though he despised being cooped up
and made it clear he expected to be part of the action every
minute. "No, can't be," I murmured as I peered at the calendar
hanging on the wall behind the fridge.

My last period was five weeks ago? Me, the original twenty-
eight-day wonder, regular as a metronome? Ignoring Alexandre's
calls, I sat down in the living room to go over the dates but jumped
up almost immediately to consult the calendar.

Could I be pregnant again? Dr. V counseled us to give our
bodies a rest, plan at least a year between babies; he claimed it
was not good to jumble them together. My pregnancy with
Alexandre had taken a toll on me. My hair was falling out. I suffered a huge sleep deficit. He'd barely begun to sleep the night
through.

Why hadn't I listened to Gabriella, who always insisted men

only paid attention to women when they cut off the sex? What about me though? I enjoyed sex.

I jumped up, fit Alexandre into the baby carrier, and ran downstairs to the pharmacy. Half an hour later, nothing. I wasn't pregnant? My breasts had been aching though. . . .

Over the next two weeks, I continued peeing on sticks. I convinced Dr. V to prescribe a *sirop* to bring on a late period. No luck.

Oh please God, no. The last thing I needed or wanted was another baby right now. I calculated it would be born in November (a Scorpio, no less). Pierre would already be in Hawaii.

He did not appear to be too bothered. Naturally. I was tearing my hair out. I got another missive from him, left on my pillow this time:

> Let me be clear: I cannot be in Paris for the birth in
> November. It's the most crucial time in the project. You can
> hire someone.
>
> How are you going to manage two babies, you ask? What's
> the big deal? My mother will help you.

Daily he repeated, "It's up to you." Every night he was occupied, flipping through yet another batch of papers he'd removed from his attaché case. Mostly he labored over projects from work, but admitted he had his own special projects and areas of investigation. *A man who had his priorities straight.*

"How will I manage with two babies?" I screeched and grabbed the papers away from him.

"We'll hire help," conceded Mr. Tight Fist. He gestured for me to give him back the reading material he'd scheduled for the night's entertainment. I considered shredding it like confetti and throwing it at his head. Instead, I meekly handed it over. I paced up and down the tiny apartment like a caged animal. One scenario I wasn't buying: one foreign lady, me, giving birth in French while an unknown nanny took charge of my fifteen-month-old son, and my husband called in after the fact to find out the sex of the newborn.

"Who's going to be holding the camera this time, Pierre?"

"Why do you have to act so freaky and emotional?"

A real crisis, not one manufactured by my neurotic brain. I called Mom and for once talked over the ten-minute limit on overseas calls. "At least it's a healthy sickness," she said, trying to comfort me.

The next night I attempted to discuss the situation with Pierre once again. "This morning I decided I would have the baby."

He glanced up from his book. "Okay."

Why was everything simple and straightforward for men? "But I wasn't comfortable with that decision."

"Why not?" he asked.

"I was psyched to have Alexandre. It was such a high. I followed all the instructions from Dr. V, and the result was a big beautiful baby boy. Now—"

A disdainful look crossed Pierre's face. He pointed to his watch. "Nine o'clock. I need to get to sleep. Tomorrow we're having an inspection at the lab." He swallowed the rest of his cognac, washed the glass, and trundled off to bed.

The only Parisian friend I told was Valentine, woman of the world, as we sat in the park munching cheese Danish from one of the Rue des Rosiers' Jewish bakeries. She tried to divert me with stories of how women in the past dealt with such crises.

"My grandmother one time tied a rope around her stomach and pulled. Another time she actually threw herself down the stairs! And she was always swallowing awful-smelling stuff."

"How many kids did she wind up having?"

"I don't know. I lost count. About ten. Or eleven. I forgot to count little Marius."

"Valentine, that's enough with the stories. Please." I had no stairs to throw myself down unless I counted the ancient, twist-ing, slippery stairs in our building. I could drag the empty baby carriage after me and tumble down one flight anyway. But what about the neighbors? And Alexandre crying hungrily in his crib with no mother but a tangle of hardware and guts stinking in the hall?

Alexandre was throwing sand at Johann and the other kids and seemed to be bawling them out. How embarrassing! I called out to him to stop. What an angry face he turned toward me! A car-bon copy of his father. Was he blaming me too? Valentine and I packed up the kids to go.

In hell, waiting to find out why and how. My lovely partner shared my anguished wait by berating me on a score of subjects dredged up from our earliest encounters. What a sweetie!

"What do I want?" he asked. "I want to build a boat and sail to every far-out corner of the world. I want to go ice skating. One day I'd also very much like to go into business with my best friend from college and drive produce in a big truck up and down the byways of France. I want to do something in my life. Surely you can appreciate that."

I understood perfectly. He wanted to do what he wanted to do, and he didn't want me to stop him.

I wanted to know if I was pregnant or not! Would I be able to get an abortion in Paris or be forced to fly to New York?

I was single-minded. Blame me. Funny girl that I was. Funny. Funny. Funny.

A fifth pregnancy test finally came back: Positive. We met with Dr. V. He could help me, he explained, as long as I had my husband's permission. On the way home, with that sour taste in my mouth, I declared, "I have to go back to New York." I'd be damned if I needed anyone's permission.

"Too expensive, Luce. Who will take care of our son? He needs his mommy."

"Naturally. He's coming with me. Like last time."

"But why not do it here? Why must you make everything so difficult?"

"I didn't like it when Dr. V said I needed the permission of my husband."

"But I give it to you. So?"

"Yes, you said it's my decision. Well, I'm not comfortable doing it here. I've made up my mind."

"Yes, okay, I get it," he agreed, after a minute. "Your mother can take care of you." *That would be a first.*

I started clearing the table. Pierre retired to the living room, Alexandre followed, all decked out in a green-and-white knitted outfit I had just made for him. They both peered out the windows as a fire engine clanged by. The same fine features, the same handsome silhouette.

What if the fetus is a girl? I'd always wanted a daughter, one to whom I could pass on my feminist ideas.

I carried on as best I could, ignoring Pierre as much as he let me, incapable of understanding his reasoning. How could he not discuss Hawaii with me, his wife, before accepting the job? I'd never understand. And now this—

"Calm down. It's settled. You're going to New York where you'll take care of it one-two-three. We can always have more babies. We're young."

Yes, I told myself I'd have a daughter one day. I was only twenty-five. I told myself I was married, a mother already, no need for guilt; I told myself, *Lucie, you are one fucking idiot!*

ele

Trip #2 to NYC

*O*n record time I readied baby and me and flew to New York. My friends were a bit surprised to see me back so soon. I kept my news to myself and headed downtown to Planned Parenthood (PP). With no insurance I could not afford the services of a private doctor or a hospital; PP was my only option. In the waiting room, I sat next to a girl of thirteen or fourteen and her mother. "Don't worry, honey," her mother said to me. "It'll be over before you know it." Pointing to her daughter, she added, "This is our third time around."

Fortunately, I did not have to justify myself. I kept repeating to myself that I was a married woman doing a little family planning. When I had another baby someday, I wanted to be every bit as excited as I was for Alexandre, relishing every step of the baby's development. I shivered—was that a movement I felt? Impossible. Too early. *Get it out!*

My mother appeared in the lobby to take me home by taxi. Alexandre and I stayed close to home for the next few weeks. I avoided my friends. Wendy, the only one I would have cared to see, was on a rare camping trip with her husband and boys. Mom taught her grandson how to sing into the cassette player, introduced him to American TV, wheeled him down the hill to Flushing Botanical Gardens for sun. Dad predictably found him too fussy or loud, or too babyish. "Can't you take him somewhere?" *What a grandpa!*

Alexandre made a friend, a giant of a kid, who joined him in the plastic wading pool Mom set up. His vocabulary expanded, though he still sounded like a French boy speaking English words. The inflection. Or could it be the "Bonjour!" that gave him away?

Talking on the wall phone to Pierre one morning in my parents' kitchen, I heard his confession: "I slept with Chita."

What! "You did what?" I clutched my stomach and almost fell off the stool.

"I wanted you to know."

"Why?"

"A man has needs."

"No. No. No. Why did you want me to know?"

". . . before you came back."

Gee. What about my needs? The rest of that day I went through the motions. That night I decided to let Grandma and Grandpa tend to Alexandre and withdrew to the basement to cry myself to sleep. Nice. I suffer for the two of us with my woman's body; he has a fling with a good friend. And she—she does this to me? *How could I have known she was asking permission to screw him when she questioned me about my feelings for him?*

Why did he do it? Is a man like him incapable of foregoing sex for a few weeks? What the hell did I know about men's needs? It was the era of free love. . . . I wasn't an overly jealous person, but we were married!

"How could you?" I asked in a hushed conversation the next day. My mother had taken Alexandre for a walk around the neighborhood. Dad was watching *Bride of Frankenstein* in the den, but he walked into the kitchen every commercial break to grab a can of orange soda or another snack.

"So I cheated with our little Mexican friend. What did you expect? You go and leave me for six weeks! You get yourself pregnant—"

"Oh, yes, all by myself!" I could feel red hot lava climbing up my face.

"You tell me it's safe, and like a fool, I believe you. Your decision to end the pregnancy, not mine."

"Lay it all on me. Sure. Like I had a lot of options. I'll get my daughter one day."

He took a deep breath and continued, "Surely you realize Chita is a friend, not a love interest. Sex between us means nothing, like bedding a cousin or a neighbor. Just mechanics. Release."

"How could I forget?" I said. "Adultery in France is the national pastime."

"Well, I wonder in that case, why you are so outraged?"

"I feel so . . . betrayed," I confessed.

"Americans are incredibly puritanical. And dishonest with themselves. Contradictory. Hypocrites! Look at the facts: a nation of cheaters!"

I tried to be logical. He liked logical. He was never going to admit he made a mistake. I walked into the bathroom for a tissue and blew my nose.

"This call is going to cost my parents a lot. . . ."

"Am I supposed to know how you'll react to things? I am a good husband. I'm young and virile. I will make some mistakes along the way. Not everyone can be like you, Little Miss Perfect!"

He waited for me to respond, and when I failed to, he added,

"There's nothing to be forgiven. I love only you. And our baby. I am not leaving either of you behind."

Was that a threat?

Winter Yields to Spring, 1977

*B*ack on Rue de la Roquette, I resumed my routine: working for the Czech dissidents, munching on Belgian chocolate bars as I cut out articles from the local papers, and trying earnestly, with the encouragement of my writers' group, to finish my first story. A woman is trapped. In Hawaii.

I vowed never to see or speak to Chita again. Why, I didn't know, but I blamed her more than I blamed him.

The highlight of my week: I had an actual grownup conversation with the father of one of the kids playing alongside Alexandre in the sandbox at the Place des Vosges. He was another foreigner like me, and judging by his accent, from a Slavic country. Bearded and a bit too thin, he wasn't my type; nevertheless, we soon found ourselves engrossed in our conversation, chatting for over thirty minutes about a very quirky book we both loved, *Tristram Shandy*. *Talking about literature, let along writing it, was so invigorating!*

Otherwise, at home and abroad, the air was clotted with tension. Everything about Pierre irritated me, every expression on his face, every gesture. In the marketplace, he'd open his little leather change purse and painfully count out *centimes*, keeping the vendor and the people queuing up behind him waiting. He treated himself to three showers a day. He refused to discuss a book or movie without subjecting it to a Marxist interpretation.

Worse, he'd argue with me about a book he hadn't even read. During our frequent arguments, Pierre wound up in the bathroom with a stomachache, and I had to lean against a wall to catch my breath. I feared the poisonous atmosphere in the home was affecting Alexandre. Seated in his highchair, he babbled at a fever pitch, determined as ever to outshout the two of us.

I was miserable, trapped, but grateful I'd resorted to PP. How would I ever have gotten away from him with two babies trailing behind me?

I shared my plan with Wendy long distance. "I'm not the type to keep my feelings hidden."

"No, you're not," she agreed.

"Nor the type to live without love, go through the motions, pretending to have a happy little family. I can't do it, can't fake it."

"You ever think about separating?" she asked.

"Who knows what that would do? Pierre would subject Alexandre to a critical appraisal of his every step. I'm grown and I can't take it. What chance would Alexandre have?"

Silence on the other end of the line.

"Wendy?"

"I don't want to tell you what to do."

"I have to give Alexandre the best chances, don't I? I'm just not sure how to go about it."

How's this for family planning? I must figure out a way to survive. To redefine "family."

The Reckoning

*C*hita was standing in the doorway.

"How dare you?" I was seething.

"Let me in, please. I brought a toy," she said, holding forth a somewhat bedraggled teddy bear. I placed my hand on her chest to stop her from entering.

Mme Karol picked just this moment to stick her friendly, finely wrinkled face out into the hall. "Hello, young lady!" she cried as she closed her door and prepared to join us.

Merde. "Mme Karol, we have some business to conduct. See you tonight. Private business," I quickly added.

Something in my demeanor cut short her advance. I watched as she reassessed the situation, finally retreating but not before blowing a kiss to Chita.

Dreading a scene in the hall, I allowed Chita to slip past me into the apartment. She threw her purse and jacket on the daybed and followed me into the kitchen. "Could you make some coffee, Lucie?"

I gave her the dirtiest look I could muster but reheated the morning's coffee in a pot on the stove. We faced off at the table.

"What is it you want?" I asked.

"You know I love you and Pierre and the baby and—"

"Evidently more than I suspected."

"Lucie, just listen. We've been good friends since you showed up in Mexico to rejoin Pierre. You helped me figure out how to terminate my pregnancy. We rode that crazy bus to Veracruz. I even taught you how to sew. We had so many laughs together." She paused to take a sip of the slightly syrupy coffee.

I waited her out. She was a moocher, once and always a moocher, and now she'd mooched my husband.

"I knew you were unhappy. You told me yourself. Remember? I asked if you cared if he slept with other women and—"

"I said I wasn't sure how I felt."

"No, Lucie, that's not what you said. C'mon. You said you didn't care what he did anymore."

"So you construed that to mean I was giving you a green light to go fuck him?"

She nodded. She clearly believed she was off the hook and dared to pour herself the last of the crappy caramelized coffee.

I inhaled a deep breath to calm myself. "Did you ever hear of solidarity among sisters? A best friend is not supposed to undermine you. You were supposed to support me in my troubles, not betray me."

"Look, Lucie, I'm going to tell you something. Sex is not that important nowadays. No one stays a virgin until they get married. That was our parents' generation and their nonsense."

I tapped my fingers on the table.

"Kids like us are living together in communes, sharing everything. I don't get why you are so upset at me. Wasn't I the only one to babysit when he was a few weeks old? I bought you that great baby harness that you can wear on your hip. . . ."

"Chita, you lived on our daybed for months after you followed us here from Mexico. I don't even know why you are here, in France. All you do is go dancing, take a few classes, and sleep with a new man every week. Oh, and drop in for dinner whenever you feel like. What happened? You suddenly had an uncontrollable urge to sleep with your friend's husband?"

"Pierre should not have told you." She stood up and gathered her belongings. "Can I say goodbye to the baby?"

"He's sleeping, Chita."

"Let me just peek in then. He's going to miss me."

At the door, she turned. "Since Pierre is in confession mode, has he told you about Bonita?"

I blinked. "Who?"

"Or the fact that he slept with Bonita during the period you were separated? You were teaching, right?"

I waited, but was forced to ask, "Bonita?"

"Bonnie Vasquez. My second cousin. She's old, about forty-five, but pretty well preserved. She's got six children, six; the oldest is in high school. Divorced. He brought her to all the gatherings and parties, but he let us know that 'Lucie' was his true love, his lady, and would be coming soon to share his life."

"I don't believe you."

"Then ask him. If he had not slept with me, he would have found a tramp somewhere. No way a man like him goes weeks or months without a woman to pound on. That's just the type of man he is. You should be happy, grateful that it was me and not some disease-ridden whore."

"Get out. Please. Just go." I felt weak, lightheaded, and leaned against the wall.

"The baby's crying. I'll get him," she said, pushing past and bringing him to me. "What's up, Good-Looking?" she asked him, tickling his middle. He squirmed to get out of her embrace and crawled to me, hugging my legs. I reached down to rub his head.

Chita looked wistfully at us both. "Call me when you want to talk some more."

Why am I angrier at her than I am at him? She's an opportunist. I knew that.

I tilted my head toward the door and mouthed, "Get out."

I was in the midst of brewing a fresh pot of coffee for myself when Chita startled me by walking back in. She looked me dead in the eye. "By the way, Mme Bonhomme, I saw you. With that bearded man. In the Marais—"

"That bearded man?" I stuttered, the blood in my veins turning to ice water. Was she going to blackmail me? I hadn't done anything . . . yet.

"That's your business. Just don't play so innocent with me, okay? I'm not buying it." Chita headed to the door with me close behind.

"Don't forget this." I tossed her jacket and purse over to her.

"We can still be friends," she said, one hand on the door-knob. "You'll get over it."

"No, no, I'm not like you." I shook my head vehemently side to side. My sins were in my head. So far.

She was snickering! I pushed her out, double-locked the door this time, and collapsed on the daybed.

Alexandre looked up from the floor where he was playing with his Legos, building a tower with some, and biting, talking to, or kissing the rest. "*V'la*," he announced gravely.

I watched him as he knocked the tower down and scattered blocks everywhere.

Should I Stay or Should I Go?

*C*ircumstances were forcing me to make a decision, months or years before I was ready. I realized I had the power to scatter us all to the four winds or dig in my heels and stay for the sake of the child. Playact for the rest of my life versus enter the unknown as a single mother.

Gabriella, drawing on her personal experience of once living for months in a car with her young son, urged me to stay in Paris where I had a place to live. No rent. A job. I could immediately enroll in a crèche, whereas in New York, he'd be too young for preschool which started at three years old. Best of all, if I stayed, I'd be able to stick with our group. This group, my lifeline, my sanity in these dreary housewife years. The group believed in me and my talent. They were confident I'd become a writer. This dream was all that kept me going in this bad, this accursed year of near death (Camille), an unwanted and terminated pregnancy, spousal infidelity, and ultimately, I suspected, separation.

Pierre would leave shortly after Alexandre's birthday. We would not follow him. I felt lightheaded at the thought of staying alone in Paris. Even worse if I imagined arriving in New York with all my valises. And a baby. "Mommy, guess who's here?" She would not be amused. Neither would Daddy, nor Aunt G, Uncle B, etc. etc. etc. I trusted my writing group to be far more sympathetic and helpful. In the States did I even have a home to return to?

Mere months to go. I pretended I had it all figured out. I did not dare dwell on the weekends when Alexandre and I would have only each other. The other French families would be *recro-quevillées* (curled up), in the fetal position, having dinner with their Mamie and Papi. Their long afternoons stretching out until *souper* (dinner) and a second meal of the same dishes, then home. *Métro-boulot-dodo* the next morning. What I imagined: morning, work; afternoon, write. My son in all-day day care. One evening per week, writers' group. Another evening, Yiddish class at the Sorbonne (Oriental Languages Department). Strolling with Alexandre through Parisian parks. I refused to take into account what I would do about sex or eventually finding a man to share my life and help me raise my son.

I was at peace, almost. A light rain was falling as Alexandre and I returned from food shopping. Last trip to New York, I'd aborted in Manhattan. First trip I talked bad marriage to one of my friends, hinted to my family, and concluded: *It's not time yet to leave him. I will know when it's time.* Now I had a deadline. I ached to be free of Pierre, to be me again, alone with my old insecurities. Free.

I pulled out a handmade book I'd made for Alexandre, illustrated with my primitive drawings, and annotated with large letters. We sat close together on the carpeted floor, I pointed and turned pages. "This is a cat. C-A-T. Can you say, 'cat'?"

Unfortunately, my son did not have much of an attention span. He was a bundle of energy, a handful, and he always knew what he wanted. He pointed at the cassette player, so I put on a cassette of French children's songs. Wrong one. Several tries later when I finally located the desired music, he grinned and climbed into my lap and snuggled. His skin, so soft, so plump. *How would I ever have managed with two babies?*

Friends

I tracked Valentine down and filled her in on my trip. I brought her up to date on my marital woes. We continued meeting in the afternoons in the park, scarfing down pastries, badmouthing men. I watched wistfully as French couples engaged in passionate kisses on street corners, in booths at the corner bistro, on park benches. When would it be my turn?

Rodin Museum

On moments of emotional turmoil, I sought out the comfort of the Rodin Museum on Rue de Varenne, an exceptionally long, lovely walk along the river from our home.

Alexandre was still asleep in his stroller when we arrived. I headed for the magnificent garden behind the house, which teemed with visitors though it was only a Tuesday. Seeing that the little snack bar was open, I waited in line for a small cheese platter and a coffee. I sat on a chair with my snack, pulled out a paperback novel, and flipped through the pages. I couldn't concentrate. My heart was beating too fast. Too much coffee? Too much life? I knew which one I'd vote for.

Alexandre stirred. I removed his hat, uncovering those tricky ears of his, prone to infection. A negligible risk, I hoped, in this temperate weather. "Do you want to go in the house? See all the pretty statues? Yes?"

He flashed me one of his signature smiles. Little white teeth. Twinkly eyes. Chubby cheeks. *Quel coquin!* Wait till the girls get a hold of him in a few years.

I disposed of my garbage, smiled back, then winked at the older gentleman at the next table who'd been eyeing me. I climbed the stairs to the main house with the help of my not-so-secret admirer, who rushed to pick up the back of the stroller. Parking the stroller in the cloak room, I picked Alexandre up in my arms and gave him a guided tour.

"Look, baby, what a funny face! See this. Or do you like that one better?" He excitedly looked from one to the other. "*Non, mon petit, faut pas toucher.*" (No, my little one, can't touch.)

Each time I entered the museum, I realized I'd forgotten how precious this space was to me. I circled the sculptures, not wanting to miss a nuance. Standing with a crowd admiring "The Kiss," I imagined we all felt the heat. What a turn-on! Drop-dead gorgeous he-man enfolding his beloved in a tender embrace. I had trouble tearing myself away. Sweating just the tiniest little bit, I glanced around and locked eyes with the gentleman from the garden. I didn't like being followed, stalked in this way, though it was flattering. The guy must have been at least forty! But he was exceptionally well groomed and dressed like a banker. If I squinted, I could spot a little of that Yves Montand cockiness in him.

Sex was in the air. Was this a trap? A test? I quickly carried Alexandre to the next room to visit another old favorite. The two hands joined in prayer in "The Cathedral" are a testament to man's belief in a supreme power waiting in the wings to intervene and to rescue us . . . from ourselves. Did I need rescue?

Alexandre was squirming and wanted to crawl around the room by himself, which was not possible in this crowd. So we stopped off in the gift store where I bought a biography of Rodin. I knew the story already. Great artist but not so great husband, he married a simple woman and kept her stashed away. On the side, he romanced a talented sculptress, Camille Claudel, and certainly contributed to her suicide. But the book was in French, filled with clear black-and-white pictures of the sculptures, and I had to have it. I paid for the book and delighted in imagining Pierre's reaction: "Twenty-five francs? Are you insane?"

A hand on my shoulder. I turned. The guy hot-whispered in my ear, "Come join me in the garden." I bet he wanted to smooch under a tree. The *blaguard*! I thrilled at the thought of being one of those couples. He was actually not bad looking. I made haste to retrieve the stroller, and we three installed ourselves in the shade under a leafy tree. Almost immediately he began stroking the side of my face and mumbling endearments, "*Mon petit chou, mon coeur, mon ange.*" Harmless enough. He sneaked in some hot kisses and even one tongue kiss. Getting hotter. He slipped his hot little paw under my blouse. . . .

My little boy, a mind reader, let out an ungodly howl, shattering the love spell. I shot straight out of my chair and smoothed down the front of my blouse. I ignored what turned out to be a full-fledged tantrum and steered the stroller out of the garden onto the street. Alexandre was right. Was this very French public display of affection the kind of educational experience I had in mind for my son? I pivoted once and waved my very confused would-be lover off. In his eyes, I read, *Are you sure?* He must have read the answer in mine. He shrugged in that charming Gallic way they all had, and moved on to a likelier, hopefully luckier, perch towards the back of the garden.

Was this the place where bored housewives came for some diversion? Sorry to disappoint you, Éric! I have some scruples left. Though it was interesting to realize Valentine's husband was not paranoid without reason. Frenchmen were apparently not deterred by a wedding ring, a pregnancy, or another man's offspring in tow.

Alexandre continued his protest so loudly heads were turning. I frantically spooned some applesauce into his hungry mouth. I prayed that would hold him for another half hour or so.

I looked both ways down the street, sighed, turned right. We set off for the métro that would get us safely back home.

That's when I realized—*zut alors!*—I had neglected to visit the "Gates of Hell," another Rodin favorite of mine. I was at the gates, wasn't I, though which side I was on was questionable. Also, which road to take out of there. Questions for another day.

Writing Prompt

I got to the writers' group, drank way too much wine, and had a good time poking fun at myself. Little did I realize what was coming towards me down the road.

Where is Ava?

Ava could not be here tonight, folks, because she has a really big deal coming through. She's been asked to write my biography. Right at this moment, she's making it with Pierre while keeping one eye open on Alexandre jumping up and down in his bed or arching his back or banging his head into the refrigerator.

Howard Hughes has paid *Dispatch* a huge sum to research the problem of French-American couples' sex lives. Since I'm the only one she knows in this category, she chose me.

By now she's seen it all: the candle routine, the scarves, the Mexican music, up, down, and around. Pisha pasha upside down and backwards.

"So what do you say, Ava?" I ask.

"I think I gave him a pretty nice screw."

What Does My Future Hold?

Next month's meeting place: a high-priced bakery in St. Germain des Prés. I arrived a little breathless, having walked the entire way, hoping to dispel some of my nervousness. I scanned the tables. I must have been early. I draped my jacket on a chair, sat, and waited, glancing every few seconds at my watch.

Gabriella, Suzanna, Ava, Ernie—surely, they knew me by now. For the past two years, hadn't they listened to my readings, short stories, and occasional poetry, offering encouragement? Though hardly role models, still, they were older than me and had lived through all sorts of situations. I was counting on them to have an insight I may have missed.

I waved the waiter away several times, but finally ordered a *café crème*. I rummaged through my handbag looking for my calendar when someone plopped down in the seat opposite me. Suzanna!

"Hi there," I said, "I was just wondering where everyone was."

"Well, I'm here," she said, pulling out her notebook. "But apparently the others are not coming today."

"Oh no. How can that be?"

Suzanna gave me a quizzical look. "Gabby has a head cold. Little wonder with all the glues and paints she's surrounded by when she works on her boxes."

"You're saying she's allergic? I didn't realize. And Ava? Ernie?"

"Ernie, if you remember, is back in the States, visiting her grandmother who just had a stroke. And Ava probably has an important meeting she can't get out of." Suzanna unwrapped a long, silk, paisley scarf from her neck. "So baby, you're stuck with me!"

I offered a weak smile. Did she suspect she was my least favorite of the authors? "What should we do then?"

Suzanna considered the situation for a moment. "I suggest we do a quick prompt and then you tell me why you're so pale."

The waiter came over to our table and addressed Suzanna, "*Café crème*, Madame?"

"At 11:15? *Non, j'aimerai mieux un coup de rouge.*"

He smiled, fetched a red wine bottle, and poured her a generous glassful. Was she really going to down a whole bottle by herself?

"What have you decided, Luce?"

"Sorry, I'm distracted. I don't much feel like writing today. . . ."

"Hmm. I've got it. Did you know I'm a psychic? I read palms," she said, folding her hand over my clenched fist and prying it open. "Okay with you?"

"I guess."

She studied my palm for some minutes, then assumed a serious business face and started in.

"Luce, your future destiny is not without some ripples of trouble. You need to tell me what you want to hear. Should I skip anything?"

"Lay it all out for me, Suzanna. I can take it," I said, not knowing if that was the truth.

"I'll start with the worst then. You will live a long time, until you're seventy-five, when you'll die of an ailment you've had for the preceding eight years."

"Seventy-five? I'll take it!" My family was not known for its longevity. My Grandparents, uncles, and an aunt died much before that age.

Suzanna rambled on about my travels and my work life before getting to what I wanted to know—my love life. She paused a long time, then encouraged by me, launched into the full report. "Luce, my girl, I see three marriages for you and two more children. See these three lines on the side of your pinky?"

Shocked, I bolted upright, but she persuaded me to sit back down. "Are you absolutely sure?" That could be good news, I supposed, though it sounded like a lot of heartache to me, falling in and out of love. I reasoned, though, that the three lines for children might be taking into account a miscarriage I'd had in Denver and the recent clinical intervention in New York. I was reluctant to ask.

"Here's the thing though," she continued. "Each marriage will be a little worse than the one before."

"Worse, how?"

"More fighting."

I swallowed. Suzanna was visibly enjoying my discomfort. I had never trusted her. In fact, I didn't like her, not one bit. She wasn't even a good writer. I bet she probably made up half of what she said. But why did she have to sound so convincing?

"Enough." I withdrew my left hand, but she quickly snared my right.

"People believe your right hand tells the story of what might have been. Did you not know that? Here I clearly see a proper housewife and mother, content in her roles. You must have taken a detour from this destiny—"

I pulled on my jacket. "I need to get back h—home now," I stammered.

"Hope my reading put things in perspective?" she asked.

"I'll let you know in about . . . fifty years, okay?" I took off down the street, mumbling, "That bitch!" At the corner, I glanced back. She was flirting with our waiter. I could hear her hearty laugh from where I stood. *Guess she's from the kick-a-dog-when-it's-down school of thought.*

I stopped off near home and purchased a very fattening slice of cherry flan for lunch. *Take that, Pierre!*

ele

Julien

ulien. His name was Julien. Would he call me? Or come by the office to visit? Should I let this moment pass? How would Éric judge me? Would Pierre even care?

I rode the métro on the way to my part-time gig doing research and writing. Not a hard job at all. Rumor had it that the CIA was mixed up in this project, but what did I care? The pay was good, and the job allowed me to get out of the house every morning and be home in time to collect Alexandre from his nanny and whiz him off, fresh from his nap, for our daily promenade.

Back to Julien. I sat on the métro reading the *International Herald Tribune* (which was in English of course) and this blond dreamboat, shades of Jeff Bridges in Starman, started talking to me (in English of course). In good ole American tell-all-to-the-lady-you-meet-lining-up-for-the-movie, the bus, the unemployment check, he let me know he was American, his mother, Jewish American, and his father, originally from Czechoslovakia. He had one younger sister who adored him and a Labrador puppy waiting for him back home in the States.

What was he doing in Paris? He had planned to spend a two-year stint in Kenya, in the Peace Corps, but that didn't work out for some reason. "I've got a part-time gig at UNICEF," he said. "Hoping to figure out my next move."

We talked about plays and literature and our favorite artists: Beckett. Sartre. Piaf.

"I saw *O' Les Beaux Jours* at the Théâtre d'Orsay last October. *Magnifique!* That head in the sand! What a play!" I said. "You know Simone de Beauvoir has it right. She and Sartre never married; they live in the same hotel but have their separate lives." I babbled on and on.

He looked at me appraisingly. We were having an intellectual discussion! His goal was not to force a Marxist interpretation on me. Or the play.

My stop was coming up. How to let him know I was married but getting divorced? I hadn't even told Pierre. How to tell him I was available, very available, right this minute a-v-a-i-l-a-b-l-e?

I gave him my work number. My luck, it turned out he knew my employers. He wanted to surprise me and stop by work. No! He'd find out I was married with a little baby at home. Not fair. He'd speak to Hadrian, my boss. And that would be that. I'd never see him again. I'd love to tell my boss to keep his mouth shut about my status but that meant explaining everything to him, and we did not have that kind of relationship. He was married to a beautiful, rich lady, like him from Prague, and aside from that one time he leaned over me when I was typing, with his hands heavily on my shoulders and his beard brushing against the top of my hair, he was strictly all business. He asked nothing about my home life, my husband and child. He only lamented that I failed to show up at any of the rallies he organized for emigrants from behind the Iron Curtain.

Julien! Perfect. I longed to touch his shoulder-length hair, to feel those strong arms around me, those strong thighs. I should ditch work and hang out with him, sleep with him. Why not? Everybody else is doing it. Including Pierre.

But—that's not me. Not how I act.

"I don't have too much planned for this afternoon. . . ." He gave me an inquiring look. All he needed was a little encouragement.

"They're . . . they're expecting me at work." Ever the good girl. What an idiot!

"Could you call them?"

Here was my opportunity. To commit. There'd be no turning back though. I still hesitated.

My stop. Boul'Mich. Julien slid open the métro door for me, and I exited. I turned and waved. The doors were closing. Heart sinking, I forced a smile. In a flash, he pried the doors open and squeezed through. A Parisian matron with color-coordinated hair, scarf, and leather purse sent a *Ça se fait pas* (that's simply not done) shake of her head our way. Seeing my surprise, he blushed a little, and whispered in my ear, "I can't leave you. Let me walk you to work." *Maybe I'm lovable after all?*

We strolled through St. Germain des Prés, down Rue St. André des Arts, past the rich people, chichi shops, the cafés, mere steps from the office where I worked. I never made it there. We stopped for crêpes and a glass of white wine, and I sneaked in a call to the nanny while he sought out the toilettes. Yes, she could stay for a few more hours. We ate and talked and resumed walking. It was a glorious afternoon.

"Do you want to see my apartment? It's cool. In the Marais." *Did I?*

How convenient! That's where I regularly hung out. I followed, crossing the river Seine, hoping he was not too near the Place des Vosges where I might run into a former teacher colleague or a neighbor or friend. Or ex-friend. I tried to keep my head down.

He was on the ground floor. I walked in and saw three small rooms, a door leading to a charming little terrace with a few dying plants. He had a big poster on the wall of Georges Moustaki! I twirled around in circles for a moment and finally sat down on his bed, covered like ours with a bright Indian print bedspread. He joined me. He smelled so good. He passed me a joint, and I inhaled deeply. I reached out and touched his long blond hair, started caressing his face, ran my finger over his lips. He carefully put out the joint, grabbed a hank of my hair, locked lips, pushing me back onto the bed. *I was so turned on!*

He was in no rush. However, I was about ready to levitate off the bed, screaming with desire by the time he penetrated me. He'd stroked and kissed and sucked on my breasts and my yoni for what felt like hours, bringing me to within an inch of orgasm until we both started screaming with each thrust, dissolving with pleasure. He finally rolled off me onto his back. We gazed at each other. "Oh yeah," he said.

"Yeah?" I asked.

"*Pas mal.*" (Not bad.)

"If you stay here long enough, you wind up becoming French," I teased.

I needed to get out of there. Quickly. I showered, dressed in the bathroom, and came out. He was lying in the same position I left him. "Julien, I have to leave you, I'm afraid."

"Oh?" He looked stunned. Did he believe I was going to move right in with him? "Where can I find you?"

I was stumped. I made up an excuse, said I was going out of Paris to visit friends in the Vosges soon. True except the "friends" were Pierre's cousins and extended family.

"Well, I can always come by the office."

"No, don't do that, Julien." I improvised. "I like to keep my private life private. Please don't say anything to my bosses."

"Can I see you again?"

"How about I come back here when I return, a week from today?"

He bounded up and walked me to the door. "You're exquisite, you know," he said, twirling my long black hair, grabbing me by the shoulders for a long, sensuous kiss goodbye.

"*A tout à l'heure.*" (See you soon.)

"Toodle-loo, Julien." I started running as soon as I was clear of his building. Once I passed Rue Vieille du Temple, I relaxed and walked slower. Man, I hadn't had sex like that in a long time. Ever? Pierre was more into demonstrating his swordsmanship technique than pleasing me. He acted like I was a nympho. Hell, yes! I floated on a wave of pleasure, committing to memory every touch and caress.

"Bonjour, Mimi. Thank you for staying. I had work to finish. You know." Great, now I was lying to my nanny. Adulteress. Liar. How much further could I fall?

Julien and I met every Thursday, the only day Mimi was available for overtime. He rarely, if ever, disappointed in the sexual fireworks department. I walked around town, purring like a kitten.

To my surprise I learned he was only twenty. He'd been kicked out of three colleges back home, not much of an academic. Yet his father was fixated on Julien becoming an engineer or failing that, an architect.

"Up to me, I'd work in an auto shop," Julien said as we walked near Hôtel de Ville. "School's not my thing. But I do like to figure out how the pieces fit together."

"Yes, you do!"

"Hell, I'd like to bum around Italy, Greece, Israel with you!" He tried to take my hand.

I looked away guiltily and stammered while saying, "You know, Julien, I'm not in the market for a boyfriend."

"I'll soon change that!" he boasted. "Anyway, my father's got me taking classes at L'Alliance Française to get my written French up to par in order to enroll in an engineering program."

I turned to face him. "Tell him no."

"You see, that's hard. I'm the one dream he has left. He never made it; he had to settle with being a draftsman. Now that my mother's left him to live with our next-door neighbor, Ruth—"

"Oh."

"Well, actually, Ruth has always been a sweetheart."

"What does all this have to do with you?"

"Lucie, did I mention my sister has Down's? To top it off, my father recently learned he has early Parkinson's—"

"Oy. Run away to India fast!"

"Not my scene, man. So that's how it is. What should I do? What's your opinion?" He blocked my forward progress by planting himself in front of me.

"Sorry, I have to get back." I wriggled out of his grasp and jogged down Rue Vieille du Temple towards the métro stop.

"Let me come with you," Julien pleaded as he jogged alongside me.

I shook my head vehemently.

"Why not? What're you hiding?" He stopped still in the street.

"I turn into a pumpkin?"

"That's the stagecoach."

"Right you are. See you next week, Jules." I kissed him on the cheek. "Be a good boy and go home now."

I was running late. Again. I decided to take the métro one stop instead of walking as I usually did. As I rushed down the métro stairs, I concentrated on reining in the bounce in my step —didn't want Mimi to start asking herself questions about my "overtime."

Leaving loose-limbed Julien and encountering my husband that night, this was what I chose to record in my journal:

> *His ramrod body bespoke a tension so profound you half expected him to snap in two like a dry twig. He was a jacked-up kind of person, primed to the max, so spare and precise a machine you wondered how he could swallow even a gulp of water. Where would it go?*
>
> *A look at his face, stretched over too broad a frame, and you wanted desperately to twang the bridge of his nose with your thumb and forefinger. What kind of high-pitched sound would you get? Could you risk it? Such encapsulated fury.*

~elle~

Infatuation

I mpossible to get Julien out of my mind. He was fresh like a newborn, like bread out of the oven. I could have sworn his blue eyes sparkled and threw off sparks when he smiled that crooked smile of his. When he approached and put his hands around my waist and leaned back to admire me, I had trouble breathing for a moment.

He was light; Pierre was dark. He was youth; Pierre was prematurely middle-aged. He was even tall while Pierre was a continental midget.

Most of all, Julien was the man I thought I was marrying, the one who swept me off my feet one snowy night and transported me to Mexico, land of intense sunlight, soccer, *pachanga* parties, and (how did I fail to take note?) rumbling volcanoes. By the time we arrived in Paris and faced down the challenges of finding jobs, friends, activities, and an apartment of our own, that man was gone forever.

How strange and coincidental that Julien knew my boss. Paris is not a small city. I never bumped into anyone I knew even when I propelled Alexandre's stroller into unknown quarters of the city. That we both chose to sit in the same métro car at the same time and that he decided to hit on me that day, seeing that I was reading an English language paper. . . .

Was this meeting *beshert*?

All I knew was that I would have given anything not to be

married with a child. If only I were a little further along in the process of kissing Pierre goodbye. I was impatient to be single again, a free agent. While waiting, I'd found myself a magnificent boy toy.

I wished I could confide in Chita. She had certainly tried my patience with her steamy accounts of the many losers she had found to date in Paris: refugee waiters, out-of-work painters, half-time schoolteachers, married men, wannabe gigolos. She had a knack, that girl, of hooking up with the worst specimens of the male sex. She probably liked being taken advantage of, I concluded, as she lent her last franc to the boyfriend-of-the-week.

Naturally, talking to her was out of the question. I couldn't tell her. I did not in any way want to be in her league or to have anything further to do with her. I was better than all that. Mine was going to be a real affair of the heart, elevated above the common experience.

I decided to tell no one.

Go Along to Get Along?

I studied Pierre as he played with his son before bedtime. He should have been a funeral director. He was proper and *serioso* and stern. A married man, a father at twenty-three, he rarely let himself jump around, have fun, laugh, or be silly. I pitied him but pitied myself more.

"What are you guys playing at?" I asked. They were seated on the rug in the bedroom, bent intently over Alexandre's new toy, a big wooden box with shapes cut in the top.

"Maman, I am showing Petit Bonhomme how to put the square block into the square hole. See?" He demonstrated, fingering the crescent shaped block, the oblong block, the circular block before selecting the square and pushing it through the hole. "*Voilà!*"

Our son clapped his chubby hands and cobbled together a short congratulatory speech in Googoogaga. When he looked up for my approval, I nodded enthusiastically but could not refrain from putting in my two cents. "Why not let him figure it out himself, Pierre?" I was rewarded with a sullen look.

"Ah, the critic has spoken and must be obeyed," Pierre mumbled as he rounded up the errant blocks and stored them in a box under the crib. "Time to go *dodo*, little man. Maman, will you join us?"

We gathered at Alexandre's crib, Pierre holding my hand, to perform the French evening lullaby. While baby sleeps, his brother assures him that Maman and Papa are busy preparing treats, cake, chocolate, and nougats for him to eat the next day:

Fais dodo, Colas mon p'tit frère
Fais dodo, t'auras du lolo.
Maman est en haut
Qui fait des gâteaux
Papa est en bas
Qui fait du chocolat
Fais dodo, Colas mon p'tit frère
Fais dodo, t'auras du lolo.

Alexandre played with the mobile of cloth animals twirling above his head and forgot to protest when we slipped out of the bedroom.

At nearly a year old, he was our little prodigy. He never stopped babbling. He knew a dozen words in English and French already and could imitate my hiccups. His motor skills were quite advanced. He could pick up rice with his fingers. Usually when I woke in the morning, Pierre would be stretched out on one side of me and Alexandre snuggled in on the other—he figured out quite early how to scramble out of his crib and into our bed every night.

Pierre sorted through his papers, and I pretended to read another chapter in the latest Michel Tournier novel, distracted as I relived the touch and smells and tastes of my illicit afternoon.

Weekend in the Vosges

We were off to the Vosges mountains to spend the long July Fourteenth holiday weekend with Pierre's ninety-nine-year-old grandmother, Mémère, his uncles, aunts, and cousins. The train ride was long and uncomfortable with an infant, especially since skinflint Pierre had booked us into second-class with no guaranteed seats. He sat on one side of the car and Alexandre and I on the other.

Halfway into the trip, our son had an unfortunate diaper incident—too many green peas in his soup yesterday?—and I was forced to stand him up naked in the bathroom's narrow sink, scrubbing his tush and legs free of smelly green goo that had gotten all the way up to his neck. *Dégueulasse!* (Disgusting!)

What an anecdote to publish in the RATP train's monthly newsletter. Would they want snapshots? *Damn Pierre!*

The old family homestead rested on a hilltop in a picturesque village nestled between two lakes. Many of the newer houses were chalet-style. The men worked as ski instructors during ski season and in various sideline industries the rest of the year. The house had no running water, no flushable toilet, no central heat, and only a heated brick to keep your feet warm when you crawled in and out of bed. All cooking was done on an antiquated cast iron coal stove. Amazingly at her age, Mémère managed to cook *tartes aux myrtilles* with thick crusts filled with blueberries much smaller but every bit as tasty as what we had at home.

Pierre urged me to take a walk with him in the countryside. "This is where I walked when I was a boy."

I would rather have talked to his relatives but went along with his plan. As soon as we were out of sight, Pierre, overcome with "needs," laid me down on the ground for a good pounding. My punishment, no doubt, for fantasizing about Julien. Minutes later, I jumped up screaming in pain, covered with red marks. "Aiee! What is this?"

"Just dust them off. We disturbed their home. They punished us!"

Ha ha. Red ants. Hardly my idea of communing with nature.

Our next adventures worked out better. We introduced Alexandre to his first boat ride on the lake and a swim at the tiny beach. He delighted in both experiences. Back at the house, we ate a quick dinner and got ready to watch the town fireworks at night. We all gathered outside the house with chairs and toys for the cousins' children. I put Alexandre to bed. It was past his bedtime, and he'd had enough excitement for the day.

I noticed Pierre's relations with his relatives were, as always, rather stiff and uncomfortable. I put this down to his being the only intellectual, the only scientist, the only world traveler, the only grandchild raised with them until he was eight then "disappeared."

The family was polite to me, friendly and curious; our differences (religion, nationality, language) were no big deal to them. Considering that they'd grown up in these Heidi-esque surroundings and had rarely been to Paris, they were surprisingly open and accepting.

When I checked on Alexandre, I became uneasy. He was still awake, scratching at his ears and looking unhappy. I picked him up. I put him down. He seemed to be getting more and more flushed and agitated. I ran outside and told Pierre that we needed to take him to a doctor. Pierre brushed me off. "Not now. The fireworks are about to begin."

Honestly? Bastard! Fucker! I didn't know what to do.

I stayed with him, putting cold compresses on his forehead, rocking him. All my instincts told me he needed a doctor. A cousin's wife came into the bedroom and brought me a thermometer. She must have overheard our exchange on the lawn. My family ran high temperatures and Alexandre seemed to have inherited this trait. His was 103.5. The cousin's wife helped me put him in a basin of tepid water to try to bring down the fever.

Pierre walked in when the fireworks were over. "How is the little ballbuster?"

"Can we take him to a doctor now?" I asked, "He's running a very high fever."

Pierre peeled off his clothes, folded them over a chair, and slid into bed. "I'm tired. We'll see about that in the morning."

I tried again. "Pierre, he needs antibiotics. He's in pain."

"Ask my cousins if they have any. And stop making such a fuss." He turned to the wall, and I didn't hear another sound from him all night.

I was out of my element. I hesitated to oppose his wishes, to involve his cousins in our family drama.

My baby whimpered in my arms all night. In the morning Pierre insisted on eating breakfast first, but finally borrowed a car and drove us to the local doctor who confirmed that my boy had otitis; his ear was white not red, meaning the infection was acute. The doctor ordered penicillin, nasal drops, decongestants, and rescue medicine in case his throat started to close up.

How could Pierre act like this? His behavior was devastating. I wanted to shout, "But this is your son. . . ."

As we bid farewell to his assembled family members, I overheard Mémère whisper to Pierre, "Be good to your wife." *Too late, Mémère. Too late.*

The Slenderest of Threads

*B*ack in Paris at the bathroom sink, I twisted the ring on my left hand one way, then the other. To no avail. I plugged up the sink and ran hot water into it. I patiently soaked my hand. Still no give. *Oh, c'mon now. Was I eating that much cake my fingers were getting fat?*

I'd been meaning to take care of this problem since I met Julien. I wiped my hands off on my jeans and opened the fridge. Last resort: a dollop of French butter. Coating my hand with the butter, I massaged the area around the ring. It was a shame to waste the butter, but it finally did the trick and off came my wedding band. What a relief!

All was quiet in the apartment. Too quiet? I dashed around, poking my head into each room, expecting catastrophe. Last week I found Alexandre balancing on the edge of the pulldown desk in the living room. I caught him as he was teetering backwards. The next day he climbed on the kitchen table and stood up, leaning out the open window. I grabbed the back of his undershirt and pulled him to safety. I convinced Pierre to install metal bars the next day. And now? Now he was seated at his little table, "reading" a book, as well behaved as any boy his age could be. Whew!

Quietly I withdrew—he hadn't seen me—and stood in the dining alcove, in the grayish afternoon light seeping in the windows. I observed the tan lines on my reddened finger. But who'd be looking that closely? Does a Frenchman even care? Julien, however, was not totally French. My guess was he would care.

I admired the ring, purchased at the New York City Jewelry Exchange. My ring. Though inexpensive, it had serious pretensions: silver-etched and very thin, you could be fooled into believing it was an antique passed down by a dowager aunt, a legacy and testament to her glory days.

I loved the ring on sight. Pierre was surprised at my choice, but he likes simple things, and he liked the $100 price tag. I agreed to forego a matching engagement ring. Why bother? From proposal to wedding, after all, was only ten days, a rush job, with Mamie flying in to represent the French family. Explanation: she booked the nonrefundable flight without checking with us first. We picked out charming cards at Rizzoli's bookstore on Fifth Avenue, hand-wrote the invitations, inserted a quote from *Le Petit Prince: Mais, si tu m'apprivoises, ma vie sera comme ensoleilée.* Loosely translated: You light up my life.

At first I delighted in declaring, "We are bound by the slenderest of threads." How romantic to imagine we got to choose each day whether to stay together or not. *Ha!*

Flash forward: Pierre never wore his simple silver band, worried it would get caught in a piece of machinery at work. What kinds of machines exactly, I couldn't fathom. In an optics laboratory? I accepted this explanation once on faith.

I slid my ring into my underwear drawer, applied moisturizer, and rubbed my finger to make the marks disappear. They were still there if you knew where to look.

I was ready for Julien tomorrow. In more ways than one. Would he notice? Had he noticed?

Trysting

I tapped lightly on his door. He opened it a crack and waved me in. Before I even had a chance to throw down my purse and leather tote bag, he lifted me—I'm a feather!—and twirled me around and around, the room spinning, me choking and sputtering with laughter. "Julien! JU-LI-EN!!"

He kissed me on both red cheeks and tossed me on his unmade bed, climbing on top of me and pulling at my clothes. He was big and brawny and . . . uncomplicated. I prayed he'd never change and wished I could stay in his room forever.

He tickled, caressed, teased. Eventually we got down to business—oh yeah—then showered together, but soon we required another shower. When the games were finished, as we pulled our clothes back on, Julien said, "Lucie, let me show you this new pâtisserie I discovered just around the corner."

Wait. I was expected back home by 6:00 p.m. I was always, alas, on the clock. I pretended to be heading back to the office. "I've got a special report I'm working on. . . ."

"Listen Lucie-Goosey, they won't care if you're a bit late. Tell them you took a late lunch or a *quatre à six*."

"No such thing, Juju," I said, taking his hand as we walked out the door. "That's not for women."

"How do you know, huh?" he insisted, putting on his most serious face.

"It's *cinq à sept*, silly, and only for men cruising the park on their way home from work."

"And who are they doing? Passing *à la casserole* with?"

Prostitutes. Aren't they all prostitutes? I puzzled over this strange French custom, shaking my head in defeat. "You've got a point there. You win. A quick snack and I'm on my way." I pulled him along the street.

Over *pains au chocolat*, we talked about his week, the usual blather about his classes and quizzes, pressure from his father, his almost-ungovernable impulse to be off to the far corners of the earth on an adventure.

"I'm not enough of an adventure for you?" I asked. *Why did I say that?*

"Sure, but you refuse to spend more time with me. Refuse to run off and elope."

Okay. We both knew he was kidding. "You know why. I don't want you to flunk out because of me." I cupped his handsome face in my hands.

"So you turned down my invitations to come to Bretagne for a sexy weekend," he continued.

"You see I've already been to St. Mâlo—"

"Once!"

He leaned in and kissed me passionately till I was all out of breath. Of course, I was kissing him back and even moaning a little. I lifted my head and glanced around nervously. It wouldn't do to run into anyone from my real life. Satisfied, I went back to kissing and nuzzling him.

He was mostly kidding around, I told myself. He was a baby, an overgrown teenager. This arrangement suited him. I pushed him gently away. He hadn't commented on my bare ring finger; he had other body parts that interested him more. "Julien, let's enjoy this perfect afternoon."

"I thought we were," he said, turning just a tad morose. We sipped our *cafés crème* together, watching the tourists wandering down Rue des Francs-Bourgeois, in and out of the little boutiques buying, as I had many times, silver jewelry, antelope leather ties, romantic all-wool Breton fishermen sweaters. Alexandre looked adorable in his pint-sized sweater and matching wool cap in blue and beige stripes. Why not? He was a quarter Breton, thanks to Pierre's father.

I picked up my purse, tote, and sunglasses and rose to my feet. "Let's go out next Wednesday night, okay?"

"You mean it? Neato!" His face lit up.

"You know what? Make it Tuesday."

"Yeah. I have a test on Monday. We can celebrate. How about I get tickets to one of those cave concerts?"

Wow. How easy. No weeklong negotiations. "You will? Good boy!"

On the métro ride home, I schemed. I'd tell Pierre I had a special writers' group meeting on Tuesday to brainstorm how to pull together an anthology, *The New Generation of Expatriate Women Writers in Paris*.

Ava actually thought Doubleday might be interested. If he refused to babysit, I'd call our Vietnamese babysitter or see if Mimi could stay on till he got home. Who said cheating had to be hard? At least I didn't wave it in Pierre's face. Unlike other cheaters I neither planned on getting caught nor on confessing.

What Julien and I had was perfect. We enjoyed each other. Oh did we! As long as he never pushed for more—and he wouldn't —we could go on like this forever. Could I ever take him seriously? He was an overgrown boy. As I told him, I was not in the market for more.

Why was I shedding tears? For lost dreams. For the Lucie who could no longer pretend to be a good and decent wife or girl-friend or mother. I was holding on with one outstretched hand to a tall metal pole in a feverishly spinning merry-go-round.

If Julien noticed my bare ring finger, he kept it to himself.

Pierre, ever the observant scientist, noticed immediately. "Where's your ring?" he asked. "Did you lose that too?"

I had no idea what he was referring to but decided to see if I could get away with a half-truth. "My fingers are kinda swollen so I took it off." I showed him my hand. As predicted, he went back to arranging the contents of his attaché case.

Is There Even a Job
for Me in Hawaii?

I watched Pierre carefully any time he interacted with our son. I tried not to think about it, but wasn't Alexandre going to miss his father terribly? How his little face lit up when Pierre walked in the door tonight! I grew up with my mother and father and brothers. No insecurities or forebodings over whether the family would remain intact. My parents' breaking up never entered my mind. How could I contemplate doing such a thing to my own son?

I gave in to Pierre's constant nagging and started searching for a job in Hawaii. Without a job I'd turn into a vegetable. But I was told it was unlikely I'd find one. Nonetheless. . . .

"Not that I regret having fallen in love. . . ." I hoped this eye-catching opening line in my job application letters would result in positive responses from colleges in Hawaii. I had to try. I sat at the fold-down desk in the living room, grinding out letters. Perhaps if I found a job there, I wouldn't mind Pierre's being up on the mountain more than half the time. Would I miss him? He'd never been much help with the baby. He seemed to exist only to comment on my poor housekeeping or my spending habits. My fear: if I had more babies, I'd never get away. Not that I regretted having fallen in love. . . .

What a mess I was in now. I realized Pierre was damaged, not his fault; he was domineering, definitely his fault. He had no male role model growing up. Fatherhood meant ditching your son's mother and starting a whole new family. I detected no sense of embarrassment or guilt in Papi. Pierre was uprooted twice: packed off to the Vosges as a baby and relocated to a Paris suburb when he was older. Pierre once shared the news with me that, for a while, he was a bully in school. Hmm. His childhood definitely took a toll on him.

But how did I ever see him as a feminist? Was I blind? Yes, I'm a feminist but I don't burn bras. I just don't wear any.

"Not that I regret having fallen in love. . . ." I heard my best friend in grad school had to go all the way to Mississippi for a teaching job. And Paris. I would not have skipped Paris for anything.

What future now awaited me? I forced my roving mind to concentrate at the task at hand: sending out queries.

A Price Too High

*O*ver the weekend, Pierre decided we three should take a train trip to Fontainebleau, about an hour away. He hoisted Alexandre into a carrier on his back and off we went. For once the weather was on our side, balmy with light breezes caressing our cheeks. Alexandre stared at the scenery, taking it all in with his huge brown eyes as we trekked through the forest. We never made it all the way to the Château, opting to immerse ourselves in nature instead.

"So, what's the problem, Lucie?"

Was he serious? I looked into his eyes and took a deep breath before answering. "I wanted to be closer to my family. You knew that." I pushed my hair out of my eyes. "What I want should count for something."

"This is an opportunity not to be missed." He stopped in the middle of the path and placed his hands on my shoulders, shaking me as if to wake me up.

I squirmed away. "Cut that out!"

"You should be on board with this move. Supportive. Happy, dammit. Stop being such a child!" His anger was never far beneath the surface. Poor man. No point in talking anymore. "Baby needs to be changed. Let's go back to that bench we passed."

I quickly changed Alexandre and fed him some juice and apple slices. We munched on baguettes of ham, chunks of cheese. Then Pierre lifted Alexandre out of his stroller and let him run around freely, sniffing at flowers, splashing in puddles, talking back to birds. Amused, Pierre and I sat in silence on the bench watching him, in perfect sync with the day.

Pierre broke the spell. "Is that all you have to say?"

"Let's hope the price for professional advancement is not too high," I half mumbled.

No way was I taking this show on the road. But . . . I promised myself I'd keep an open mind, right? We three kept up our act of spending a pleasant enough afternoon in the country-side. The question was: How long could I keep up this charade? For life?

Confidences

*W*as this really happening to me? I headed downstairs and walked to the corner café, relieved to be out of the house. Gabriella was already seated at an indoor table, smoking a Gauloise, flipping through the latest edition of *Elle*.

"Sorry to keep you waiting."

"Catch your breath. What's up with you? You look terrible."

"Nothing much. Just needed to get out."

She raised an eyebrow and waited, expecting more. More fodder for her blasted boxes. When I remained silent, she added, "I ordered you a red wine," and slid the glass towards me.

I lifted my glass and sipped the warm liquid to indicate my approval. Should I dare confide in her? Probably not. She was hardly trustworthy, but I felt like a cannonball was resting on my chest. Was I wrong to take myself, my needs, and aspirations seriously? It was true what Pierre said. I'd always just loved the sound of my own voice, particularly when speaking French.

"So what did you want to talk about?" Gabriella asked. "It sounded urgent on the phone."

I sighed and stared into a corner of the pressed tin ceiling. Approaching thirty with five ex-husbands, Gabriella was not exactly a role model.

When I failed to say anything, she flipped through the magazine to show me a fur coat. "One day I'll have one like that."

"Oh?" I sipped at my drink and averted my eyes. "Horribly

expensive but very chic," I muttered. "What's the occasion? Are you planning to take a new lover?"

Gabriella, amused, leaned back in her chair. "Silly, I'll make it myself. First, I'll start on a mini model for my figurines, you know, and put it in one of my dioramas." *Could I hide out in one of her creations?*

7:45 p.m. already. The little monsieur must have been coming out of his bath about then—I'd miss reading him a story. I stifled another sigh, ordered more red wine for each of us, and pretended to be listening to Gabriella's account of a fight she'd had with a lady in the *boulangerie*. "That poor woman couldn't believe what she was hearing. I was cursing like a damned fishwife!" Gabriella was laughing with tears coming down her cheeks. "How dare she swipe the last slice of flan?" Gabriella was guffawing now. "That poor woman'll think twice before trying that again."

A Gabriella original story, meaning outrageous, but no doubt true. Again I asked myself if I could trust her or anybody. The French would never discuss what happens at home with anyone outside the family. I felt guilty for even thinking about it. I started tapping my fingers on the table.

"Don't you want to know how it turned out?"

"I've no doubt you got your flan."

"Did I! And I got to meet the cutest baker who came out of the kitchen to check on the ruckus."

"No! Are you going to see him?"

"Ha. We'll see what opportunity arises." She stopped talking for a moment. "My dear Lucie, pardon, but you seem . . . agitated tonight. Are you unhappy, dear?"

"What? No. You know what happens when I drink too much coffee. Today I believe I overdid it."

Gabriella was no idiot. Early on she declared her dislike of Pierre. Surely, she'd noticed the tension between us. She reached a large bejeweled hand across the table to cover my own and said in solemn tones, "If anything ever happens to that husband of yours, you know, Lucie, you can count on me." Aha! I suspected she had an itsy-bitsy crush on me. She was bisexual after all.

Settled: no way could I confide in her. Who else was there though? Not Mamie. That would just awaken her past traumas. She risked losing all of us as it was. . . .

The Lafontaines? I shivered as I imagined letting them know that we might be breaking up. The patronizing looks. The strained silence. The incomprehension—they've been married forever.

"No, it's settled," I said aloud, to my dismay.

I got to my feet, left enough francs to cover the whole tab, and walked her out to her car. "See you next week at the meeting. Remind me not to drink so much coffee, will you?"

"Whatever is worrying you, Lucie, in ten years will seem insignificant."

Once she'd pulled out, I took a last stroll around the block. The streets were still buzzing with traffic. What it came down to was this: I was ashamed, deeply ashamed at my failure to make this marriage work, and ashamed that I yearned to leave Pierre and take his son from him.

I'd have to figure this out for myself. What worked for Gabriella would not necessarily work for me. By this time next year, I might be one of the company wives, hopefully one with a job. If not, Pierre could be persuaded to make me another baby. After all, I needed a daughter.

I'd get her one day too. Just not now. Someday?

I had to play along and keep my cool. Though he rarely listened to me or took my concerns seriously, it was up to me to make him listen and understand what he was doing to our little family.

I climbed the twisted stairs and entered the apartment. Both Bonhommes were asleep on the bed. I lifted Alexandre, kissed him on his forehead, and laid him down in his crib, positioning his stuffed animals within easy reach. I fetched the cognac bottle and poured myself a generous shot. Finally, I cracked open the window to let in some fresh air and climbed into bed next to Pierre. The buses and *vélomoteurs* rumbled by, and an occasional drunk howled from the alley, but by this time I was three sheets to the wind and dead to the world.

Flap

Wednesday, we writers gathered in Ernestine's apartment. When my turn came, I nervously read the opening of my very first story, entitled, *The Flap of a Single Wing*:

People seem to expect something of me that I can't deliver.
So I've succeeded in withdrawing to a place where there's
only me and a wall of sea facing me. I devote hours
searching for a break in the wall through which a savior can
step. The sun bleaches my brain, my braids, turns my
eyeballs white. I crawl about in the sand, stretch out my
long neck. I've become more lizard than wife.

Gabriella asked where I got this idea.

"I'm basing this story loosely on a couple Pierre knows, a fellow scientist on the project."

"Is that what you're doing?" Gabriella winked.

Oh—

The others were intrigued and urged me to keep working at the story. *I'd be working at my life at the same time.*

In my spare time I continued trolling for jobs in Hawaii. Victory! One interview set up! The dean of a private high school planned to be in Paris in a few weeks and wanted to interview me. Why wouldn't they take me as a high school teacher? I'd taught freshman English at the university level after all. Maybe my decisions would be made for me.

Company Wife

To put an end to Pierre's constant nagging, to his "Get on board, dammits," on a chilly Saturday morning, I schlepped to a pool party for the future company wives held at a house in Neuilly. My first impression, staring through the smoky sliding doors leading from the deck to the interior of the house: fish-dead faces floating sideways on the surface of the living room. Unreal. I entered anyway, my son in my arms, sat down, found a cozy spot, stripped to the waist, and plugged him in. Sarah, the homeowner, seemed to have at least six children charging around from inside to outside and back again. A group of teenagers sprawled in a corner of the living room planning a camping and hitchhiking tour of Europe, a big deal, for that fall. Two rowdy little boys played outside on the swing and the slide, threw balls, and let the dog run after them.

Sarah sat useless like an empty vase waiting for someone to fill her. Vacant, vaguely polite, vibrating to the voices around her. After feeding Alexandre, I deposited him in the kiddie corner where the youngest were building towers of bricks and running a broken-down train over crooked wooden tracks. He flashed a delighted smile my way and turned and grabbed a loose brick from his neighbor. "Play nice," I said, as I skedaddled back to my spot near the refreshments with nary a glance backwards.

Sarah's oldest daughter, one of the teenagers plotting adventures, jumped up and came over to where the mothers were sitting. In a stage whisper, she said, "Mom, I'm sure one of these ladies would like to join a gym with you? Or take a cooking class. There's one starting up next month right here in our neighborhood." She looked around at us, pleading with her eyes for us to back her up.

Meanwhile, I could hear her friends in the corner busy laughing and hugging each other, giggling over adventures they were sure to have, adventures to keep secret and not tell their moms about.

Gee, remember Wendy and me—ten years ago? Just like them. Hearing some shrieking, I jumped up and removed Alexandre to a giant playpen set up near the windows which overlooked the pool and yard. I placed some thick cardboard books in his hands and returned to my observer post, watching the women watching the girls. *Ten years from now, will I look like one of these women?*

Sarah's daughter was still chirping about tennis coaches, yarn stores, art history classes. Sarah listened like a tired vegetable, an eggplant in the middle of her own living room. Blonde patch on top, the rest roundish, settled into the rug. *She was only forty, for heaven's sake! Her face without angles, without light—could it be no makeup?*

I squirmed uneasily and filled a pretty porcelain plate with cheese and crackers. Next time I moved, I was going for the wine.

Sarah's daughter, defeated, rejoined her circle of friends. We sat in silence until one of the other women in the room, Claudette, took the floor, holding forth a ten-month-old girl. "*Qu'elle est vilaine!*" she confided.

Though her fourth, she'd never seen such a monster for waking in the night, playing, screaming, squirreling all over the house. She woke not once, like mine, but ten times. Claudette's face was weather-worn, tight. She was sucked out, reedy, and bent like an old straw. Not much left to her but a voice. And she talked, more than the rest of us, blinking, gesticulating, sighing.

Ten years ago, she completed medical school, met young vigorous Felix—who was still young and vigorous—and sat on her eggs till they hatched. Meanwhile she hatched herself too, into a homemaker. The others claimed she was happy not working; they also whispered she was cracking up.

I scanned the room for a happier role model. These were women who played the game. I focused on Barbara, blonde, ponytailed, and tall like a model, with triplets she admitted she didn't enjoy raising. After nine years of waiting, she finally landed a job teaching at the university. She'd been at it a month or two. A dream come true. Except that now, like the rest of us, she was slated to be shipped to Hawaii, courtesy of Telescope Corp.

Hawaii. I was overcome by seasickness each time I asked myself if I was really going. I made believe I was. New York, Mexico, Paris—not even four years of trotting around after my husband. Yet this puppy-dog vocation held no attraction. I had such hopes for myself. Two steps from writing my dissertation yet I couldn't wait to leap into the arms of a visiting Frenchman and cry, MUSH! The Arctic, the South Pole, wherever you go, I go. My life was finally going to begin, in a big way.

Barbara, Claudette, Sarah, the others . . . it was hard to read enchantment on their faces. Boredom seeped through their masks of patience, endurance, sacrifice. But why should that matter? *Don't consider me, Jack. I'm only an accessory. C'mon kids, it's time to pack up!*

Fear, I experienced waves of fear as they talked of where they'd been, always spectators, never actors. Hard to believe that

most of these women had not learned to speak French—or Spanish—or Japanese—despite years of living abroad. *It's not all right,
girls!* I wanted to shout. *Why do you do it?* But who was I? As the
afternoon wore on, I found out—apparently, the only one young
enough or rebel enough to begin to voice a timid, *"No. I won't go,
no!"*

After consuming three glasses of wine, just following the
cues of those around me, I realized it was time to go back home
and prepare for the banquet that night. We dressed our babies
and corralled the older kids. We thanked the hostess, Sarah,
though she hardly seemed to register our departure.

"See you tonight. See you in Hawaii."

You bet your life. Enough was enough. I pled "stomach virus,"
packed Pierre off to the banquet, curled up on the daybed, and
finished reading the latest Romain Gary novel.

ele

The Home Fires

_I_ suspected we knew our time together was limited.

"Didn't I tell you this morning to cook me a hot meal tonight?" Pierre asked as soon as I came in the door.

Saturday, and he'd gone into work for an "important meeting."

I glanced around the living room. He'd already removed his shoes, lined them up by the door, and stepped into the pair of slippers he kept nearby. I proceeded, shoes on, into the bedroom to change and spotted his open attaché case parked outside the closet. He'd apparently extracted a scientific journal and brought it into the kitchen where he sat in the dying light, ramrod straight, awaiting my return.

"I've been waiting thirty-five minutes. I'm hungry, you know."

I poked my head into the kitchen. He'd taken several items out of the refrigerator. On a cutting board near the sink were a minced clove of garlic, two precisely sliced carrots, and a small bit of green pepper and onion. A head of lettuce drained in a colander. I pictured him bringing the lettuce to the sink and bathing each leaf lovingly in a slow trickle of icy water.

"Oh, you started dinner. Thanks." I hurried back into the bedroom to change into my at-home wear, inadvertently tracking dirt in on my platform shoes. Trying my best to ignore an evil look from him, I threw myself into the closest chair. "Whew, it's hot out there. How do you stand it? I can't believe no one has air conditioners. Can we at least get a fan?"

My Frenchman shrugged in a way I used to find adorable.

Now I was tired of the whole charade. I dared to ask, "How's it hanging, baby?"

If looks could kill.

What next? I grinned and walked over to the cassette deck to put on the new Bob Dylan tape. Loud. Louder. Loudest. I opened a window to let in a cool breeze.

"Mind telling me where my son is?" he asked.

"Oh, the greatest thing. I found this day care place, a cooperative, where I can leave him for an hour or two as long as I take my turn babysitting for the kids of the other moms." I looked at my watch. "Another hour yet."

"What do you know about these people? This is crazy. My mother will watch him if you need to go on an errand."

"No way, she's not careful enough. Her whole family is a little too lackadaisical in that regard. Remember that your aunt with that awful scar down her neck fell into the fireplace when she was a toddler? With a whole room of relatives supposedly watching her and—"

"That's enough! Mamie's his grandmother. She knows what to do."

I retreated to the bathroom to wash up but not before adding, "I am not leaving my child with her. End of story."

"You're impossible."

Minutes later I came out of the bathroom and stood at the kitchen table, determined to change the weather in our tiny apartment. "Pierre, let's go out tomorrow night—"

He held up his hand. "We'll see. I'm hungry. I worked today. Remember?"

"Okay, got it. Let's eat." I pulled two mutton chops out of the fridge and quickly breaded and fried them in olive oil.

He poured us each a glass of red wine and we sat down to our meal. Always a fast eater, I finished first and cleared the dishes away.

"Why do you have to be so cute?" he asked, standing behind me at the sink.

"Just comes naturally!" I answered, pulling away from his embrace. I grabbed a sweater from the back of a chair and headed out the door.

"And so *casse-pied* at the same time?" he called after me.

"Me, a ballbuster?" I smiled prettily as I gamboled down the stairs. "I'll take that as a compliment."

I had wanted to try out a new persona. Fun but exhausting.

~ele~

Desperate to Be Published

*I*n an effort to distract myself from all my frightful imaginings, I worked up the nerve to call Ava to ask if she could possibly assign me an article for *Dispatch*. I heard she'd done this for Ernestine. Ava agreed, asking that I pick up this new book from the office, arrange to interview the author, an American, and submit an article, half book review, half interview. I was ecstatic! My first bona fide writing assignment.

I quickly read the book, met the author in her apartment, and managed to record our talk. Way before deadline, I wrote it up and presented it to Ava. But to my dismay, she was less than ecstatic with the end result. "Make it stronger," she advised. Okay, look, she was the editor, not me. I tweaked it some more. "Again, not biting enough," she declared. My pride was hurt, but I resolved not to give up so easily. Indeed, after a few drafts, she appeared satisfied with my work. "Look for it on page six of the next issue. Wednesday." Oh, joy!

Wednesday Pierre came home early with an expensive wine to toast my success. Sweet of him. However, I was crying when I let him in the door. On page six there was no mention of my name, no article, nothing. I'd been unable to find the article on page six or anywhere else in the newspaper.

He flipped through the pages. "Where is it? I don't understand. Maybe it's for next week?"

"No, *pas du tout*. I know what she said."

"Is this a kind of sick joke?"

"Of course not. Ava's my friend."

"Call her. Right now." He passed me the phone, which he had finally agreed we could afford.

She took my call. On the phone she was brief and very businesslike. She confessed the reason for pulling the article was that the publisher did not like the subject. Of course not! The female orgasm! "He pulled the article at the last moment. Look, that's what happens in the business world, Luce. Get used to it." I hung up the phone.

Seeing my tear-splotched face, Pierre suggested we go to our favorite Chinese restaurant, the Empire Celeste, in the Latin Quarter.

"I'm not the least bit hungry."

Alexandre woke up from his afternoon nap, and I went to tend to him.

"C'mon Lucie, let's focus on other more important things." Pierre was trying to help, but I wished Julien were there to comfort me. I'd been neglecting him, yet I was the one who felt neglected. Writing that article had taken up so much of my time. I made a mental note to go see Julien soon.

"No thanks, Pierre. I'm sorry you had to leave work early."

"Well then, maybe I'll take my son out for a walk."

The bottle of Beaujolais Nouveau sat in the middle of the kitchen table, in hopes of better times.

I spent the next week crying when no one was around. My dreams of being discovered, a sham. My father tried to tell me I was no "real writer" when I was fourteen and bragging that I had written my first Western for the school magazine. Why hadn't I listened to him?

A letter arrived postmarked Hawaii from the dean who had interviewed me in Paris weeks before. I thought the meeting went well. My services were not wanted?

The heavens had spoken. No published article, no budding journalism career, no staying in Paris? No teaching position or any other type of work materializing in Hawaii. No opportunities to explore back home either, not that I'd tried. How would a single parent support herself here, there, or anywhere? What now? Was I doomed to be a company wife? No—I felt an urgency to get away from this man. Before it was too late. Late? Define. Before there were more children, more property, more experiences shared between us. Before he got worse. Or I did.

Qu'est-ce que c'est, le divorce?

Four years . . . only four. Strange how entangled we were. A baby. I guess that made a huge difference. My choice to sit and write a treatise in my journal or try to escape, which my body and soul were telling me to do.

Confronting the Man

"So what's the verdict on my leek and potato soup?" I asked at dinner.

"It's got carrots in it!" He disapproved but spooned another noiseless sip into his mouth. "Not bad, though. By the way, have you seen my jeans?"

"Your favorite pair?" He meant the ones faded and torn, with shredded cuffs, holey beyond repair, that I dumped in the trash a few days ago. *Uh-oh.*

"Lucie, the ones I change into every evening and wear all weekend."

"No, I . . . uh . . . don't think so. I bet you sent them out to the laundry." A bad liar, I kept my face averted, went over to the stove, and helped myself to another bowl of soup. "You're schlurping again!" he complained.

"Sorry. That's how we eat soup in the States." *Get used to it!*

I served the main course. The only sound, the traffic outside and my still-quite-audible schlurping.

"I cannot believe that about your fellow Americans. Do they also have such a messy plate at the end of the meal?" he asked, pointing to my plate littered with tiny fish bones, errant peas, buttery smears of potato puree.

I peeked at his plate, knowing what I'd find: bones stacked in one corner, plate otherwise swept clean. "Listen, Pierre, can we talk?"

"And what exactly have we been doing?" he asked, exasperated with me already.

"A letter came from Hawaii today."

"Yes?"

"No. I didn't get the teaching job."

"Not possible!" He clenched his fists and slammed his hands down on the table, squeezing his eyes shut. Recovering quickly, he took my hand. "Don't worry. My salary will be enough for us. You can write. . . ."

"And the three evenings every week when you don't come down the mountain and I'm alone with a toddler?"

"You're not the only one there. You met the other mothers. They are all like you, educated, and all supporting their husbands because—"

A wife follows her husband?

"A wife follows her husband!"

I got to my feet and took a deep breath before continuing. "The fact is, I know what I want, Pierre. I've figured it out. Finally. I want to have a career, write of course, *and* be a mother too. I'm not staying home doing laundry, cooking, or cleaning. Or spreading my legs when you happen to walk in."

"No need to be vulgar, Lucie."

I cleared the table. "I don't need any more babies, and that's all there is to do over there. Watch. I predict most of the couples will divorce—"

"I don't like you when you're so unreasonable, so intransigent." He was on his feet and approaching. I instinctively backed up.

"*I'm* intransigent?" Squeezing past him, I untied my apron and threw it on my chair. "Do you listen to yourself? Does any opinion but yours count?" I slipped into my light jacket, which I'd left hanging on the bedroom doorknob.

"What are you doing? Where are you going now?" he asked. You're not going to leave the kitchen like this?"

Alexandre called from the bedroom, "Maman."

"Lucie?"

"Get the baby. You're the father, aren't you? You can do it. And you know what? If the diaper's dirty, change it! He doesn't care who does it as long as he's clean and dry."

I headed for the apartment door. He reached out and grabbed my arm. "What are you doing?" he asked.

"I'm leaving." *Am I?*

"Leaving?" I caught a glimpse of a frightened white-faced little boy in place of my husband, a note of panic in his voice. Quite unexpectedly I was overwhelmed by a tsunami of pity, coming at me full force. I stared at his face, beneath the bravado and posturing. I mourned his inability to change. Any love I once had for him had been washed away, leaving only tears and pity in its wake.

"I need to buy a copy of *Le Monde*. I forgot to get it earlier today."

"I have no time to read it now. . . ."

"It's for me. For me to read." I slipped away, ran down the stairs, heart thumping. I turned left on Roquette and decided to walk halfway to République and back, a long enough walk to sort out my feelings.

Forty-five minutes later I charged back up the stairs, thinking, if I broke my neck, I wouldn't have to confront him. The door was unlocked, and I pushed it open to reveal Pierre and Alexandre on the floor playing with an assortment of toys.

"Maman!" chirped my son.

Not bothering to look up, Pierre asked, "Back so soon?"

Why was he always smirking?

"Yes!" I perched on the edge of the daybed. "I have something to tell you. Chita came by. She practically forced her way in. In case I wasn't upset enough by your philandering, she made sure I saw the whole picture."

I'd gotten the attention of the elder Bonhomme. I paused for effect. "I know you don't schlurp your soup or scatter fish bones over your plate, but you're not too fussy about where you park your penis, are you?" I struggled to keep the quiver out of my voice.

"Lucie, really! Your son!"

"Bonita. Sound familiar? Why didn't you feel compelled to let me in on that confession? You were bonking her the entire time I was in Rochester studying for my orals? You took her everywhere with you. Everyone knew her as your girlfriend? What the hell?"

I worked hard at keeping my voice level so as not to alarm the baby, who raised his head to look at me and then went back to sorting out his blocks. Pierre was busy turning colors and seemed frozen in place, turning a block over and over in his hands. "Pierre! Put him to bed. Now." The men disappeared into the bedroom. When Pierre emerged, he said, "Before you start in again, how about letting me answer?"

"There's no answer I can live with. What? You had needs? C'mon. You humiliated me. Everyone in Puebla knew I was being deceived, pitied me most probably. . . ."

"Not at all. Don't forget we weren't even married and were separated by thousands of miles for more than half a year."

"So I ought to have slept with the jock upstairs then? I was certainly horny enough. Somehow, I thought we had serious intentions about each other. It never occurred to me that . . . Why didn't you feel the need to confess about Bonita? Huh?"

"How would you know?"

"So I couldn't find out, meaning you didn't have to tell me? Obviously, you trusted Chita to keep her mouth shut."

"Chita is a friend, I told you."

The indignity of it all. "I misunderstood you from the beginning, didn't I? You just want to do what you just want to do. The public, be damned!"

"Lucie, we can get over this. We love each other. You're just having a bad time adjusting to our plans—"

"Our plans? Yes, you would see it that way. But I'm looking far and wide for my plans. Don't be too surprised when I figure out what they are." I pushed away his hands reaching out to me and took my journal with me into the kitchen. I poured myself a cognac and sat down, intending to scribble out my life.

He interrupted. "We might as well get everything out on the table, *n'est-ce pas*?" He sat down opposite me. "Yes, I admit I slept with Bonnie for the five months we were separated. Chita introduced us. There was no way to hide it. She was part of our group."

I put my head in my hands. But I knew all this. "How could you humiliate me like that? Tell me everything. Go ahead. I can see you're not finished." That's when I had a brainstorm. "The secretary too? Fernande? All this time you've pretended she was dating Bernard."

"And?"

"Bernard never likes any of the women we present to him, does he? No. Why? How can that be? Because he's gay! A homosexual. How do I know? Gabriella took one look at a photo of him we took at his party and said, 'Wake up, Lucie! The secretary is his beard. She allows Bernard to pass for straight and friend Pierre to operate without too much subterfuge.'"

Softly Pierre said, "I know about . . . Julien."

"Ju—what?"

"I forgive you."

My throat was drier than chalk, my tongue, a swollen, useless body part.

"Frequenting café s in the daytime? And so close to home. Not very wise, my dear." He wagged his finger at me.

Was this some kind of joke to him? Had Chita continued to spy on me? The ingrate!

"I knew it wouldn't last, so I said nothing. But really, you're not good at this, Lucie. Out in public like that. Shame on you! And with such a boy!"

Dinner threatened to come up on me. I jumped up and went into the bathroom to wash my face and compose myself. I knew I might as well face the music, but I felt so exposed.

Sitting back down at the table, I decided to take the offensive. "Fernande, that secretary, is your lover then?"

Pierre paused before answering to take a swallow of water from my glass on the table. "Yes."

Whywhywhy?

"At first she resisted my charms." He rolled his eyes. "Anyway, I think she has broken up with me."

"What about that blonde amazon?"

"Gretchen? Well, you know how it is, six weeks on a sail-boat. . . ."

I wanted to kill someone. I wasn't particular whom. Crime of passion. Would I have to serve a prison term? If I were him, I'd be very careful.

"Take it easy. Gretchen resisted my charms. She's engaged to a guy in Philadelphia. And quite old-fashioned."

"Otherwise, you would have boffed her too!"

"As I said, she resisted my charms."

"I'm confused. Let me get the tally straight. Bonita in Mexico, Fernande in France, a flirtation with Gretchen. Chita!"

A light bulb blazed bright in my head. "So that's why you never have time to help me with the baby, why you leave me alone, why—"

"I'm French. These romances have nothing to do with us, our family, our home. You cheated too." He glanced at the wall clock. "I've got to get to bed. Give me a kiss and let's forget all this." He leaned down and tried to give me a peck on the cheek, but I was too quick for him and pulled back in time. "Okay, if that's how you want it. *Bonne nuit*."

I stayed at the table until past midnight, trying to assign blame. "You started it. You're some kind of sex maniac! I only did it because I was lonely. . . ."

I crept into the bedroom. Neither the noise from the street nor my ranting had disturbed Pierre's untroubled sleep. I thought about waking Alexandre just for the company. Instead, I returned to the kitchen, collapsing at the table for a few ragged hours.

I had nothing left. No illusions. I felt so broken.

The Center Does Not Hold

*T*hings were going along swimmingly for little Lucie C. L. Bonhomme. No pressure. No decisions to be made—just the realization that any move I made next would have earth-shattering repercussions for me and my son, and I suppose, Pierre. Which was the road not taken? Which road was I meant to take? There likely would be no do-overs.

Why wouldn't anyone help me? I couldn't recall the last time I had made a decision. Anger and anxiety combined to keep me up at night. Weekdays I continued on in my sleep-deprived way, taking the bus, crossing the lovely Pont Neuf, always a delight for the senses, climbing three flights of stairs, arriving at the office. Today the scent of freshly brewed coffee filled the air. Surprise. My boss was here. He was a rare visitor. He was puffing away on his pipe—a little early in the morning for that?

He waved me in. "Lucie, over here." He forced a smile. I threw down my bag holding the five daily newspapers I had to read and reduce to a digest and collapsed a bit winded into the nearest chair.

He started pacing and taking his pipe in and out of his mouth. What a disgusting habit! I noticed his wife then, standing in the kitchen area. She was not the friendliest of boss's wives. We never engaged in conversation, and she almost never came into the office. I was on high alert.

"I am afraid we will not be needing your services any longer," he began. "The board is quite happy with your work, your weekly tracking and compilation of the Soviet bloc dissidents' activities, the monthly newsletter you put out, but—"

"Just tell me why."

"Let's just say they're no longer willing to disburse the funds necessary to carry on this particular project."

"Can't I just—"

"No." He was a portly older gentleman and loomed above me. "It's perhaps for the best, no? You'll be able to spend more time with your child. And your husband. He'll surely be happy to have you at home."

What? No!

The boss's wife stepped into the room.

I get to my feet. I always knew I was too well paid for this gig. Suppose the rumors were true and the CIA was behind this operation? I stuttered, semi-coherent, "I . . . understand." For once I deftly sidestepped the boss's hug by whipping out my hand, forcing him to shake it. I decided to ignore the wife. Undeterred, she followed me out to the stairway. "You never even came to *one* of our rallies," she said.

I slowly walked down the flight of stairs to the street and began wandering aimlessly around St. Germain des Prés. Oh well. Another day. Another loss. Number three. I was cursed.

A thought: Could Julien have told them about me?

Lucie Girl, you have to start fighting back, figuring things out for yourself, like how you're going to leave your husband now.

Julien?

I stopped by Julien's on the way back. I'd been avoiding him, but today I was in need of comforting. He flung open the door at my knock. "Oh . . . you!"

Instead of stepping aside to let me enter, he blocked the doorway. I darted under his arm and nervously danced around his apartment, babbling on about a sick family member. . . .

"I don't buy it," he declared. "Not for a minute." He gestured toward the still open door. "You need to leave."

I'd been avoiding eye contact but risked it now. Stepping in front of him, I said, "Julien, you're right. There might be more. I mean, there is more. But I can't involve you. I wanted to tell you how much I enjoyed . . . you know . . . say goodbye . . . tell you I care about you." I expected a reaction, an argument, a plea. I got . . . indifference?

"Yeah. Lucie, I have a class assignment to prepare. I'm going to show you out—"

He backed me toward the door, but I put a hand on his chest to slow him down. By this time I was crying. "But Julien. Julien!"

"Listen, Lucie," he said, grabbing my arms. "When you didn't reappear, three weeks went by, then more. What I was going through! Were you lying unconscious in a hospital? Were you even alive? You know I'm just a stupid American. Finally, I could stand it no more. I asked my father to check in with your boss . . . blushing now won't help your case."

"Julien, let me explain."

"What for? I know everything, okay? And I'm sick to my stomach about this whole affair. Know why? I have no intention of being like my father."

"Why bring him into this?"

"Will you keep quiet for once? My father has kept a mistress for years, all the time he's been married to my mother. And three guesses what he'll do if my mother dies before him. He'll go out trolling for a newer model, right off the factory floor, for sure a woman younger than I am."

Tears streamed down my face as he again pushed me toward the door. "Can you give me one last hug? I really need a hug; I'm having a bad time, and—" *God, I'm pathetic!*

He shook his head violently. "You cannot stay here, Lucie."

"No, of course not." A sad little sob escaped me. As I turned to go, his arms slipped around me and held me tight. I relaxed into his embrace. He whispered, "Lucie, I hope you straighten out things in your marriage. You're a bright and beautiful lady. You should fight for your happiness."

"But I need you now," I insisted.

"Goodbye, Lucie," he said, walking me out. "Have a good life."

I stood planted for a moment in his doorway. He jerked his head in the direction I should go. I took the hint.

"And tell the truth," he yelled down the street after me before he slammed his door.

As I turned the corner, I almost collided with a sleek young French student sporting a trendy backpack, dressed elegantly in shades of black and a silvery gray. Going on instinct, I hid beneath the awning of a shoe store and let a few minutes pass. Emerging from my hiding place, I peeked around the corner.

Sure enough, Mademoiselle tapped lightly at the door I had just exited, and Julien let her in. Before the door closed, I heard tinkles of laughter from her and one whooping noise from him.

I led my weeping self to a bench in a corner of the Place des Vosges.

How would I manage without Julien? I intercepted a few questioning glances, but no interference from the other mothers and nannies present. After a bit, to the horror of the others, I approached the fountain closest to me, scooped up a handful of water, and washed my face. With no tissues, I had to let it air dry. I noticed one mother grab her child's hand and forcibly walk him away from my vicinity. Because what's the one cry heard most often in a French playground? *Faut pas te mouiller!* Don't get wet!

I started laughing and hiccupping. Okay, now I was a certifiably crazy person. I swept my eyes over the scene. My imagination or were people leaving? Hordes of them, hastily gathering up their belongings, their kids dressed up like mini executives in leather and suede, wheeling their stuff the hell out of there.

I found a new bench. Julien was right. I stunk. To high heaven, as my mother would say. What the hell was wrong with me? Since our arrival in Paris, I'd gotten more and more depressed, unhappy, itchy. Crying from room to room. I had a baby not as a cure-all or a balm to heal our marriage, but because I yearned to be a mother and feared my opportunities were shrinking. Yet I had more than an inkling that my marriage might not last.

Were things really this bad? Was it me? Was I nuts? Here I was living in this glorious city with its soul-catching architecture, its picturesque alleys, its classical concerts in vaulted churches, its incredible cuisine. I was speaking the French I learned in high school and college, translating, teaching, writing. I had given birth in French! With the Lamaze team! How many people could say that?

I'd married my French sweetheart after "shacking up" with him in Mexico. Weren't we a pair of happy lovebirds, taking weekend road trips to Veracruz, Oaxaca, Mexico City? My only problem in those days: how to get him to marry me. What a delicious challenge. He warned me once that he could eat me up, destroy me if I let him, which had happened with his college girlfriend. So I read up on Virgo males. Yikes, was he one! The monomaniacal dedication to staying on task, the high intelligence, the rigid morality? And the incessant picking away at scabs, the domineering nature, the perfectionism. Still, I convinced myself that I alone could handle him. Fix him. Make it all up to him. Yet the day he asked me to marry him, I actually felt a little letdown. Why? I had chased him, cornered him, and captured him. I was getting what I wanted. My subconscious knew better. His scratch indeed proved worse than Braveheart's.

Back to Julien. Why had I never stopped to question my treatment of him? His rights. His feelings. He certainly did nothing to merit such disregard. I was ashamed of my selfishness, my neediness, my dishonesty. Judging by my replacement in black and gray, at least I didn't seem to have done any lasting damage.

Of late I'd taken to having imaginary conversations with my imaginary French psychiatrist, and I slipped into one while crouched on the bench. Pierre spoke deprecatingly about Americans and their shrinks—he'd never entertain the idea of marriage counseling.

Hence I rehearsed scenes of confession instead. I never considered seeking out a real live doctor—I'd have to talk to him in French, and I was not sure I could communicate all the nuances of the situation and certainly not the mindset of a semi-liberated New York Jewish woman.

"Dr. Arnolphe, I'm not a bra burner, please believe me. Yes, I agree [*do I?*] American women, those feminists, are going too far . . . Just tell me what to do."

"Start behaving like a proper wife, for starters," he says. "What are you wearing when your husband arrives from work?"

"Wearing? [*I'm wearing my favorite ripped blue jeans with the embroidered butterfly covering up the hole on the upper right thigh.*] Uh . . . oh . . . I always look nice."

Dr. A throws me a skeptical look. "That's a good start." He puffs on his pipe. What a cliché, I know. "Take me through his homecoming if you would."

"Homecoming? He does come home. Eventually." I start to squirm around on the hard seat.

"Humor me," insists the good doctor.

I force myself to sit up straighter on the fold-up wooden chair. "An hour before, I shower and apply makeup, lots of lipstick. [*The doctor is nodding.*] I dress the baby in a colorful outfit I've knitted, and myself in a dress Pierre likes. I wear high heels and stockings."

"Go on."

"I kiss him hello?"

"Two cheeks or three?"

I'm fidgeting like mad and glancing around the room, looking for answers. "Depends."

Doc screws up his face. He disapproves of my answers. I start to lose it.

"Depends?" he prompts.

"If he's been a complete asshole, I just nod at him and go back to my reading."

"A book? What book is more important than your husband?"

"One like *Le Deuxième Sexe*." I daren't look at his face. "Pierre will want to take a shower, but I'll jump up and block the bathroom door, inundating him with the day's horror stories till he has to back up or push me out of the way."

"I don't see. Horror?"

"The toilet's backed up, Alexandre threw up, projectile vomiting it's called, the tape recorder's busted, and I forgot to go shopping for baguettes. His mother came to the door, and I didn't let her in. . . ."

"What? *Ça se fait pas!*"

"Well . . . then he'll push his way into the bathroom, bathe, dress, and take a plate of grapes and camembert and stale bread with a glass of wine over to the table, not bothering to open the leaf on either side. I'll drop Alexandre into his highchair and go back to pretending to be reading my book."

"No dinner for your husband? Unheard of," rages Dr. A, standing up, all portly and white and old, and gesticulating madly. "What a bitch!" escapes his mouth.

"Yeah, that's me all right. A real bitch."

But I never managed to tell him how Pierre refused to take us on vacation other than to a chicken farm his friends run near Grasse, refused to babysit while I trained to become *une interprète*, and refused to renounce his philandering ways.

I intuited no help from Freud or his followers. If only we

were in New York City, my brothers or my father or Wendy maybe could have talked some sense into Pierre. But as things stood. . . .

The young matron at a neighboring bench jumped to her feet, yelling, "*Pas dans la bouche!*" (Not in your mouth!) All heads turned her way. She rushed to the fountain where her toddler had just dunked his rubber duckie in the water and was about to put it in his mouth. Whew! She made it in time. Catastrophe averted!

I pushed damp hair out of my face and got to my feet and stretched. The remaining mothers and nannies and unemployed men averted their faces. I walked over to the café near the Victor Hugo Museum and chose to sit at a small outdoor table. The waiter appeared. "*Un verre de vin rouge, s'il vous plaît.*" (A glass of red wine, please.) After downing it, I asked for another: "*Encore.*"

I was strictly a one-drink cheap date. Who cared if I held my liquor today? I caught a man lounging at a neighboring table giving me meaningful sidelong glances. He motioned for me to come over and sit with him. I politely demurred. When he persisted on persisting, I slammed my hands down on the table for emphasis, almost toppling it, and let loose: "*Va te faire foutre!*" What a useful phrase, one I'd learned early on, containing the French f-word and guaranteed to put an end to any and all harassment. The waiter wiping down a nearby table winked at me approvingly and presented the poor lecher, who was just acting like a typical Frenchman, with his bill.

Boy, did that feel good!

ele

Who Am I Really?

*A*nd that's when it hit me: I was not a passive woman trotting obediently after her husband. True, I'd carried this image around in my head for years, that I needed a man to "mold" me. I hoped to meet him before I had done too much on my own. *Well done, Lucie!*

How had I forgotten my father used to call me "Daddy's Little Rebel?" My fantasy lover and I would share pivotal memories and *side-by-side* sketch out our futures together. At just the opportune moment, Pierre materialized by my side, stepping straight out of a François Truffaut movie, a dead ringer for the hero, Antoine Doinel. Strong, sexy, self-assured, confident. He knew where his footsteps would fall.

The years I spent waiting to meet The One, I hadn't been idle. I'd been a serious grad student. I'd indulged in a love affair or two. I was no slug, crawling about in the weeds. Why did I feel I needed rescuing?

I did have goals all along: wife and mother. Not enough? Somehow and somewhere I would have a career too. And be a writer. Yet in one fell swoop, I'd lost my writing career, my Paris job, and for extra kicks, my lover. My marriage would no doubt come next.

Weaving slightly, I made my way home. My feet knew where to go. Once there, I refused to meet Mimi's questioning eyes. Instead, I scooped up my son and hugged him to my chest, inhaling the fresh scent of his hair. "Go play with your fire engine. I'll be right there," I said as I put him down. Smart boy, he obediently trotted off to the bedroom.

It's my fault too, I intended to tell Pierre that night. "You were right all along. You're not the marrying type. I'm not sure I am either."

I brewed a fresh pot of strong coffee after Mimi departed, gulped down a scalding cup, and joined Alexandre on the bedroom floor. He was babbling on about something. Sounded almost like a lecture!

I'd made mistakes. It wasn't all Pierre's fault. I pretended to be a passive, easygoing person, a follower, good wife material. I believed that malarkey. *Anything you want, my dear, any kind of marriage. Sure, leave the babies with me and travel around the world. Just marry me. I'm twenty-four already and my parents treat me like an old maid.*

He was like a movie star to me. He loved me. I must have loved him. He might still love me.

I knew I was a fake. How could I be a college professor? Could I reel off quotes by famous authors? Uh-uh. My colleagues did every day at lunch. Little old Lucie. Panicking and pacing when I thought about what I would do when I finished the program. The older English Lit grads were sending around hundreds of curricula vitae to colleges in less-than-ideal locations for a New York Jew. Could I land a job? Even before reaching that stage, I had to put in more time, years, two, five, seven, researching and writing a dissertation. I'd had enough. I was bone tired of being poor, with no decent clothes, and no boyfriend.

The year before I met Pierre, after being awarded my master's, I chased a guy out to Colorado, telling fellow classmates I was all but engaged. For months I had been exchanging letters with Kenny, a Jewish guy from Boston with his own very delicious and sexy accent. Sounded like a Kennedy. Letters, be damned! Within the first week we both realized how unsuitable a match we made. I returned to Rochester, tail between my legs, and enrolled in the doctoral program. What else could I do?

My father's words still stung. My only value had to come from being a married woman. I was nothing if not the chattel of some man.

I was not honest. With myself. With Pierre. He knew himself much better than I knew myself. And I'm the introspective one!

Here's what I knew: "Paths are made by walking." I read that somewhere. Exactly. Time for me to walk.

The collapse of the marriage wasn't Pierre's fault at all. Or only half his fault. My hand on his hand. I did not have the nerve to take him on, defy him openly. He was too strong, and I was too scared.

Ah—that sweep of hair over the perfect forehead, the fine features, the square shoulders, the athletic V-shaped torso. The world-is-ours approach to life. Yes, that seductive accent. A boy named Peter from Brooklyn would never have had the same effect.

Alexandre approached and crawled into my lap, snuggling close. Had he seen my tears? Heard my sniffles? He was counting on me to do the right thing. If I dared to do what I wanted, what I had resolved to do, would I ever make it up to him?

Try, Try Again

*A*va had been avoiding me since the female orgasm fiasco at *Dispatch*. Determined to swallow my pride, I followed her out of the next writers' group meeting. As she stopped to light up a Gauloise, I pounced. "Ava, I'd like to try again. I know I can do it. Please give me an assignment."

"Can't you see I'm busy?" she snarled. Undeterred, I cupped my hand around her lighter; she leaned forward, closed her eyes, inhaled, then blew the smoke out slowly. *Is there such a thing as a nicotine orgasm? Maybe that topic would be palatable for the publishers?*

I ignored the smoke and refused to let my eyes water. She was forced to acknowledge my help with the slightest of nods. I grabbed her free hand. "I am asking for your help, Ava. I really need this. You know the troubles I'm having. It would mean so much to me to see my name finally in print—"

Shaking loose of me, she took off down the street, turning to yell back, "Call me at four tomorrow." Ava came through and assigned me a piece! I decided to drop everything and work it to death. I could not afford to fail again.

I'm a Writer!

My write-up was published! Page two. At last, a clip to establish me as a serious writer. My task was to interview women who earned more than their husbands and explore the effects and repercussions on their marriages. In our circle alone, I located four women willing to share their personal stories with me and with the world, providing I supplied them with pseudonyms.

Ava uncovered four other couples for me to talk to. I had an amazing time though I had to spend many hours in the library pulling it all together. But I had more free time than ever—no job and no lover. Mimi loved the extra hours of babysitting I threw her way. And this time Ava only had me rework the piece three times.

"You have the right instincts to be a journalist," she said. *Wow!* She promised to line up more work for me.

My next topic: the success and failure rate of mixed marriages, as in Franco-American couples. I'd already learned that chances for a marriage lasting increased if the woman was French and her husband, American. Not a shock. What red-blooded American boy wouldn't want to be spoiled silly by an attractive and attentive, exceedingly well-groomed wife, who respected his authority and accepted her role? A wife who could cook and clean, manage the household finances and the children, and share her recriminations about men only with the women who huddled in the kitchen at every social event, bitching and moaning amongst themselves?

I had to be sure to keep my own prejudices out of the article, which would not be easy.

Dining with the Lafontaines

I continued to hunt for an ally among my French women friends. Mostly we saw each other in the company of husbands and kids.

On a cool afternoon, Pierre and I travelled out to the suburbs to visit the couple who had been the guinea pigs of my culinary experiments and never once complained, the Lafontaines. I agreed to leave Alexandre at home with his grandmother.

We sat down to a multicourse lunch expertly prepared by the missus. Midway through, Pierre abruptly rose to his feet and, without a word, walked out onto the terrace. Husband and wife exchanged a look, and the husband went to join him. My stomach gave a heave. Were they going to talk about our difficulties?

I avoided looking at the wife. Instead, I picked up a magazine lying on the coffee table and pretended to be absorbed in a *Clair Foyer* bouillabaisse recipe. For the last two years, I'd longed to find out what went on behind Mme L's placid exterior. Did she like being a woman? Why couldn't she just lift a corner of the tapestry and let me take a peek?

I pulled my head out of the magazine, caught my breath, and plunged in. "When did your youngest cut his first tooth?" Damn! And damn if she didn't proceed to tell me. I died a thousand deaths. Coward! Without a word to either one of us, Pierre walked back in with her husband. They moved the table to the terrace, poured more wine, tried to get at the heart of the artichoke. The four of us discussed cinema and politics and food, talking to fill up the time until the last train to Paris was due to depart.

"Do you think Mitterrand has a chance in 1981?" asked the husband.

"Let's hope so," chimed in Pierre. A heated debate of French current affairs followed: the death of Pompidou, the presidency of Valéry Giscard d'Estaing. Realizing they'd left me out of the conversation, they asked, "How do you think Carter is doing?"

Women have no valid political opinions. That's what husbands are for. To guide the poor creatures.

"Sorry," I responded. "I haven't been following American politics of late." I paused to let Pierre jump in. To be truthful, I was far more interested in the capture of serial killer, Ted Bundy, a handsome devil; the rehabilitation of Patty Hearst; and the release of a movie about my favorite comic book hero, Superman. Woody Allen was big in Paris, but the Parisians laughed in all the wrong places, making it imperative that I see *Annie Hall* again next time I was in New York.

On the train ride back, I remembered I did not like the majority of French women. They intimidated me with their practiced putdowns, glares, snipes at my accent or my clothes or my ways. Yet I envied them in a backward lobe of my brain, envied their act, their playing the game as well as they did. Sure, they were insecure too, and afraid, which made them secretive. I understood but still could not identify with this culture, which was so entirely buttoned up. All façade. I needed a confidante. Ideally, someone to tell me what to do. A guru?

Most Frenchwomen never asked themselves any questions. How did they manage that feat? They accepted everything their neighbors accepted, everything their men urged them to accept. They were happy and I was not. I failed to accept my assigned role. Who was I to put them down? Yet—how did they manage to be stupid and unseeing? How come they liked to live like this? Nothing was ever wrong at their house. They put their babies on the potty before they could sit up, slapped them around if they made in their pants, tied their hands behind their backs to prevent them from feeding themselves and staining the carpet. The girls they dressed in short dresses, the better to get sand up their cracks in the sandbox, and clogs to facilitate falling when running. Little girls soon saw that movement was out, sitting pretty was not. Weekends chez Mamie or shopping or cooking or building a country house or a garden. Bringing boss his coffee.

Was this what it was all about? Unhappy faces in the métro. Tired, strained faces. Tight lips.

I knew these women suffered. Their lives were hard, their men were hard, they were bound like Gulliver with tiny ropes and cords, conventions, rules, taboos. No breathing space. When they laughed with the boys' off-color jokes at the office, they were double knotting the Lilliputians' ropes.

How to forgive their pretentiousness? They'd insulted me and hurt me with their assumptions and prejudice, which were not even theirs. Would it hurt them to be honest for a change?

I was unable to talk to them, unable to see through all the murk. And I could no longer wait for them to come out naked either.

I'm going to have to come out naked all by my lonesome.

Floralies

*H*ow naïve of me to imagine I could lay out my troubles yes-terday at a get-together with another couple. The hostess was better prepared and much better suited to give a heart-in-mouth recital of her baby's dental woes.

At our meeting I brought Gabriella and the other writers up to date on my predicament. I explained my desire to make a clean break from Pierre while Alexandre was still young. First, they encouraged me to stay in Paris where they argued I already had an apartment, a part-time job, babysitters, and them. And the start of a writing career?

"I lost my job."

They reversed position: Why not go to Hawaii where I'd be alone most of the time while Pierre was up on the mountain? I could focus on writing a novel. They were still confident I could knock one out in eight months. Or might it be better to return to New York and take up a career as a teacher or administrator? *Ugh. How could I live in Queens again after seeing Paris? How you gonna keep them down on the farm after they've seen Paree?*

I nevertheless dedicated a week to envisaging this last sce-nario. I'd always had a love-hate relationship with New York. Everything seemed more difficult there: commuting by bus and train over an hour to a job, finding a babysitter, meeting men at singles mixers, making new friends, dealing with my not-always-loving family. I had to admit my chances of finding a decent job in New York were probably better than if I stayed anywhere else.

After nearly four years in Paris, in some respects I had settled in quite nicely. What remained was to figure out the fastest way out of this dreary marriage. But Paris, the city of Paris? I liked Paris. Who wouldn't? In all my calculations I failed to consider long-term career prospects or envision how I'd manage as a single parent in France with no family around other than my mother-in-law.

Pierre, baby, and I awoke on a Sunday morning rather late for us: 7:00 a.m. As I set the table with fresh bread and croissants, butter, jam, and coffee, I stared out the wooden casement windows at a scene I would never tire of: Rue de la Roquette, dressed in her Sunday finery: streets swept, shops closed, grates firmly in place, only a lone walker here and there sampling the crisp morning air.

We sat down to eat, and before Pierre could formulate an escape route leading to the swimming pool, the laboratory, or the photo lab, I hatched a plan. I passed Pierre the jar of blueberry confiture and innocently suggested, "Suppose we go to Floralies? Alexandre's old enough now to appreciate the zoo." I'd already been there several times with Valentine but did not let on.

Pierre frowned, deep in thought. *Oy vey*. He finally lifted his head to wrest the butter knife from me and spread a bit more jam on his toast. He reached over to the counter and turned on our little radio to listen to the weather forecast. Satisfied that the weather would be warm and balmy, he said, "Why not? You'd like that, wouldn't you, Petit Bonhomme?" By way of response, Alexandre let more oatmeal dribble down one side of his mouth. I giggled. Pierre fixed me with an accusatory look. He's a baby! I wanted to shout, but I obliged by fetching a washcloth and cleaning off his little rosebud mouth. I even wiped down the highchair.

My heart beat unevenly in my chest. I now had a venue, a calm and beautiful public place, the Floralies, in which to share my insights on our marriage and our future. No more stalling!

Pierre packed a sleepy boy into the child carrier and hoisted him onto his back and we set off, hardy pilgrims, to explore the suburbs. The trip was quite effortless. We boarded the number 46 bus at the corner of Roquette and Boulevard Voltaire, our wait a hell of a lot shorter than it was at this spot when I was in labor. A mere thirty minutes later, we disembarked at the Bois de Vincennes, situated in a neighborhood where all kinds of trees and flowers and green grasses sprouted, and concrete was seemingly banished. Alexandre swung his head from side to side; his feet beat a rhythm on his father's back. "What do you say, old man?" Pierre asked him, reaching back to tickle him. "What exactly is he looking at, Lucie? Tell me."

"Everything, the colors, nature, the people. . . ." Crowds of well-dressed Parisians strolled up and down the long boulevards ringing the park. Large immigrant families picnicked on the grass, and couples lounged in cafés reading newspapers, sipping cafés crème, people-watching and munching on croque-monsieurs. I closed my eyes for a moment, relishing our immersion in a Monet painting come to life.

"But what specifically? I can't see him, you know."

"Okay. Well, he's done flirting with that man over there," I said, pointing to a tattered old man seated on a turned-over crate, eating peanuts. "And now seems absorbed by that red squirrel shimmying down the tree trunk."

"He's wants to go closer, doesn't he? Can you pluck that yellow flower?"

"Sure." I brought the flower close to Alexandre. He wrinkled up his nose and turned his head away.

"I guess he won't grow up to be a *parfumeur*."

"Or botanist," I added. "He must take after me." A city girl, I could barely distinguish one flower from another.

"Lucie, walk this way," Pierre demanded as I veered off to the right, from habit heading towards the Parc Zoologique.

I was accustomed to following orders issued by Monsieur Bonhomme, but today I had reasons to stick to my original plan. "Pierre, I saw a sign behind us, indicating the zoo is that way."

Pierre pulled a map out of his pocket, consulted it, and nodded. Our little family veered right.

I loved this zoo. Small but delightful. Walkable. We visited the bears, the big cats, the seals. We saved the best for last—the elephant. She rested against a back wall of her enclosure with only a low three-brick-high barrier separating her from the crowds. Valentine and I loved to linger here, relishing the expressions on the older kid's faces when the elephant slowly turned her massive head around to gaze back at them. *Uh-oh. My mission! I still hadn't said a word.*

Pierre announced, "I'd like to sit in the sun," and steered us over to an area at the front of the zoo where we found an empty bench right below the gibbons.

"Pierre, we need to talk . . . about . . . our future." I stumbled over the words.

He released the baby from the carrier and held him in his arms, turning Alexandre around to show me his broad smile.

"What about?"

How to start? Every discussion we had those days quickly morphed into an argument. He'd insist we were not arguing but discussing. I couldn't agree less. On this sun-drenched afternoon, I was not looking for an argument, just honesty.

"Lucie? Be careful you do not ruin a beautiful memory for our son."

Great. At that very moment the gibbons decided to put on a show, the best in town. In the trees directly above us they staged their ballet—brachiating wildly through the air, from branch to branch, swinging distances of up to fifty feet, and standing up (to take a bow?) to walk on their hind legs with their arms raised—accompanied by their amazing vocalizations: whooping, barking, whistling. What a fantastic show, truly. Too bad I was not in the mood to enjoy it.

Pierre handed Alexandre to me. Too much sensory input. He had succumbed and slept through the performance. Pierre jumped up, head craned back to get a fuller view of the gibbons' antics. He talked for a while to a man with three school-age kids, patting them each on the head before returning to our bench. He caught me nervously biting my cuticles and wagged a finger at me to get me to stop. Oh, that was effective. He was taking a line out of my parents' playbook. Shaming had never worked on me. I was still sucking my thumb at age ten.

Was that how he'd encourage his son when he was older? If he grew up with a father like Pierre, nothing he did would ever be right. His self-confidence would be nil. Pierre would destroy him. Look what his constant criticism had done to me, an adult. Another reason to leave him.

I took my hand out of my mouth. When I failed to otherwise respond, Pierre suggested we head home. Of course, Alexandre and I followed his lead.

I gazed out the window of Bus 46: the snarling traffic, the few intrepid pedestrians who dared to cross the wide street where there were no traffic lights or stop signs, no lanes. Just keep moving like you know what you're doing, I wanted to advise them.

What I planned to say to Pierre: You know it's not working. Sure, we can stay together for the sake of our child, but what kind of home would we be creating for him? *Decided then: Alexandre and I will stay in Paris.*

Truth

The truth was I no longer loved Pierre. The only emotion I could access was a deep well of pity. He couldn't change, wouldn't change, and would only get worse as he aged. He had no insight or interest in psychology. Soul-searching was not his bag.

My mother had always said, "It takes two to tango." My father liked to reply, "In marriage you must agree to agree." Wrong? Right? Yes, I played into a scenario our culture reinforced: strong, virile male rescues beautiful directionless maiden. Now I wanted out of that scenario. *Was it my fault I didn't know who I was at the beginning?*

I still did not know exactly where I wanted to be. I had trouble imagining myself waking up in the morning and planning the day for my child, let alone myself. Did I have that strength? If I went back to the States, how could I furnish an apartment, find a job, fashion a life for the two of us? More likely I risked sinking into a deep purple funk, unable to extricate myself. Whatever I decided I had to make sure I did not risk hurting my child. I would have to make the right decisions for two now. Or three.

A full-time mom once again, I resumed my old habits. As I paid for my pastry and stowed it in my bag, I admitted: this is not what I want. I can eat this stuff day and night without touching the profound unhappiness at my core.

Sure I blamed Pierre. He fooled me by acting the part of a poet, looking the part certainly. Yet as soon as we touched down in Paris, he morphed into a kind of domestic tyrant and left me feeling useless, stupid, incapable. I reminded myself now that I ran my life just fine before meeting him. Well. . . .

With Alexandre buckled into his stroller, I embarked on marathon walks throughout Paris, obsessing over the decisions I had to make. Not religious, I nevertheless prayed for guidance.

The Brake

*A*fter dinner, Pierre camped out in the living room, Alexandre in his crib, and I propped myself up in bed to write. After a while I tiptoed out of the bedroom and slipped Pierre a paper on which I had listed all the reasons we were never meant for each other:

You are a doer; I am a thinker. You worship order; I thrive on a certain amount of chaos.

Nonsense mixed with a sliver of truth. I waited, silent. Even with the windows closed, the noise from the street was deafening, particularly those damn motorbikes. Why weren't they outlawed? I stood rock still, remembering the quiet of our place in Mexico, the multicolored flowers in the courtyard, the smells of cooking cream of carrot soup, mole, and goat stew. I could still hear the laughter as Pierre and our roommate traded jokes while Chita and I studied dress patterns.

I heard a rustle of paper and came back to the present. Pierre had picked up a copy of *L'Humanité* and was catching up on the latest communist propaganda. The paper I gave him? Tossed on the floor. To my surprise, he offered no counter arguments to anything I had written. Part of me was hoping for a rebuttal or even a declaration of undying love and devotion.

As we undressed before bed, he took my arm and squeezed it hard, whispering, "You are a brake. You delight in holding me back." A bit stunned, I followed him into bed where instead of stretching out on his back and positioning my head on his shoulder, he turned over to face the wall. In the old days, I would have rolled him over to face me and pleaded, "Talk to me." But now. . . ? He'd opened the window, unleashing the discordant caterwauling, the plaints of all who were imprisoned at the Bastille down the block or at La Roquette and finally interred at Père Lachaise cemetery. The symphony of the streets.

A brake? Me? I'd failed to get on board with the whole Hawaii thing. I believed the welfare of the family trumped that of the father. Shoot me.

I remember a photo taken in the Instituto's lunchroom in Mexico. Me, in my white peasant blouse embroidered with vibrant threads of red and green and yellow, staring over at him, wondering why he was staring down at his plate, sullen and brooding. Ah, he's in another one of his moods. Good thing I knew how to manage him.

Our communication devolved into lectures and harangues and even implied threats. "You can't take a boy away from his father," he insisted.

Still deathly afraid to spell things out, I practiced in front of the bathroom mirror. "I'm staying. For the moment. I'm not going to Hawaii with you. Your son and I, neither of us is going."

Coming Clean

"Pierre, stop eating!" I commanded. We were alone in the apartment. Here was my chance. Pierre shook his head as if to say, Can you believe this crazy woman?

"Now! Drop it!" I gestured towards his utensils.

He reacted by rolling his eyes, but he put down his fork, clearly taken aback by my tone. "What now? Histrionics? Can't you ever be quiet?"

"Like a mouse? That's what you need. A plain, uncomplaining mouse-wife who—"

"Look, Luce, I'm tired. I have no energy for your whims tonight."

I picked up a knife, a dull butter knife, and wondered what might drive a woman to plunge it into her mate's throat. The mess alone she'd have to clean up! Herself. Not my style. I put the knife down on the countertop and turned to face him. "This marriage, it's no good. Surely you know that." *What a dark, brooding scowl!* "You don't like being tethered—"

"Tethered? What is that word? I don't understand."

"Forced to stay in one spot with one woman."

"I only did what every young Frenchman does or dreams of doing. And if I remember correctly, you yourself—"

"Whatever!" I yelled. "Can't you just shut up for one minute?"

He ignored me and directed his attention back to the delicately scented mutton chops his mother had taught me to prepare. *Why was I still cooking for him?*

I picked up the knife again. It felt good to run my fingers over the dull edge while I gathered my forces and tried to figure out how to penetrate that mask of his. Suddenly it came to me. "I need my freedom. This is not working for me. It's not your fault—or not entirely. We are too different. You're right; I *am* a brake. I wish it could be different. Come out and let's talk about it like two adults."

He picked up his fork and resumed eating. "What's for dessert? Did you pick up some fruit? I told you we needed fruit."

"No," I admitted as I stared into his condemning face with the knowledge I'd fallen short once again. I took a deep cleansing breath and let the truth out into the universe: "I don't love you anymore."

I saw the pain register on his face, his too-white face. "I'm so sorry," I whispered.

He got to his feet and headed for the bathroom where he locked himself in. I waited outside the door, but he stayed so long I began to worry. Would he swallow pills or do bodily harm with a rusty razor blade? I hated that I'd probably forced him to relive painful scenes of separation dating back to his childhood. He was fragile. I knew that. But he wasn't eight years old any longer.

"I wish it could be different. . . . Come out and let's talk about it like two adults."

"F—you, Lucie! Leave me alone!"

I retreated to a kitchen chair.

Just a minute! I'm feeling sorry for what he's going through? What kind of dope am I?

After a lengthy wait, I put on a light jacket. "I'm going to fetch Alexandre from Valentine's. Try to compose yourself. We don't want to frighten him."

No answer. By the time we returned from Valentine's, Pierre was nowhere to be seen.

The Brake

*A*t breakfast Pierre reappeared. *Which girlfriend had shel-tered him for the night?*

He announced he had no intention of changing his plans. Alexandre and I could remain in Paris if we liked. For a while. "Do you want me to get you a house in the suburbs?" he asked.

We have that kind of money?

"The suburbs? No, not really." We had no car. I had never driven in Paris. Who would I know in a new neighborhood? "I prefer to remain in familiar territory, close to my friends."

"You'll join me in a few months," Pierre did not fail to add as a footnote.

I'd made up my mind but was quaking inside. I could not seem to stop second-guessing myself and trying on different outcomes for size. Tilting one way, then another, like a dreidel on the verge of toppling over.

Was the best course of action to return to the family hearth in New York to take advantage of extra pairs of caring hands, of as-sistance which would surely be needed? I felt confident I had good friends there who'd be delighted to have me around to play with them and eager to participate in Alexandre's toddlerhood and beyond.

If I acceded to his wishes, gave in and followed him to Hawaii, I'd have to make sure not to have more babies, for how would I ever leave Pierre with two babes in arms?

Two years ago, I coldly calculated that I had to get a baby out of this marriage or risk missing the opportunity to be a mother. Given a second chance at motherhood, with no one to share the agonizing decision with me, I opted out. But no way could I stay under the yoke for years as Pierre became even more demanding, unbending, selfish, old, and crotchety with no possibility of changing. One baby to nurture. Another—a daughter?—in the pipeline for me in the distant future? *I did not calculate what that would take, nor my guilt at removing my son from a father who clearly loved him.*

Who'll Be Crying Last?

"You'll be crying last. Your turn will come." I sniveled from room to room. Lately I'd lost the ability to plug up my tear ducts.

He remained seated with his nose stuck in a physics book. "Lucie, stop acting like such a child!"

The list of our differences I slid under his nose. My avowal? He had not deigned to reopen the discussion. Other matters took precedence: the dingy laundry, the inadequate meal preparation, how I insisted on spoiling the boy. Endless Virgo criticisms.

He and I continued our farce: He beelined to the bathroom during arguments; I rested against a wall, taking deep breaths. We were at an impasse. He refused to concede his error, his neglecting to consult me before accepting the job in Hawaii. Seeing my outrage, he repeated over and over, "A wife follows her husband." As if that explained anything.

I decided to heed advice given me earlier by Gabriella: "If you continue to sleep with a man, no matter what you say or how you act, he will not believe anything is wrong." I stopped sleeping with Pierre. The more I pondered our sex life, the less I wanted him to be the one giving me pleasure. I vowed to remain celibate until I was clear of him.

"A man has needs," he intoned. The old story. I bought it once, twice—in the past. Now I hardly cared. Line up the bimbos!

He squirmed away on another six-week sailing trip. "*Papa*

est parti en bateau," I announced to my child, a line I would have recourse to many times in my future. Each time, confused, Alexandre swung his head around a room, trying to locate his father.

Sailing? I guessed he was trying to get it in before he shipped himself off to Hawaii, a state not exactly known for being land-locked. Why not wait a few months? Perhaps the air in our home was turning too toxic, even for him. But his son? Pierre willingly surrendered whole weeks in which he could have bonded with his son, been there when he reached a few more developmental milestones.

Surely, Pierre delighted in these changes. Did he not need to be on site to witness them? Was this a father thing? Or was he just accustoming himself to long periods without his son?

I wondered if that blonde, Gretchen, was accompanying him. In any case I was treated to another foretaste of what single parenthood would be like, all responsibility falling to me alone. Terrifying, but I calculated Pierre had been absent a total of six months this last year between sailing, skiing, and business trips. A little birdie whispered in my ear: *You might as well get credit for being a single parent.*

꒰Ꙭ꒱

D-Day

D-day arrived. Pierre departed for the airport in the early
morning. I stayed behind with Alexandre. Pierre kept up
his stoic act, hugging the baby one last time, kissing me on the
cheek. Then he was gone. A deadly silence prevailed.

Things could have been worse. Thank the heavens above I
was not pregnant and due to deliver alone. I resolved to ease into
my new role as a de facto single mother. I had no fears of staying
behind in a foreign country with a baby and not much of a support system. My only concern was how to get away from him. I
acted as if I'd be joining him in Hawaii at an ill-defined distant
point in the future. Did he believe me? Did he care? I honestly
did not know. After all his master plan, which he clearly articu-
lated in Mexico, was that I have the babies and he roam the
world, stopping in once in a while for a visit.

In my bones I knew the marriage was kaput. *Fini*. Over.

Till the end Gabriella continued to urge, "Go to Hawaii with
him, Lucie. You'll have plenty of time to write while he's screwing
around on that mountaintop." Sure, this tactic worked for her.
She'd gone from living out of her car a few years ago to shacking
up with a senior British bank official who allowed her to use his
living room as her atelier. When those arrangements went cold,
she entered into a lesbian affair with a Romanian lit prof to en-
sure a roof over her head. In her present incarnation, she was
convincingly enacting the role of a middle-class woman with a

top-level business executive husband, the compleat housewife, albeit on her fifth marriage.

Pierre was not an evil person. I loved him once. I'd always thought of him as a quality person with good values, morals, highly intelligent. . . .

That first morning the weather was uncharacteristically warm and sunny. We walked through the Marais and wound up outside an appealing jeweler's window on the Rue de Rivoli. In the window I spotted a lovely pewter necklace, a choker featuring a row of birds craning their necks. On impulse I pushed the stroller inside the store.

The old Jewish man behind the counter greeted me. Taking in my small triangular head scarf, which swept behind my ears and knotted on my neck, my unruly dark curls and fair skin, he bent over the counter to whisper in my ear, "Yid?" I glanced around the store. No one else in sight. An old habit from the war, perhaps? I nodded back, my Ashkenazi Jewish looks now center stage. I had gotten used to strangers on the street pulling me aside. "*Juive?*" they inquired. I assured them that their eyes were not deceiving them. But when they asked, "*Israélite?*" I shook my head no, meaning, I am not an Israeli. My mistake. *Israélite, Juive,* Yid were all synonyms for Jew.

Once we concluded with the formalities, Mr. Lev, the jeweler, smiled. He brought out trays of earrings and bracelets, but I remained transfixed by the necklace. I rarely purchased anything for myself. Not accustomed to haggling, I paid full price. "It's called *Le Paon Boudeur*, the Pouting Peacock," he said as he prepared to wrap it up. *Back in New York, jewelry does not come with its own name!*

"No, please, help me put it on." I leaned over the counter as he fastened it around my thin neck. Alexandre stroked the metal, looked back and forth between the man and me, and grunted his approval. I owned a piece of real jewelry now. No need for me to ask permission to make the purchase or justify it to Pierre.

"Bonne journée, Monsieur."

"Bonne journée, Madame."

We took our leave of Mr. Lev and embarked on a rambling tour of the Marais, walking this way and that, circling back on ourselves, crossing the street whenever and wherever. I was quite dizzy with power. Confident. I was going to make this work.

Without Pierre to direct me, to micromanage my every step, I began to see Paris, experience it in a new way, and love it even more.

For the next three months, Alexandre and I stared at the amazing architecture as we crossed the bridges over the Seine, climbed to the top of Notre-Dame to visit our favorite gargoyles, or stopped in the Latin Quarter for a giant lamb souvlaki right off the spit. Not infrequently we circled back to Île de la Cité, lining up for a passionfruit ice cream cone.

At night when Alexandre glanced at the front door anxiously, waiting for it to open and reveal the face of his father, I worked at distracting him with picture books and stories I made up on the spot. If he started complaining, I stroked his back and repeated, "We're going to be all right, Petit Bonhomme. Just you wait." My euphoria did not last.

Sundays were the worst. I pushed the baby carriage through empty streets and deserted playgrounds. It was family day in France, everyone gathered around the dining room table, with no room for us. Camille had never resurfaced, and we'd had no news about her whereabouts. Another woman, Valentine's pretty neighbor, who had gained at least thirteen kilos in recent months, reappeared at the playground, showing off her new skinny self. *That must have been some diet she put herself on.* Valentine whispered that Welfare came at night to take the new baby away. What? The woman was pregnant all along, and despite being mothers ourselves, we had been hoodwinked! Valentine told me it wasn't the first time this woman had relinquished her rights to her children. Well, *sacré bleu*, we'd all kept up a true French façade!

Valentine remained steadfast, almost the only one aside from Mme Karol who checked up on me. My large circle of friends? Gabriella? The other writers? If I was able to get a babysitter and join them for a meeting on the other side of Paris, great. Otherwise, they did not appear keen on working within my limitations and tuned out if I dared mention my need to work around babysitters, mealtimes, doctor appointments, etc. Traitors! Naïve me, believing they would feel a bond, a responsibility, a desire to help out. They went about their own lives, and I rarely heard from them. The joke was on me.

Mamie visited every two weeks, but I no longer allowed her to clean the apartment. We prepared and ate a meal together. She repeatedly proclaimed, "Pierre doesn't count for me anymore; only Alexandre."

I returned to the co-op nursery I had previously located, one where mothers dropped off their children for a few hours, providing they'd accumulated "credits" earned from watching other mothers' children. After a few visits, I had to take Alexandre to the doctor, who diagnosed him with pinworms. I concluded the nursery was not as sanitary as it should have been and quickly opted out.

With a little effort, I found a job in an international school: receptionist! I wondered if I were the only receptionist in the world who'd read Moby Dick all the way through. I called my sitter Mimi to give her the good news. To my shock she informed me that she was splitting from her husband and moving back to Normandy. Crap! I dashed around the quartier collecting names posted on bulletin boards. How could I find another nanny as trustworthy and reliable, as lovely, as she was? I interviewed the gay friend of a gay colleague from my teaching days. This guy was flamboyant. I was not proud of my prejudice but couldn't surmount my fear that my son might mimic his mannerisms.

Fortunately, I found YaYa (Lucia), a young mother who left her own toddler behind in Guatemala to make her fortune in Paris. With her I asked only that she speak to Alexandre in English or French, not Spanish, fearing he would never learn to talk in any coherent fashion. I headed out each morning for my new job on the other side of Paris, started making friends with the teachers and principal, and returned, as before, in time to hang out with Alexandre in the playground. The job afforded me a little income to supplement what Pierre sent me—I could manage for a while.

Letter from Hawaii

I opened a perfectly folded blue aerogramme from my husband. I read it over several times. *Oh yeah, this was going to get me to change my mind!* Who was he kidding?

Hawaii, September 1978

Chère Lucie,

In France, a wife follows her husband. I've told you that. More than once. But you fail to listen. I mean, what's the big deal? Who wouldn't want to live in Hawaii?

You say you want a career. All of a sudden you don't want to be "just" a mother. Weren't you the one insisting you needed to stay home with the baby? He's two years old already—why haven't you put him in day care? It's good enough for all the other mothers. Not you. Didn't I tell you to get his name on the waiting lists before he was born?

I'm tired of hearing how you're bored or isolated or whatever. The whole thing was your idea. "I want to have a baby in 1976," you told me when I asked about your goals a few years ago. You have your baby. Now what?

Can't you understand this is an incredible opportunity for me? To be working on constructing the largest telescope in the world. Does that mean anything to you? It's an international effort. And they chose me! It's my dream job. Not to mention the location and the surfing and the sailing and I'll be able to work on my photography. I've already set up a lab.

Be happy, goddammit! Okay, I get a little out of control. One time I grabbed your wrists. Big deal! Just trying to make you see. You go into that business about the use of force, and how Jewish women (like you) never allow themselves to be abused in any way. They just walk out. You must be joking. I wonder who's getting abused here.

Now you say you'll join me . . . I left a month ago. When you got pregnant again, I told you I wouldn't be there for the birth—a crucial time in the project. (And it is.) You could have hired a nanny. How were you going to manage two babies? Figure it out, I said. I left the decision entirely up to you.

We can always have more babies, Lucie, we're young. Be a little logical. You two can come over next month when I'm settled in a bigger place. Surely you wouldn't take your son away from his father.

I'm excited about this job, working with Bernard and the others. We're up on the mountain most of the week and come down about once in two weeks. It's an altitude thing. You're probably discouraged because that job interview for teaching school here did not result in an offer. Big deal. Why give up so easily?

You say funding ran out on that PR job with the dissidents? Time to move on. Can you understand now why I didn't discuss Hawaii with you earlier?

Listen to me. I've decided to cut off all payments to you at the end of this year. Time to grow up, my dear.

Je t'embrasse, Pierre

What?! He couldn't just decide not to support us. An idle threat surely. Right? He didn't know about my new job, which was a good thing. I reread the letter. No "I love you." No "I miss you."

Was it my imagination or was he not trying very hard? Did I care? My pride was hurt a little, but overall, he made it easier for me to live with my decision.

~ele~

Saving Mme Karol

*A*s I lay half-reclined on the daybed, I heard a little scratch-scratch noise from the wall behind my head and wondered what Mme Karol was up to. Cleaning her Russian eggs, polishing her husband's picture, or just plain dusting?

Alexandre started clamoring for food or his mother's full attention, so I gave the noise no further thought. However, the next night I realized I had not seen her that week. It was probably the lack of companionship *au chocolat* that alerted me to a problem. I knocked on our common wall but heard no answering reply. Not even a scratch.

I swung Alexandre onto my hip and ventured down the hall where I thumped on the door. No answer. Peculiar but perhaps this was her day to visit some of her friends in the countryside. Three different families came by to collect her during the week, and I'd never been able to sort out who was who or to gain any insight into her schedule.

I returned to my apartment and went about my day. Late afternoon I decided to try again. This was the time she would normally be home already and working on her dinner. I left Alexandre in his crib napping and banged on her door. No response. An uneasy feeling washed over me. I knew she had a bad heart. . . .

I decided to try the door and it was open! I called out her name, "Mme Karol? Are you here?" I heard a weak response and quickly headed for her bedroom. "Oh my god!" I whispered. She was stretched out on her bed, dressed in a long antique lace dress she'd often told me she intended to be buried in. "What's wrong?" I hurried to her and grasped her hand, very clammy and slick to the touch. Next, I felt her forehead. She was burning up. "Mme Karol, dear, where's your telephone?" No answer. I rummaged around and finally I located it tucked under some magazines. "I am going to call for an ambulance and—"

She lifted her head and uttered one word weakly, "Never." I remembered her irrational fear of hospitals. Very old-world style, she believed if she ever entered a hospital, it would be a one-way trip. She swore that hospitals killed people and preferred to trust in her morning calisthenics, her borscht, and her good humor to get her through. She was so committed to this vision that she regularly refused invitations to spend the night at her former employers' houses. She would die in her own bed or die trying.

I looked around the room frantically. How to balance her wishes with helping her American style? I realized I did not have any contact information for her and did not know the names of any of her friends. I wondered if I could get Pierre on the phone. But he was no doubt up on the mountain. I would have to handle this myself.

I filled a basin with cool water and placed a compress on her forehead. "I'll be right back," I announced, and scurried next door to check on my son. Luckily, he was still napping. I went back to her place and called our pediatrician for advice. He was on vacation. Desperate, I dialed SOS Médecins and they promised to send a doctor over immediately.

Within a half hour, Dr. Eng arrived and took stock of the situation. I explained her unwillingness to be removed from her bed. Considering her age, he did not find that surprising and agreed to work with us. He did a full body exam, drew blood, and prescribed a general antibiotic. She gave up protesting and lay limp in the bed. The doctor promised to return the next day and advised that I keep her hydrated in the meantime.

I was no nurse but could remember my mother taking care of us three children when we had chicken pox and measles. I knew Mme K must be uncomfortable lying there in days-old damp clothing. I knew what I had to do.

A half hour later, I had Alexandre set up in his playpen in Mme Karol's small sitting room, far enough away from her, I hoped, to be free of contagion. We ate a simple dinner and then I spread some of his toys out for him to play with. I gave my patient a sponge bath and managed to find a clean nightgown to change her into. She nodded her approval. Her temperature seemed to be going down a bit and she drifted off.

I sat on a kitchen chair and worried about how to manage everything. First, I needed to call in sick to my job in the morning. I wouldn't cancel YaYa but use her to take care of my son, feed, diaper, and entertain him, while I tended to my neighbor. Hopefully one of the friends would come by to see her or call her. I packed up Alexandre at seven and put him to bed. As for me, I slept in dribs and drabs on the daybed, getting up every hour or so to check on my neighbor.

Dr. Eng returned the next afternoon to announce that Mme Karol had a bacterial infection, potentially a serious problem. He brought along a more powerful antibiotic and predicted that she would need bed rest for a week. He said he was cheered by a noticeable improvement in her breathing.

By the end of the sixth day, Mme Karol was up and observing Alexandre's playtime activities. She even made soup for us all, and I supplied the rest of the meal. I took her into our apartment and helped her shower, surely a treat.

By week's end she was back to normal. I arranged to return to work. She shrugged off the whole nightmare in typical Mme K style: "I'm made of strong peasant stock. Never forget that. Yes, I'm over seventy, but still strong, strong, strong."

"I'm going back to my apartment now," I announced, heading for her front door.

"Darling girl," she said, turning me around and giving me a hug. "I won't forget how you took care of me. But I need to teach you how to make some good Russian soups to add to your repertoire."

"I'd like that. See you later for *tisane et chocolat*."

"I'll be there."

"And don't forget to bring me the names and addresses of all your friends. In case there's a next time."

"Next time just let me lie there. I'll be ready to go."

"Fat chance!"

Camille Resurfaces

So there I was in the street near Sevres-Babylone, on my way to my annual gyn exam with Dr. V, when something in the walk of a woman ahead of me caught my eye. The woman was beautifully dressed, wearing a black Persian lamb coat, though the day was rather warm, with a long colorful scarf expertly knotted around her neck. My heart beat wildly in my chest as I shortened the distance between us. Could it be?

An equally elegant older woman shepherded her around, actually pushing on her back to keep her going. I hesitated. What if I were wrong? Then I heard her speak.

"We're going to be late again. Dr. Molnia doesn't like it when you're late. Cami, c'mon!"

I crept up alongside and stopped directly in front of them. "Hello, Camille," I said. She smiled weakly and put her hand on my arm. "Lucie."

For her mother, however, this reunion held no interest. She tugged roughly on her daughter's other arm.

"*Arrête, Maman!*"

"Can we get a coffee?" I asked. Camille locked eyes with her mother, who jabbed at her wristwatch. Camille turned back to me and whispered, "Lucie, meet me in that café across the street. In an hour." I watched as she resumed her slow almost tottering walk to her doctor's office.

I cancelled my own appointment, walked around, and did a

bit of window shopping before installing myself at a little table in the café. An hour and a half ticked by, and she had still not appeared. I finished nursing my café au lait and headed out, running smack into her. She pointed to her mother across the street and sighed. "I'm on a tight leash. . . . It's no fun. . . . Listen, I have one thing I must say to you: They are not worth it." Her voice was quavery—I strained to make out her meaning. Close up, I noticed streaks of eye makeup smeared on her cheeks. She must have been crying.

"They?" I asked.

"Jacky, Eric, Pierre. All of them."

Her face: Whatever she'd gone through was etched on its once-perfect surface. She looked to be almost thirty. She interrupted my appraisal by presenting her cheek. I couldn't believe we were forced to say goodbye before we'd even started. There was no way for me to delay her parting. "A kiss for Chloé," I said.

She turned away and I heard her mumble, "When I see her."

Oh no. Her life, what had it become? Had she been judged an unfit mother? Poor, poor girl. Poor Chloé. Any time I was in that neighborhood I kept my eyes peeled but never ran into her again.

Crisis Mode

Next, Alexandre came down with a fever. We got in to see the doctor, stocked up on antibiotics, and I called in sick to work. First day back at work, a panicked YaYa called me at the office to report that Alexandre had been running around the apartment in his usual hyper fashion, when he fell and cut his lip on the corner of the daybed. She hadn't been able to stop the bleeding and pleaded with me to come home immediately.

The train ride was forty minutes; I jumped in a cab instead. By the time I arrived, the bleeding had stopped. Mimi would have been able to handle the situation herself.

A few days later, Alexandre was literally bouncing off the walls. YaYa confessed she'd had a tough day with him. As I prepared his dinner, I couldn't fail to notice he was rubbing his left ear a lot. I rushed him over to the pediatrician. As I suspected, his ears again. I knew the drill: another round of different antibiotics coupled with nose and ear drops which never seemed to do much for him.

From the moment Pierre left, he had been sick more often than not. The night after he received the measles vaccine, his temperature peaked at 105 degrees and his body broke out in an angry red rash. I convinced his doctor to make a house call in the middle of the night. After examining Alexandre, the doctor asked, "Madame, has your baby ever been put in the hospital for a fever?"

"No, why?" I answered as ice water replaced the blood in my veins. Taking in my white face and shaking hands, the doctor instructed me to fill the bathtub with tepid bath water. We put him inside. After ten minutes his fever came down slightly. The doctor picked up his bag and made for the door.

"Keep doing what you're doing," he said as he slipped out of the apartment.

Don't leave me!

One night while the pediatrician was attending a conference out of town, I had no choice but to call SOS Médecins again. A baby-faced doctor arrived and appeared quite concerned. Alexandre's tonsils and adenoids were abnormally swollen. "*Vegétations*," he called them. "Here is a bottle of rescue medicine. Give him seven drops on his tongue if it looks like his throat is swelling shut."

"And then?"

"Get him to the hospital, of course."

He left me clutching the thin vial tightly in my fist. I closed the door, deposited the vial in the medicine cabinet, and sat down on the edge of the daybed, trying to still my trembling hands.

I started to get the message: Paris was no place for a single parent. I had no reliable help, no backup, no family. Mamie was not the only family member I wanted my son to know. Where were his uncles and aunts, grandparents, and cousins? Back home.

I was shocked to learn my writing group, my lifeline, was breaking up too, everyone heading off in different directions, following their whims or their boyfriends and husbands to the next posting. Gabriella was off to Hungary to do research on a nonfiction book. Suzanna's husband was being transferred to California. Ernie decided to study screenwriting in the south of France. Ava was tight-lipped about her future plans. If she too left, would I get any more writing assignments?

I refused to throw in the towel just yet. There had to be some way to wring success out of this new lifestyle. Then. . . .

~ele~

The Last Week

*M*onday: The day I almost lost my baby. I left him with Mme Karol to run down to the store for fresh butter, slipping him a hard candy on my way out the door.

Why on earth did I do that? When I returned to the apartment twenty minutes later, Mme Karol was bent over, hands on knees, out of breath, and I could hear Alexandre howling in his crib. "Madame," she said once she managed to catch her breath, "you almost lost your son!"

"What?" I ran to pick him up and comfort him. She followed.

"He was choking on that candy you gave him. I grabbed him and turned him over and shook him by his legs. I thumped him hard over and over again on his back. Over and over. Finally, the candy shot out of his mouth."

"Omigod. . . ."

"Madame Lucie, you might have come back and found both of us dead!"

What was wrong with me? I'd endangered my child. Where was my judgment? My mind flashed on all the times I'd run out, leaving him alone napping in his crib. All my worries: What if I got run over by a car or *vélomoteur*? Who would know that he was alone starving in his bed? Yet what choice did I have?

I was going to have to do better. A lot better. Or wind up like Camille.

I brewed a pot of chamomile tisane for us. Mme Karol ran back to her apartment and returned with chocolate, which she insisted was good for little children. No argument from us. We broke off little pieces and sat silent in the kitchen, taking in the sweetness of life.

Tuesday: My immediate supervisor at the international school, a well-preserved French divorcée of about forty, bawled me out in front of an assembly of parents. I didn't make enough copies of the agenda, she claimed.

Damned mimeograph machine! I wheezed every time I got too much ink on my hands. She acted like I was a threat of some kind. Huh? And there I thought I was a contributing member of the staff. . . .

Was I in danger of being fired?

Wednesday: As I was on my way back from the post office, attempting to cross Rue Basfroi, a man jumped off the curb and grabbed the handlebars of the stroller. I shrieked bloody murder! Poor guy—he was only trying to help me over the curb. I was ashamed of myself.

Thursday: The toilet broke! I had no idea how to fix it. It refused to mash up anything anymore. Nothing further will be riding down those ancient Parisian pipes to the sewer. I did not feel up to looking for a plumber; I couldn't handle it. I knew my limits. If Pierre were here, he'd know how to unplug it. Why wasn't he here? I was just a woman and wasn't supposed to know about these things.

My solution was to emulate Mme Karol and a few others on

the third floor: Use a bedpan and then dump it in the hall water closet. *Gross!*

Today I had a crying fit at work. I couldn't seem to stop. I hid out in the basement toilettes for a half hour.

No contact this week from Pierre. We were approaching the cutoff date. I didn't want to fall for his bluff. I had stopped sleeping. Alexandre and I were not going to survive on my pittance from the International School. No other part-time jobs were in the offing.

Friday: This was no way to live. I splurged on a long long long-distance call to my folks.

Au Revoir

*O*ver the weekend, I committed to a new plan of action. No more procrastinating. No more back-and-forth. My nerves couldn't take any more. "Home is the place where they have to take you in," eh, Robert Frost? We were about to find out.

I packed my most beloved books, a dozen at a time, into small boxes. I carried down a box, fetched Alexandre and strapped him into his stroller, and made the first of many daily pilgrimages to the post office several blocks away. Off my books flew on yet another transatlantic flight.

I needed to decide where everything was to go. All my baby paraphernalia, clothes, extra diapers, creams and ointments, and toys I donated to the pinworm nursery. One day Alexandre sat contentedly astride his favorite toy, a shaggy orange doggie-on-wheels; the next, it vanished from the apartment. Strangely, he never said a word as all his toys disappeared one by one. On transatlantic flights you couldn't take much. You were forced to leave most of your life behind. In fact, France did not allow you to take more than the equivalent of $1000 out of the country. I had my son—what more did I need? What did he need? I told myself he'd be better off away from a cold-blooded father like Pierre.

Finally, I alerted all my friends and acquaintances to the situation and managed to rent out the apartment to my gay friend. I left him a blank check with the understanding he'd call in the roto-rooter guy up the block.

I walked up and down those mean streets. . . .

Rue de la Roquette was a mean street, a dirty twisted rope snaking around the edges of smudged tan-colored buildings. One end tied to the Bastille, the other secured to the graves at Père Lachaise. In between, Frenchmen and foreigners endeavored to exist, between Liberty and Death. The fumes on the street from buses, mopeds, autos, and the garlic-eating public contributed to the heavy, overbearing atmosphere. The screeches reminded one of the jungle a city really is. I could never have lived on this street. How would I have breathed? For me, once it was a gentle cow path I dreamily trod back and forth to my job in a foreign country, to my dollhouse of an apartment, and to my adoring husband. The French were the natives; I got to be the foreigner. That much at least had not changed.

I bid farewell to my writer friends by hosting in my apartment the last writers' group meeting I would ever attend. I followed another one of Gabriella's amazing recipes and served up a delicious garlicky roast beef. We promised to stay in touch while knowing we would not.

I called a few people I'd never miss to advise them of my leave-taking. I kissed and hugged and cried real tears with Valentine and Mme Karol, most aggrieved to be leaving them. "You saved my son's life," I told Mme Karol, and turned to Valentine, "and you saved mine."

"Will I ever see you again?" asked Valentine, all round eyes and turned-down mouth. "Of course you will," I responded, not knowing if that was true or not.

"Oh, Madame, I am sorry you are going," interrupted my neighbor. I hoped she'd give me one of her Russian dolls or painted eggs as a memento, but she didn't volunteer, and I didn't dare ask. In any case, no way could I ever forget her.

Would I ever see them again? My dearest friends. I vowed to return not once but many times. Paris was in my blood. Mamie, I invited to visit in the spring. She had not commented on the split. When I told her I was returning to New York, she simply said, "*Ah, oui.*" No questions asked. My heart was breaking for her.

I kept busy making checklists and taking care of business quietly and methodically. Three months from the time Pierre left, the day after Alexandre's second birthday, Eric, Valentine, and Johann accompanied us to the airport. Even Eric gave me a hug, no doubt thrilled to see me go.

"*À la prochaine*," we shouted. "See you next time!"

ele

Heading for Home

_A_lexandre screamed and fussed during the entire flight as if he knew what a big change was in store for us.

I finally landed safely back home in Queens, New York, with a toddler in tow. My mother had transformed the basement of their house. She'd found a secondhand crib and installed a small refrigerator and stove in the laundry room for our use. We had two rooms, a bathroom, and a "kitchen." She seemed happy to see her grandson, less happy to see me.

"Where is the Fisher-Price explorer bus I asked you to buy and have waiting?" I asked.

"Oh, I figured you would get it when you got here."

"But you don't understand. I gave away all of his toys!"

"Oh well," she shrugged. "Too bad."

Reality began to dawn. My parents, never the most nurturing or understanding, had been less than delighted to hear we planned on a prolonged stay. But I knew they'd not refuse me. I intended to clear out the minute I could afford my own place.

Poor little Alexandre found himself transported to a place he had visited only once before. Everyone spoke his mother's language. He recognized few people. Gone were his friend Johann, all his possessions, our daily routines, his home, and of course, his father.

That first week when I tried to drop him off at a nursery for a few hours in order to do some apartment hunting, he threw a megawatt tantrum. The director outright refused to take him. I briefly alluded to our situation, my need to secure housing and a job, but she was adamant. Furthermore, she advised me not to leave him anywhere for a while. Two whole months? Of course, she knew what she was talking about. I realized then I was the one constant in my son's life, and he had no intention of letting me disappear.

Letters from Pierre arrived regularly. And checks. He was enjoying his work and hanging out with his comrades in science; he spent his free time exploring the Big Island; he complained about his forced celibacy. Well, he hadn't let my absence bother him before. He professed to miss me and his son. He sincerely hoped I had a plan, and that I knew what I was doing. Behind my back he talked to my parents about me. I overheard their whispered telephone chats: "When is Lucie going to come to her senses?"

One morning I pushed the stroller into the neighborhood library, plunked Alexandre down in the children's storytelling circle, and retreated to a carrel with my notebook and a pen. Maybe writing about my dilemmas would help me think more clearly—it usually did.

Story of the End of My Life

So after all that, I swung my baby onto my hip and walked away from storybook endings. I wasn't born to them.

"I wish I could have gone without dying," I said.

Yes . . . that would have been nice.

I strode past La Bastille down Rue de la Roquette to Père Lachaise and dug a hole. Love, marriage, baby carriage, in went the Romance shelves of the Vleigh Place library, my whole sixteenth summer's reading list.

*Pierre, "love of my life," followed, the poetic soul so long
awaited. He had flitted into my room belatedly, Peter Pan,
danced a few steps on tiptoe, leapt, sang, and shouted,
lifted me and whisked me out my window, a happy victim,
flapping my wings. I tossed him away now with a mere flick
of my fingers. Down he floated, lighter than a whisper.*

*I kicked in a footful of Paris before leaving, lifted out
Alexandre on all fours.*

*I walked. Out of Never-Never Land of the mind. Out of the
Old World which was my new world into the New World
which was my old world. Which was my world? I was
looking right and left.*

*I walked. I walked. Over hill, over waters. Where could I go?
Mama! (Mama, he cried. Mama, I echoed). I returned to the
womb which was only once a womb and never again, too
bad.*

To Grandmother's house we went.

How was I doing really? *Moi?* Strangely, I felt like a crusader em-
barking on my journey. At the end of 1978, at twenty-eight years
old, I found myself with no money, no job, no apartment, no
profession, and no man. I'd taken an incomplete in grad school
only to get an F in marriage. I'd reenrolled in life as a single
mother, not knowing exactly what that entailed or what price I
might have to pay.

And yet . . . my whole life was before me. Pierre wasn't
around to drag me down anymore. I had gotten away from him. I
had gotten away with it.

Hallelujah!

Epilogue:
Two Months Later

I unpacked the crates. Five. Nailed shut like coffins. Maybe they were never meant to be opened?

Clumsy, I pried and pulled off pieces of lid with a pair of borrowed pliers. Pierre, observing the end result, would have said, "A woman must have opened these crates."

I'd often thought over the years of stumbling on a place where our beautiful Mexican dishes could be unpacked, never imagining a basement in Queens. I lifted out one sculpted piece after another, caressed the curves, the puckered lips, the knobs. Such artisanry. No doubt months of work went into these dishes with their blue-gold-orange-green-rust-black-ivory design, their flowers on a garden wall, their birds and bows. They were bold, womanly, unquestionably Mexican. A woman's dishes.

I lined up the three pitchers, a stout soup tureen, a sugar bowl, and a creamer and placed them on the cracked linoleum floor. I stacked plates and bowls, saucers and cups. What did they all add up to?

Five years ago Pierre referred to "our dishes" with a sly smile as we conferenced in a corner of the Talavera pottery factory in Puebla, Mexico. He said, "No matter what happens, you can keep the dishes."

I thought: *Even a travelling man has to rest his weary feet.*

I swept up the shrouds of straw and splinters and headed for the shower. The water washed away nothing. I tightened my bathrobe, finished my tea, and washed my cup. I'd placed the dishes on the highest shelf of the cabinet. I opened the cabinet, closed it. Memory and desire. Five years. . . .

I looked around my home. Two months back and it was shaping up; textured beige curtains, photos on the walls, a small rust-colored rug make it homier. If I dyed the spread a warm brown, perhaps my brother's old bed would look more like a studio couch.

I tiptoed into Alexandre's room, our old den. "You've got the most beautiful room in the house," I'd told him and he believed me. At his age he believed everything except my answer to his daily, "Where's Papa?"

"*Papa est parti en bateau.*" A fishing trip, I said. I reasoned he couldn't tell the difference between six weeks and two months. Wrong. He was not buying it and asked anew every morning.

I bent to kiss him goodnight and silently retreated from his room. What now? How to be responsible for his life and my own without Pierre to tell us what to do? How had I, a middle-class woman, one highly educated and an all-around pretty smart cookie, wound up in my parents' basement alone with a baby?

I switched on the TV. Pierre disliked American TV. I listened to the audience laugh, but after four years in France, my humor was no longer American and not yet French. I was bored and restless.

Something was clinking in the laundry room/kitchen. Spooky. I crept in, with visions of little trespassers, little Mickeys and Minnies playing tag in the darkened kitchen. The noise was coming from the cabinets where I'd stored the dishes. The dishes had been very cold—maybe I shouldn't have washed them in hot water?

For lack of something better to do, I shut off the TV and rewashed the dishes in warmer water, dried them with a chamois cloth, restacked them in the cabinet. There I was, restarting from scratch.

Tinkle, tinkle, clink. *Out with them*, I thought. But those dishes were expensive. All these years the dishes had stayed stacked in a corner of my parents' garage, too fragile to risk further shipping, and anyway, we were always on the verge of moving. What did we need fancy dishes for with our kind of life? Too cumbersome for a souvenir. Too heavy.

I called Katrina, a potter friend in Soho. "What's up with these dishes?" I said as I held out the phone and made her listen.

I braced myself for the answer.

"We say, in potter's terms, that the glaze doesn't fit the clay," she explained. "You'll get hairline cracks, crevices, and in a few years, rough edges and holes. You will cut yourself and the dishes won't be healthy or particularly sanitary."

Stunned, I thanked her and hung up the phone. She rang back. "If they're still tinkling after five years, they made a bad job of it."

We never fit, Pierre and I. Master potter, reluctant clay. All we had together was the hope, that moment in Mexico, whispering in a corner of the factory.

Late the next night, I sat in the dark with an apple and a cold glass of wine when I heard pounding on the garage door. I slipped through the door from the bedroom to the garage and pulled up the garage door. Wendy, my wise old friend, whose hobby happened to be collecting displaced persons, or persons likely to be displaced, came in. She was always happy to listen to my "ironies," my talk of blasted hopes over a glass or two of wine.

"Did you know," she asked, "that I have an entire set of Rosenthal china that sat in my father's house for twenty-three years? With all the serving pieces?"

"Why?" I asked, then stopped to consider her depressive husband, her long but unsatisfying marriage, her two sons nearly grown.

"I've never had a home."

"But you've got a lovely apartment," I protested.

"A home!" she insisted.

I thought of how she and her husband conducted their separate lives and loves.

"But you know," she added, "I've never forgotten they're there."

When was I going to come to my senses? My parents refused to babysit. They decided to charge me rent—$150—the moment I found a job. I asked Wendy to drive Alexandre and me around one afternoon. That's all it took to locate a garden apartment near Jewel Avenue, a mere ten-minute ride from my parents' house. The rooms were cold and bare.

On a return trip from Hawaii to France, Pierre stopped off to cosign on the Jewel Avenue lease. He believed in giving me enough rope with which to hang myself. More than a little shaky, I made a couple of big purchases: a sofa bed followed by an expensive oak wall unit. Now I had to stay.

And stay I did.

But after three months' separation in Paris, three more in New York, Pierre's patience abruptly snapped. He started calling me every hour: "Lucie, where are you? Everyone is asking me that. Your behavior is extremely embarrassing. Childish. What do you have to say for yourself? Where is my son? You cannot keep him from me."

"He's getting to know his family—"

"I AM HIS FAMILY! I AM HIS FATHER! I'M THE ONLY FAMILY HE'S MISSING!"

"I can't leave. I have responsibilities here. My parents are getting older. . . ."

"Listen to me now. I am sending you plane tickets. You'd better be on the plane. You'll be sorry if you screw me around."

These phone calls unhinged me. A student therapist I consulted helped me understand Pierre was only trying to get a reaction out of me, reduce me to tears. She helped me see that he didn't care about any of my responses. "Oh."

I stopped answering the phone. Questions from Pierre like, "What are you doing about Alexandre's education?" were destined to remain unanswered.

We had an amicable separation according to Pierre—no need to make it legal. Nevertheless, my cut-rate lawyer warned me Pierre might try to abduct Alexandre when he was in New York for a scientific conference. I spent a week pacing the floor, not letting my son out of my sight, sending my blood pressure through the roof.

Pierre arrived in New York, assuming he'd stay with my parents. We picked him up at the airport and deposited him at the 42nd Street Y, with the foreign students, the hippies, the almost homeless. He was incensed. I refused to let him spend time alone with Alexandre. Amazing, but I no longer feared to go against Pierre's wishes.

May I never again be in thrall to a powerful man.

"Whither thou goest—" he said.

"Sorry!" I answered.

Once back in Hawaii, his next move was to sue me for divorce and custody. He lost the custody battle, failing to convince the Bronx-born judge that New York was too dangerous a place to raise a child. I didn't even need to use the card I withheld . . . that Pierre was a communist!

We divorced. I was awarded some child support. Despite the fact I'd quickly moved out of the ancestral home, a semi-hostile environment, my parents were continually on my case. "Be a teacher." I tried some subbing, but in my heart of hearts I knew I did not want to spend my life inside a school. I'd graduated. Instead, I decided to find my own way.

Pierre had to content himself with sending for his son every summer and calling him sporadically during the year. At the end of every summer visit, he issued a report, very clinical and cold, on our son's "progress." His latest serious girlfriend was Chinese, and her family was vehemently against their daughter dating a Caucasian divorcé. Ha!

I went out on a date with my hairdresser. I promised myself I'd find a job, a better job, eventually a career, and one day, live a writer's life. I'd learn to take responsibility.

When Alexandre complained, "You're not the boss of me," I knew how he felt. I hugged him and comforted him and gave him choices. But he was two; I was a lot older. I relished the feeling of being in charge of my life. Again.

Pierre got what he wanted too: a telescope in Hawaii.

Epilogue:
Ten Years Later

"*N*othing lasts forever," says my mother.
Well, it can feel like forever.

Once I get over the euphoria of being back in my own country, with my own language, and my own deep understanding of how our culture works, I face a giddy decade of going it alone. I try my hand at teaching junior high, proofreading business manuals, doing clerical work in import-export firms. I depend on sitters rather than my parents to make it through the tough years. True, I do feel like a crusader, but a tired one at best.

Nothing lasts forever. . . . I stay up until midnight to nail the tracks of Alexandre's first train set to a piece of plywood; run alongside him, breathless, as he gets his balance on a two-wheeler; read him *Le Petit Prince* and *The Beast of Monsieur Racine*; watch him sing and dance in "Oklahoma," herd him and ten other ten-year-olds to "The Gods Must Be Crazy" and then off to Eddie's Sweet Shoppe for birthday sundaes.

Along the way I learn to install convenience outlets by tacking wire from my living room stereo to the outlet in my kitchen. I refinish old desks, lay linoleum tiles, hook up VCRs. (Well, actually, before I open the instruction manual, Alexandre announces, "Look, Ma, it's easy!")

I also chase a mouse out of the house (lie: I drink a whole bottle of red wine and sleep with all the lights on). I awake in the middle of the night to kill a few roaches, try to explain that Tom, Dick, or Harry won't be visiting any more, help make recordings to send Papa, drag Alexandre to nature hikes and antique fairs and museums and Lincoln Center Young People's Concerts. Instead of shopping malls, we take trips to Mystic, Williamsburg, the Jersey shore, and one ten-day trip to his hometown, where we drop in on Mamie, Valentine, and Mme Karol. Mamie agrees to accompany us to restaurants (a rare treat for her). She enjoys showing off her grandson to the neighbors and baking individual pies for him alone to sample. Valentine invites us all for her signature couscous while sneaking sidelong looks at me.

"What?" I ask.

Eventually she confides that she misses the old me. "Where did the rebel go?" How to tell her there's no longer anything to rebel against? I ask about Camille—there's been no word. Eric is cordial enough, content to know our trip is of limited duration. Could he still be worried about my influence on his wife? Mme K is the same lovable creature with a few more wrinkles perhaps. She must be nearing eighty-five, but she's as fun and spry as ever. She delights in seeing Alexandre so grown up and brings special Belgian chocolates for him to enjoy.

Here's the setup: I teach our son about expressing his feelings in words and writing, and taking others into consideration, and being adventurous and daring. His father takes him surfing in Hawaii, rappelling in the mountains, skiing in the Vosges, rafting in Idaho, and backpacking in Iceland.

Every summer I pack Alexandre off to Hawaii. I joke that Pierre is in charge of the Greater Outdoors Club; all the rest falls to me. Alexandre returns every September with a healthy tan but looking rather pinched. It takes him a week or so to decompress and return to his usual boisterous self. Meanwhile I am left with the mundane tasks of making a home for us, earning a living, dealing with sprained ankles, ever-present ear infections, allergic reactions, his temper tantrums, and my meltdowns. During the year, there's only sporadic communication between the two Bonhommes. When I could use a man beside me, there's only . . . empty space.

I'm convinced my French-American baby is a lawyer in the making or an artist, architect, public speaker, sailor. He's bursting with ideas and projects and has endless confidence in his future. I am doing a good job raising him and putting my own needs second. *And he sleeps through the night!*

The day I turn thirty-four, I take a handful of clips to the local newspaper and plead for an assignment. I get turned away. Undeterred, I haunt the managing editor for months until I get a green signal to go. I interview local businesswomen, ride shotgun with a female sea captain, and bring Alexandre with me when I accompany a sailing instructor for a day out on the Sound. An inauspicious beginning, but I am determined. My interview with a banker who's discovered that golf is a good networking tool for women makes it to the front page. What a thrill! Within a few years I see my bylines on articles appearing in New York's major newspapers and magazines and trade journals, and my work goes national, then international. *Thank you, Ava.*

I'm asked to write a business book and I deliver. One summer, on my own, I interview women across the country; the next I sequester myself in a friend's cabin in Maine and write a book, *Single Parents Are the Strongest People in the World*. My book wins an award! I move out of Queens, buy a co-op on the water, commit to an even longer commute into New York City, but to a profession which guarantees a steady salary.

However, the men I encounter in my single days are uninspiring and unwilling to get involved with a woman and her child:

Gregory is enrolled in dental school, hasn't got a penny, and, I suspect, is cheap to boot.

Paul treats me like a wailing wall. His big complaint in life: He can't find time to open his mail.

Andy has a wart on his you-know-what.

Micah, at forty-five, confesses he's never had more than two dates with the same woman.

Jerome never comes back for his hat.

So, yes, I am lonely; yes, my friends are generally too busy hopping around Manhattan to art shows, concerts, and dances to bother with me. I'm on the lookout for a writers' group where I can find my people once again.

All along I jokingly tell Alexandre he must alert me if he spots a good-looking single teacher. I confess to him I'm not good at picking out viable prospects myself. Lo and behold when I'm thirty-five, after almost ten sex-starved years of singledom, Alexandre's social studies teacher takes a fancy to me—I can tell by the fact that our open school night session extends into the next morning.

Ben Cooper is everything Pierre is not: A mensch. The boy next door. Born in the Bronx, he speaks my language. He's solid, supportive, sweet, sexy, Jewish. He loves me, he loves Alexandre, and cares about our welfare and our happiness. Divorced himself, he knows the pain, the unmoored sensation, the disappointment in oneself that follows a marital split. We find a new home in each other, and there's no need for it to be exotic. And he loves my cooking!

I vow to celebrate our union and work hard at not causing him any grief. A few months in, we're already picking out wedding invitations.

Everything I ever wanted—motherhood, career, love—has come my way.

How did I get to be so lucky?

Acknowledgments

This book was a long time in the making, and I wish to thank everyone, especially my husband, Sheldon I. Hanner, for reading and critiquing snippets along the way and encouraging me to keep at it.

Special callout to: Sarah Lawrence Writing Institute teachers Pat Dunn, Jimin Han, and fellow writers and beta readers, Susan Curran, Dvora Rabino, Thea Schiller, the Somers Westchester Writers Workshop, Barbara Josselsohn and her writing groups, as well as "Ava," "Ernestine," "Gabriella," and "Susanna" from our original expatriate writing group, and all my lovely French friends and acquaintances. And the glorious city of Paris, which I will always regard as my second hometown. A special thanks to Martine Hahn Arenella for looking at my manuscript through the lens of a French native.

About the Author

Janet Garber is a native New Yorker who's nurtured a lifelong love affair with France. Living there in the 1970s put her romantic notions to the test. But she still dreams about Paris, strolling the boulevards, crisscrossing the Seine, people-watching in one of the grand cafés in Saint Germain des Prés.

She's published both nonfiction and fiction, dozens of short stories, essays, and a comic novel, and taught literature and composition at the university level.

Book Club Discussion Questions

1. What was the reader's very first clue that Lucie's powers of perception were faulty?

2. Why was she in such a rush to be married?

3. What did happen to her poet-lover?

4. Which scene was your favorite? Your least favorite?

5. Did you sympathize with Pierre or agree with his feelings about spoiled Americans?

6. Do women today have an easier time of it blending ambition with romance?

7. Were there characters you disliked? Those you felt were given short shrift? What were your feelings about Julien?

8. Did Lucie make the right choice on her second trip back to New York? Why was Pierre not involved in the decision-making process?

9. Did Lucie make the right choice at the end? Was she right to worry about the effects of her actions on her young son?

10. Have you experienced a story like Lucie's? Were your conclusions the same?

If you enjoyed the book, please take a moment to post a brief comment on Amazon or Barnes and Noble to help me spread the word! And you can always find me at www.janetgarber.com. I'd be happy to add you to my subscriber list.

Now you know what it was like to live in Paris in the '70s! Hope I didn't make you too hungry.

A bientôt!

Later—

SELECTED TITLES FROM SPARKPRESS

SparkPress is an independent boutique publisher delivering high-quality, entertaining, and engaging content that enhances readers' lives, with a special focus on female-driven work. www.gosparkpress.com

The Long-Lost Jules: A Novel, Jane Elizabeth Hughes, $16.95, 978-1-68463-089-9. She thinks he's either a nutcase or an eccentric Oxford professor. He thinks she's the descendant of Henry VIII's last Queen, Katherine Parr. They both harbor deep secrets, but their masks slip as they join forces to investigate the mystery of Queen Katherine's lost baby—endangering their hearts, their carefully constructed walls, and possibly their lives.

Charming Falls Apart: A Novel, Angela Terry, $16.95, 978-1-68463-049-3. After losing her job and fiancé the day before her thirty-fifth birthday, people-pleaser and rule-follower Allison James decides she needs someone to give her some new life rules—and fast. But when she embarks on a self-help mission, she realizes that her old life wasn't as perfect as she thought—and that she needs to start writing her own rules.

That's Not a Thing: A Novel, Jacqueline Friedland. $16.95, 978-1-68463-030-1. When a recently engaged Manhattanite learns that her first great love has been diagnosed with ALS, she is faced with the impossible decision of whether a few final months with her ex might be worth risking her entire future. A fast-paced emotional journey that explores whether it's possible to be equally in love with two men at once.

The Sea of Japan: A Novel, Keita Nagano. $16.95, 978-1-684630-12-7. When thirty-year-old Lindsey, an English teacher from Boston who's been assigned to a tiny Japanese fishing town, is saved from drowning by a local young fisherman, she's drawn into a battle with a neighboring town that has high stakes for everyone—especially her.

The Cast: A Novel, Amy Blumenfeld. $16.95, 978-1-943006-72-4. Twenty-five years after a group of ninth graders produces a Saturday Night Live-style videotape to cheer up their cancer-stricken friend, they reunite to celebrate her good health—but the happy holiday card facades quickly crumble and give way to an unforgettable three days filled with moral dilemmas and life-altering choices.